THE RAGE WAR BOOK 1

PREDATOR™

INCURSION

TIM LEBBON

TITAN BOOKS

PREDATOR™ : INCURSION

Print edition ISBN: 9781783298334
E-book edition ISBN: 9781783296392

Published by Titan Books
A division of Titan Publishing Group Ltd
144 Southwark Street, London SE1 0UP

First edition: September 2015
2 4 6 8 10 9 7 5 3

This is a work of fiction. Names, characters, places, and incidents either are used fictitiously, and any resemblance to actual persons, living or dead, business establishments, events, or locales is entirely coincidental.

A CIP catalogue record for this title is available from the British Library.

Printed and bound in Great Britain by CPI Group (UK) Ltd.

Did you enjoy this book?

We love to hear from our readers. Please email us at readerfeedback@titanemail.com or write to us at Reader Feedback at the above address.

To receive advance information, news, competitions, and exclusive offers online, please sign up for the Titan newsletter on our website
www.titanbooks.com

For Howard and Caspian

PROLOGUE

LILIYA

USS Evelyn-Tew *(decommissioned)*, *Alpha Centurai*
September 2351 AD

The sounds echoed, deep and heavy, thudding in her chest like death's metronome. For a crazy moment she thought it was the vibration of music, and she found herself subconsciously tapping her finger on her cot's frame. But when she heard the screaming and chaos, the bloodletting and explosions, she realized the truth. The pounding was the ship's heart beating its final moments. Her plan had worked, and it was time to enact its final phase.

For all Liliya knew, she might be the last living thing on board the USS *Evelyn-Tew*.

Apart from *them*.

Unarmed and alone, she worked her way down from the accommodation deck to the laboratory levels. Slipping into an open doorway, she closed it behind her, and hid in the shadows as someone or something passed by outside. She heard heavy breathing, gentle hissing, and the fear pressed in deep. Remaining there longer than was really necessary, she again found herself questioning her orders.

Look at what they are! See what they can do!

One of the creatures had found its way onto the accommodation deck and caused chaos. Liliya heard the assault—the startled shouts, the beast's heavy hiss, gunfire, and screams—and then she saw the results of that attack, stepping around the wet, open things that had once been people. There were at least seven of them, although the bodies beneath one bunk were so tattered it was difficult to discern how many had died there. She had probably known their names.

I disabled the failsafe, I let them out, and now—

But it was not her place to question her orders, nor to doubt. She was there for a reason. She had never once let Wordsworth down, and now was not the time to start.

It was strange, walking through the laboratory ship when it was all but abandoned. Usually busy, the quiet corridors echoed with distant sounds, and the *Evelyn-Tew* boomed and groaned as its acceleration continued. Liliya knew where the ship was heading. In any red-level emergency the automated response was to plunge into the closest sun. Burn everything.

There could be no risk of escape.

Except she had changed everything. In her mind, a countdown had already begun.

Reaching the junction of three corridors, she looked the way she needed to go and didn't want to go there at all. The lighting systems in the staircase were flickering and failing. It could have been a result of the ship's emergency procedures, or maybe there had been damage down there due to someone's interactions with the escaped Xenomorphs. Hesitating only briefly, Liliya started down the first staircase that led to the lower decks.

I should have done it sooner, she thought. She'd been aboard the research ship for almost a hundred days, and in that time she had settled in as part of the crew, blending into the background, performing her tasks well but not too well, being friendly but not making friends. The longer she stayed, the less people noticed her. It was invisibility she had been seeking.

Yet if she'd fulfilled her mission sooner, she would have been away from the *Evelyn-Tew* by now, and perhaps everything would not have gone so wrong. The shouting, the shooting, the screaming might never have happened. The crew might have escaped.

Perhaps.

But with the Xenomorphs chaos was inevitable. Whenever samples were obtained, whether live specimens, eggs, or embryos, everything eventually went bad. They weren't meant to be contained and studied, and these creatures reared from samples captured on LV-178 were destined to go the same way. Order was not in their nature—they were creatures of violence and blood. The universe was a jagged place wherever they were found, with cruel, sharp edges.

On the next level the lights flickered again, luring her on. A dull glass shape winked from the wall. A communications point. She brushed her hand across the screen and a schematic of the ship appeared. STATUS glowed softly. Liliya touched the light and watched it fade out. In its place, a warning appeared.

She held her breath as she read it again, even though she didn't need to. Her memory was photographic, her recall total. That was why Wordsworth had chosen her above all others for this task. Different people were on alternate missions across this part of the Human Sphere, but he'd told her that this was the one that mattered most. This was important. What she took from the *Evelyn-Tew* might mean the difference between the Founders' triumph and their demise as a dark, forgotten footnote of history.

According to the warning, she had even less time than she'd feared. The ship had been set on an accelerated suicide trajectory, due to impact the star Alpha Centurai in under an hour.

Liliya closed her eyes and breathed deeply.

They're right, she thought. *These creatures should not be allowed to—*

A crackling sound echoed in from the distance, like a velcro flap slowly being opened. It was followed by a shout, the words unclear. Shooting, then screaming.

Liliya hurried to the head of the next staircase and started down. Her descent was cautious, senses alert for movement or sound that might mean danger. She only hoped she could still find what she had come for. Ironically, with the Xenomorphs escaped and rampaging, the laboratories where they had been kept might be the safest place on the ship.

The staircase ended and she emerged into a lobby area with several corridors leading away. Something bad had happened here. A body sat propped against the far wall, one arm bent unnaturally and blood spattered around it. A weapon lay close by. A grille in the floor had been smashed upward, and darkness from the space below seemed to flood out into the corridor.

Liliya moved quickly away from the scene, a story she would never know. Good or not, she hoped the person had died quickly.

She was now on the laboratory deck, and through the next set of doors she came to the first security point. Any hope that the doors had been smashed, or even left open, were instantly dashed—but she had been prepared for this. As she took the small tool kit from her pocket, a dull thud pounded through her feet, followed by a booming sound from somewhere far away.

That was an explosion. She blinked and tilted her head, listening hard. If something cataclysmic had happened, and the ship started to break up, she'd have to get to the docking hangar or an escape pod, and her purpose for coming here would be lost.

The floor vibrated a little, but nothing else changed. The ship's beating heart persisted as the engines continued to cycle up.

Whatever had caused the explosion was distant, and no business of hers.

At least not yet.

Pulling out a decoder, she got to work on the locking mechanisms. While the device worked at the combination, she wielded a set of fine calipers and a filament knife, and started turning over the first of the deadlock's tumblers. The mixture of electronic locks and an old-fashioned deadbolt system should have been enough to keep out intruders, but Liliya was trained. And she was special.

Less than a minute later the doors slid open and she was inside the main laboratory compartment. This entire central section was enclosed within a giant, reinforced, pod-like structure—a hull within a hull, its systems and conduits self-contained, designed to prevent whatever was kept inside from escaping. Yet she had left a trail of faulty failsafes, and the Xenomorphs had found a way out.

Passing the first of the airlocks leading into Lab 3, she glanced through thick diamond-glass at the interior. The labs were in disarray, with several bloodied and torn bodies slumped in one far corner, and a wall blasted open at the far end.

Lab 2 was filled with smoke. She could see little inside other than a few smeared handprints on the window's interior.

Between Lab 2 and her destination, Lab 1, lay the main storage sphere, its walls thicker and stronger even than the ship's outer hull. She hadn't dared tamper with anything here. Death sat inside and, ironically, the source of terrible life.

The queen.

Liliya had only laid eyes on her once, and the memory provided a palette of nightmares she should never have been able to dream. Even being this close set her skin crawling, her blood cooling.

She hurried past the blank, heavy doorway, and sensed an awful awareness beyond.

Does she know what's happening? Will she try to break free, rip away from her birthing sac?

Liliya berated herself. She had to focus, and the queen wasn't her aim.

Lab 1 was still secure, and she again had to use her lock-picking skills. As the door whispered open she pressed back against the wall, listening for the screech, waiting for the violence. But all was quiet.

She slipped inside and got to work.

It took her less than ten minutes to access the mainframe, bypass a series of defense protocols, and commence download of all the information she sought. Three minutes later, the records were scorched from every hard disc, data cloud, and quantum storage fold on the ship and beyond. Liliya became the sole bearer of every scrap of research the *Evelyn-Tew* had carried.

The scientists on board had come a long way. In the past few years they had learned more about the Xenomorphs than had been discovered over several centuries prior—and now she had stolen it all.

It was a heavy weight, but she bore it for Wordsworth... and everyone else. Now her most important mission was one of survival.

Her plan had been to take one of the ships from the docking bays. There were several shuttlecraft there, as well as a decommissioned Colonial Marines dreadnought-class vessel ostensibly acquired for protection. But some of the lower decks were burning, and as she approached the docking bay she heard shooting, screaming, and the unmistakable screech of a Xenomorph.

So she decided to take her chances with an escape pod.

Over a mile long and half a mile wide, the USS *Evelyn-Tew*

was a decommissioned Colonial Marines destroyer built to carry many more people than now crewed her. Bloody evidence showed that the Xenomorphs had depleted the science crew, yet she could only assume that others had escaped. She hoped at least one secure escape pod remained behind for her to use.

Two hundred yards and one level from the nearest lifeboat bay, she heard them. Whispering. Scratching. Brushing along the corridor wall ahead of her, around the corner she was approaching. When the overhead lighting flickered she saw them, too, dancing shadows flitting and shaking as different lights powered on and off.

Liliya paused and froze, becoming as motionless as possible. Ten steps behind her lay a door, but there was no guarantee it would be open. Fifty steps further back was a bulkhead door. If she turned and ran she might make it—or she might not. Even if she did, there was no guarantee that she'd be able to close the door before it, or they, took her down from behind.

Blinking rapidly, she tried to decide her next move, and the shadows burst around the corner.

"I told you I heard someone!" the man said. There was a woman with him. He carried an old model of pulse rifle, and she was holding a carving knife in each hand. They both looked terrified.

"You're from the canteen," the woman said. "Liliya, right?"

"Right. You?"

"I'm Kath Roberts. Engineer. This is Dearing." She didn't offer his profession, and Liliya didn't care. It was clear that neither of them knew how to use the weapons they were carrying, and the need in their eyes was dreadful. The need to be helped, and led.

Liliya couldn't give them that, but they could all work together, and maybe that way they'd survive.

Do nothing to compromise the mission. The voice in her head was Wordsworth's, the words her own, speaking what she knew was the truth. *They'll be a danger to your task. They'll want rescue, and not what* you *want. Not to disappear.*

"I have to help them," she said softly, and she saw Dearing's frown as he heard her. Maybe he thought she was mad.

"You seen any of those things?" Roberts asked.

"One. I hid away."

"It didn't smell you out?" Dearing asked.

Liliya shrugged. "That's what they do?"

"Yeah. We think." He glanced aside, then back the way they'd come. "If you were heading for the lifeboats, you're too late."

"They've all gone?"

"From Dock C, yeah. Dock A was destroyed in an explosion, and B is venting atmosphere, and D is almost half a mile away toward the stern. I don't think…" He trailed off.

"You know we're on a suicide trajectory, right?" Liliya asked.

"Suicide?" Roberts' eyes went wide, her face turning pale.

"The ship's going to crash into the sun," she said, then added, "Come on. There's one chance."

"What chance?" Dearing asked, but Liliya didn't say. Partly because she didn't trust him or Roberts, and her knowledge was power. But also because she didn't know how great their chance might be.

There were emergency escape pods in a bay beneath the officers' quarters. They were each built for one person. She had no idea how many might be left.

There was a dead woman in the stairwell.

She was spread down the stairs. Her uniform identified her as a ship's officer, flight deck crew, but there was little else to distinguish her from the other dead people Liliya had seen. Torn flesh, ripped clothing, splintered bones—in death, at least, the Xenomorphs made everyone equal.

I caused that.

She shoved the thought aside.

Stepping gingerly past the mess, she tried to place her feet on dry parts of the stairs. There weren't many. The woman had been caught making her way down toward the escape pods, and there was no saying whether the creature that had killed her had continued down, or come up from beneath.

"Step carefully," she whispered back at Roberts and Dearing. "Don't slip." There was plenty to slip on. But they made their way down to the landing and around to the next flight, and then they were in a gently lit lobby area, with several comfortable seats and a drinks machine in one corner. The lighting was low-level faux daylight, expensive to maintain and generally reserved for the plusher parts of ships. It was obvious that they were in the officers' section.

Roberts waited to be told what to do. Dearing shrugged, holding the pulse rifle in one hand.

"Which way?" he asked.

Liliya recalled the ship's layout and zeroed in on the escape-pod bay. It was another level down, but close. She turned away for a second, listening, stretching her senses, trying to make out whether danger was close. Life support hummed. Distant thumps shivered, seemingly gentler down here, as the ship's drive continued their acceleration toward the star. No more screams, no more gunfire or hissing creatures. That was no comfort.

It might mean that everyone else was dead.

"Come on," she said. "We don't have much time."

Leave them, Wordsworth's voice said. *The mission is all.*

Yet saving these two people might mean rescuing some small facet of her soul.

They followed her down another level. Access doors to the escape-pod bay were stuck open, the electronic lock beside them a smoking mess. Someone had already blasted their way through.

"Oh, no," Dearing said.

"They might not all have gone," she said, but already she was thinking ahead. Calculating time and trajectory, supplies, and life-support potentials. Balancing saving the two people with her against the successful completion of her mission. *I've come so far...* she thought. She couldn't let herself down now.

They reached a circular room with seven round doors, each leading directly into a pod dock. Access was designed to be quick and easy in an emergency.

"Shit," Roberts whispered.

"Only one left!" Dearing said, and Liliya wondered whether he knew what that meant. She turned around. He was already stepping back from them, lifting the gun, not quite aiming it at her but ready to swing it up at a moment's notice.

"You don't need that," she said, staring him in the eye. He paused, just for a moment. Then he backed away three more steps until he was pressed against the soft bulkhead beside the access to the remaining escape pod. Here in the officers' compartment, they even dressed the walls of the emergency bay.

The ship's engines pulsed again through Liliya's feet, and she wondered if the others sensed it as well. Probably not. There was a lot she could perceive that would escape them. Dearing's increased heartbeat, the dribble of sweat at his temple, and the whitening of his knuckles around the pulse rifle's trigger.

"Dearing…" she said.

"They're only designed for one person," he said. He looked back and forth between Liliya and Roberts, as if trying to decide who might come at him first.

"There are a dozen other ships in this system at any one time," Roberts said. "We'll be picked up in a matter of days. It'll be cozy, but all three of us can get in there."

Yet that's not what I want, Liliya thought. *I don't want to be picked up—not by anyone but the Founders.* She should have known better than to bring them along.

Dearing lifted the rifle.

She was fast, but probably not fast enough.

"Roberts is right," Liliya said. "It'll be tight, the launch will be rough, but three of us can last in there for days. You think they wouldn't give the officers enough food and water? You think they don't consider a bit of comfort?"

Dearing glanced to the side and touched a panel on the wall. His eyes were wide with the excitement of imminent escape.

"You can't leave us here to die!" Roberts said.

"There are more lifeboats aft," he said.

"That's half a mile away!" she shouted.

"Quiet," Liliya said firmly, but it had already gone too far. There was a dynamic here that she hadn't perceived, and Roberts' next statement exposed it all.

"Don't I mean anything to you?" she asked.

Liliya took a step forward as Dearing's face dropped. He saw her, and drifted the gun barrel in her direction.

She heard the scattering, scampering sound as one of the things came at them. It had been following their trail, perhaps homing in on the sound of their voices. She didn't think Dearing had heard it yet. She had moments to react, and in that time everything rushed in at her.

The risks she had taken to be posted on the Evelyn-Tew, *the favors that had been called in, the machinations behind the scenes by Wordsworth and the other Founders.*

The responsibility she bore, the importance of the information she now carried on her person.

The disaster and deaths she had caused by effectively releasing the creatures.

The implications if she didn't succeed.

Every part of her fought against what she did next. But her commitment to Wordsworth was greater than her own strength, instinct, or the moral code she had developed through her life. His dedication to his cause was absolute.

Liliya stepped behind Roberts, grabbed her beneath the

arms, and shoved her at Dearing.

The pulse rifle boomed. The woman jerked once, hard, and slammed back against her. Liliya kept her footing, threw Roberts again, and followed. Dearing staggered back against the wall with the bloodied, dying woman splayed against him. As she slid to the floor, one hand grasping at his clothing and leaving a bloody trail across his chest, he freed the rifle from between them and lifted it at Liliya.

She slapped it aside. Something broke in her hand, and the rifle clattered to the floor, sliding across the bay and coming to rest beside the door through which they entered.

A shadow danced beyond, hard limbs and dark hisses.

"What the fuck?" Dearing shouted. He wasn't looking at Liliya's face. His eyes were wide, staring at her torso, and as she glanced down the pain signals hit her at last.

She cried out, more in desperation than agony.

It couldn't end like this.

It wasn't right. It wasn't fair!

Pressing a hand to her wound did nothing to prevent the white fluid from spewing across the floor.

"Jesus Christ!" Dearing said.

Liliya took advantage of his confusion. She dragged him aside with her free hand, exerting all her strength. He tripped over the body of his lover and sprawled on the floor, just as a shape filled the doorway.

She didn't look. She knew she didn't have time, and if she was to survive she had to execute every movement, every moment, with complete efficiency. She stepped over the dead woman's leg, pressed the panel on the wall, waited an agonizing eternity as the escape-pod hatch spiraled open, grasped at its edges and—

Dearing screamed.

She looked—she *had* to look—and saw the Xenomorph standing astride the fallen man, one limb piercing his shoulder, the other pressing down on the small of his back. It crouched low, curved head sloping down at its struggling prey, and as he screamed again its teeth lashed out and smashed his skull apart.

Liliya hauled herself into the pod and slammed the execute button on the wall beside the door. The hatch slammed shut. Something struck the other side, hard, and then a roar shattered her hearing and became everything as the escape pod's mooring bolts blasted loose and its propellant ignited.

She should have been strapped into the single seat, protected against the immense acceleration. Smashed back against the closed hatch, Liliya let herself give in to the white-hot pain at last.

As unconsciousness fell, she welcomed the release into blessed darkness.

Between blinks Liliya snapped awake and reality rushed in. A low whine issued from her, an uncomfortable moan with every breath. Pain brought her back. She was alone, and Roberts and Dearing were dead.

"No," she said.

She had caused their deaths, even if she hadn't pulled the trigger on Roberts or smashed Dearing's skull apart with her own teeth.

"No!" She shouted this time, voice deadened by the small pod's soft interior, and she knew that she was right. There was nothing she could have done.

Not if her mission was to survive.

The escape pod shook for a few more seconds before its thrusters cut out. Weightless, Liliya shoved herself slightly away from the hatch and held onto the seat, swinging herself around, pulling herself down, fixing the strap around her waist and the restraint over her shoulders. Her blood misted the air and formed into droplets, milk-like bubbles that drifted in the disturbed atmosphere.

Her stomach hurt, but what hurt more was the idea that it all might have been for nothing. Once secured in the seat she settled her frantic thoughts, running a calming program that leveled the peaks and troughs of her human personality. It was a process she disliked intensely—Liliya was over fifty years old, and thought of herself as human. Initiating support protocols pulled her out of that pleasant fantasy. Yet it was a necessary evil so that she could assess damage— both to herself and, more importantly, the information she had stolen.

Launching internal diagnostics, she quickly focused attention on the area of her wound and the associated components. It took less than a second to reassure herself that her internal hard disc was undamaged. A fragment of bone had been blasted from Roberts' ribs by the pulse rifle charge. It had entered her stomach and passed out through her side, missing vital internal systems and barely skimming the porcelain surround that protected her hard disc.

Though breathing wasn't essential, Liliya still gasped a sigh of relief.

Everything was on there. Not only what Wordsworth had asked for, but everything for which the *Evelyn-Tew* had been designed. All that research. All those hours, days and years of analysis, experimentation, trial and error... and the errors had almost ended it all.

The Company had come far. Their research into the Xenomorph samples from LV-178 had advanced further than anyone could have imagined, or hoped for. Though the strange species was still an enigma, the information now contained in Liliya's hard disc shed more light than anything that humans had ever discovered before.

Soon, the *Evelyn-Tew* would crash into Alpha Centurai. If they weren't already dead, everyone on board who still retained an inkling of the research would be destroyed.

Liliya had already confirmed that in their desperation to escape, anyone who might survive in the jettisoned escape pods had not had a chance to take any of the precious research with them. She possessed the last known copy, and she was taking it to Wordsworth.

Confident now that treating her wound could come later, she examined the escape pod's computer and assessed its limited flight capabilities. In such a catastrophic situation it was pre-programmed to take her to the nearest planet, moon, or asteroid, but she initiated a manual override. There was still seventy-three percent of an engine burn left, and she estimated that it could get her up to point-oh-four light speed. That was enough. By the time any rescue ships arrived, she would be gone from their scanners. Lost to the void.

She composed a short, coded message for the Founders, then set it broadcasting on a twenty-hourly loop.

When she blinked she saw Roberts blasted back against her, Dearing's head taken apart by the beast. The human part of her—the strongest part, and the side she had been promoting for as long as she could remember—hated what she had done. However human she felt, though, she knew that she had been built to last a long, long while.

As long as was necessary.

After repairing the damage in her stomach and sealing the wound, Liliya initiated the burn, then settled down to pass some time.

1

JOHNNY MAINS

Southgate Station 12, Outer Rim research facility
March 2692 AD

Lieutenant Johnny Mains never got used to seeing them close-up. Alive or dead, a Yautja was a weird-looking creature. Ostensibly humanoid, yet there was so much about them that was so inhuman that traditional classification systems just didn't seem adequate.

Freaky bastard, he thought. That described it well enough.

"L-T," Cotronis said. The corporal stood beside him, close enough for their shoulders to touch. She was still breathing hard. He saw the splash of blood across her bald head. Human blood. He never really got used to seeing that, either.

Mains raised an eyebrow, but he could see the truth in her eyes.

"Willis didn't make it," she said. She blinked quickly, sweat running into her eyes and tears running out.

"Probably a good thing," he said softly. "Messed up like that, Brian wouldn't have wanted to go on."

"You can't say that," Cotronis said. In private, with only other VoidLarks in earshot, none of them used formal military speak, and no one pulled rank. They'd been out here together too long to require false monikers to display deep respect.

"I can," Mains said. "I've known him for a long time. Longer even than you."

"And Lizzie?"

He'd seen Private Lizzie Reynolds go down fighting when she'd taken on the first of the two Yautja. She'd been protecting a man and two young kids, and she'd got a few good shots in with her nano-rifle before the alien took her head.

"She died well," Mains said. "She died fighting."

"So what now?"

Mains sighed, then turned away from the dead Yautja. They'd have to put it on ice and send it back with what was left of the station's crew. The Company rarely got its hands on such a complete specimen, and there was still so little known about this enigmatic species. He couldn't help admiring their martial abilities. He couldn't help hating them, either. Willis and Reynolds weren't the first troops he'd lost to them, but they were the first of the VoidLarks to be killed in action.

"Let's do a full sweep of the station," he said. "Take Faulkner and Lieder and make a few circuits outside, secure a perimeter. I'll get Snowdon and McVicar to tie down the base's interior."

"Right." Cotronis sounded uncertain, even fragile.

"Sara?" Mains said.

She looked at him sidelong.

"You fought well. We all did. We lost two, we took down two. You know that's a good result against these bastards."

"I didn't realize we were keeping score."

He reached out and grasped her upper arm, squeezing through the combat suit. She smiled. Then Cotronis left to muster the troops, leaving Mains standing beside the Yautja's corpse.

Its left leg flickered in and out of focus. The third blast from his laser rifle had severed its hand at the wrist, and the control panel it wore on its forearm was sparking and spitting. He knew well enough to disable its weapons systems—Snowdon, more knowledgeable than any of them in Yautja tech, had done that—but the dead alien's stealth field was still cycling, as if to take it away from death.

Mains shoved it with his boot and its head lolled, tusks clacking against the floor.

The 5th Excursionists, nicknamed the VoidLarks by Mains on their first day out from an Outer Rim drophole, had been patrolling space beyond the Outer Rim for a little over three standard years. In that time they had only interacted with other people on three occasions. This was the third, and the most traumatic.

The death toll among Southgate Station 12's scientists and support staff was still being ascertained, but initial reports suggested the pair of Yautja had stalked, hunted, and killed at least seventeen in their two days on the ground. Ten of those were indies, mercenaries hired by the station commander to provide protection. Mains knew there were more bodies yet to be found. They hadn't yet discovered either of the Yautja's nests.

When they did, there would be trophies.

It could have been so many more. The research station maintained a permanent population of over a hundred, and almost eighty people were gathered in the canteen, being looked after by the commander and the remaining few indies. Shocked, traumatized, still not really understanding what had happened, or why, they were preparing to be sent back deeper into the Human Sphere. Where, Mains didn't know, nor did he care. Away from here was all that mattered. This place was tainted now, and though it wasn't like Weyland-Yutani to waste anything, Southgate Station 12 would likely remain unoccupied for a good while.

Mains checked his combat suit's status. There was no damage. Laser charge on his sidearm was low. His com-rifle ammo and charge were at eighty percent, and his shotgun was a reassuring weight on his back. It was a fully restored antique, but it had saved his skin ten years before on Addison Prime when his unit was sent in against a rogue Marines outfit. He'd been a corporal then, and it had been his first firefight against other trained soldiers. He'd held his own, and when his suit's CSU went down and all his weapons went offline, it was the shotgun that had saved his life.

"L-T?" The voice buzzed from the comm implant in his ear.

"Yeah, Snowdon."

"Sir, the base commander wants to talk to you. He's demanding to know what happens next. Sir."

Mains smiled. He could hear the nervous tension and humor in Snowdon's voice. She was a good fighter and an experienced soldier, but she didn't take any shit. Especially from people they'd just lost two friends fighting to protect.

"Tell him what happens next is, he sucks my dick."

Snowdon snorted laughter. "So, shut down the base?"

"Yeah, that'll do. Tell him to commence shutdown. Whatever it is they do here, it needs to be closed up ready for them to leave, say, a day from now."

"Yes, Sir. So we'll be leaving soon after that?"

Mains turned away from the Yautja corpse, the blast holes in the walls, the stark laser scars across the ceiling, and looked around. It was a large dormitory, set up for a single family with sleeping area, a dining compartment, and a recreation corner with holo-stage gaming consoles that rivaled some of the hardware they had on the ship, complete with comfortable seating.

The atmosphere controls leveled the temperature comfortably, and low-level lighting made it feel almost like home. Someone else's home, sure, but that was good enough.

The dormitory was almost as big as the whole rec room on their ship, the *Ochse*, and the rest of the base was just as expansive, with freshly grown food from a green dome and a leisure complex that included pool and gym. He could see the allure of staying here for a while. He could feel it, and he hated that. Mains's concentration was already slipping, his alertness relaxing, and the temptation to slip into some undefined period of rest and relaxation was strong.

"You know we will," he said to Snowdon. "This is an unusual attack, and I want to get back on-station as quickly as possible. That Yautja habitat might be gearing up for something more. Something bigger."

"They've never launched anything bigger than this," Snowdon said. She lowered her voice. He could hear conversation in the background, the scared survivors. "Come on, L-T. A day here after the civvies have fucked off, swimming and eating and relaxing."

"You'd like that, wouldn't you, Snowdon? Seeing me skinny-dipping."

"You know it, L-T."

"Tell the Commander to stay there. I'm coming down to speak to him. You and McVicar tie down the rest of the base, post lookout drones, make sure we're safe and sound."

"Yes, Sir! Right away, Sir!"

"And if you're there when I arrive, I'll beat the shit out of you."

"You and whose army? Sir."

Mains grinned. He liked Snowdon. He liked all of his VoidLarks—they were a family, friends, and that was why they were so good at what they did. Few other people could remain so isolated from human contact for such long periods of time. All Excursionists were the same, but Mains naturally thought the 5th, his VoidLarks, were the best.

The impact of losing two of their family had yet to truly hit home.

"You're not going to escort us?"

"Not unless there's a good reason," Mains said.

"Good reason? How about twenty-three bodies? Is that good enough reason?"

Mains glanced around the canteen at the stunned survivors. Men and women, there were tears and blank stares, shivering people and those who still could not believe. There were also several children, some of them huddled into their parents, a couple sitting side by side, bereft. Maybe they were the orphans. Mains felt bad for all of them.

A few indies had also survived, weaponless now, shorn of any semblance of control. They weren't to blame for the massacre, but Mains still couldn't bring himself to exchange words with them. If they'd been better trained and equipped, and more inclined to prepare for what might hit them this far adrift on the Outer Rim, perhaps they would have put up a more effective defense. Perhaps. But the past was done with.

"You think we should take this somewhere else, Commander Niveau?"

Niveau glared at him, but all his anger and bluster was hiding his own terror. He was in charge of this research base. He could never have anticipated the horror that had come to visit.

"But… it's seventy days to the drophole—at least—and our orbit's taking us further away all the time."

"Good reason to start soon, then," Mains said, keeping his tone even. "Please? Your office? Your people need to rest, eat, get strong for the journey. We can discuss everything else in private."

"For Christ's sake!" Niveau shouted. He was shaking, ghostly pale rather than flushed with anger. "You're supposed to be here to—"

Mains turned his back on the commander and faced the

survivors spread around the canteen, aware that most of them were hanging on his every word. He and his unit had arrived here to save them, after all, and now they were waiting to see what happened next.

Niveau fell silent, and Mains heard the creak of a plastic chair as he slumped down.

"Six hours," he said. "That's how long you've got. In that time you need to put this facility into hibernation. Gather any data and information you need to take back with you. Pack your personal gear. Flight crew, pre-flight checks on your *Apollo* transport commence in thirty minutes." He nodded at the indies. "You gather the dead. Seal them all in coffin suits, put them in the *Apollo*'s hold, show them the respect you'd expect for one of your own. My people will isolate and secure the Yautja corpses. They'll be going back with you."

There was a flicker of unease at this last statement, but Mains could see the trust the scientists and their crew held for him. That was good, that was right—but to get that, he'd had to turn his back on their authority figure and effectively usurp him.

Before sending them on their way, he had to put that right.

I never signed up to be a politician, he thought, and he turned back to Commander Niveau.

"Your office?" Mains asked. It wasn't really a question.

It was a sparse, functional space, with no luxurious trappings. A holo screen framed one wall, and data danced and jumped across it as they entered. Mains glanced at it, but it made no sense to him. Niveau viewed the screen for a moment, then muttered a command and shut it down. He sat in a chair behind his small desk and turned to Mains.

"That display back there—"

"Brian Willis was thirty-seven years old," Mains said. "He was a private, passed over for promotion several times in the regular Colonial Marines because of a supposed rebellious attitude. He was in the 17th Spaceborne when I recruited him. The unit's nickname is the BloodDoves, and Willis never really fit in. He wasn't rebellious, he was curious. He didn't like... order. Orders were fine, but he wanted to look beyond the next posting to some mining habitat or asteroid research station.

"He wanted more, so he came with me. Left behind a wife who didn't really understand his wanderlust. She's never even left Earth, so I guess you can figure how different they are." Mains knew that everyone out here was different. Working close to or beyond the Outer Rim, at the furthest extremes of the ever-expanding Human Sphere of influence in this small corner of the galaxy. It took a certain kind of outlook.

"He died trying to lead a Yautja from a room where a couple of the indies were protecting one of your scientists and her family. If the Yautja had broken in and clocked the weapons, it would have killed them all. Probably quickly, because in the heat of the hunt they usually kill their prey as efficiently as possible. But we know that *some* of them can be sadistic.

"It might have been slow."

"You've made your point," Niveau said.

"Not yet. Not until I tell you about Lizzie Reynolds. Young kid, really, this was her first posting beyond the Sol system.

Spent her first few years wearing a Marines beret on board Charon Station. It was General Bassett himself who saw the potential in her. She was a loner who worked well with a close unit. Sounds like a contradiction, but it really wasn't. Lizzie wanted to see further, and go as far as she could, and she never once told me that she wanted to go home. Ever. Far as Lizzie was concerned, we could have patrolled the Outer Rim forever.

"We provide a service, Niveau. Lizzie knew that, and she died doing it."

Niveau nodded slowly, and his eyes were wet. He was still shaking. Chances were, he'd continue shaking until he showered, ate, stripped, and was settled into his cryo- pod for the ten-week journey to the drophole.

He's lost people, too, Mains reminded himself. *A lot more than me.*

"I'm sorry," Niveau said. "I'm sorry for your dead."

"Yeah… and I'm sorry for yours."

Niveau stared at him for some time, as if readying to say something else. Then he pulled a control pad across the desk, brushed its surface, and swiveled to look at the display rising on the holo frame.

"Facility status," he said. "My people are working quickly. Look, those blue areas have already been shut down into hibernation mode."

Mains sat down in a padded chair, sinking into the cushion. What he wouldn't give for a drink right now. But an urgency was growing in him, a need to get moving. He wanted to speak to his people again, and soon. Compare notes and thoughts.

And more than anything, he was keen to send a message back to Excursionist HQ and get their take on things.

The VoidLarks had been surveilling a Yautja habitat beyond the Outer Rim for a little more than a year. It was a huge artificial vessel, several miles long, orbiting a star in one of the countless unexplored and uncharted systems beyond the Human Sphere. He was as certain as he could be that the Yautja who attacked this facility had not come from there.

"It's good that your people are efficient," Mains said. "They need to keep busy. There'll be plenty of time to think about things later, and mourn the dead. But for now, I want you all away from here."

"I've been here seven years," Niveau said. "We're doing important work. Genetics, medicine, using bacteria mined from just under the surface of the asteroid. This is one of only five places we know of where it exists. But… I never thought anything like this could happen. Never."

"It's space. Nothing's ever safe. If it's not something you know that kills you, it'll be something you don't."

"Nice outlook," Niveau said.

Mains shrugged.

"So why can't you escort us?" Niveau asked. His voice was low, quivering slightly. The fear was real, the void of space suddenly deeper and darker to him than before. He'd become too settled here, in this place where comforts distracted from the promise of the uncaring, infinite vacuum.

"Because we're doing something important, too," Mains said. He gestured at the blank holo frame. "You'll understand that. You know what Excursionists do?"

"Of course. Patrol the Outer Rim. Escort Titan ships as they move beyond the Sphere and build new dropholes."

"That's the easy part of it, yeah, but expansion isn't easy. For the past year, maybe a bit more, my VoidLarks have been keeping an eye on a big Yautja habitat that's been drifting past this sector, hanging around a star system several light years beyond the Sphere. It's pretty inactive, seemingly without purpose, and it's never seemed much of a threat. Nevertheless, that's our job. We're not just an escort service for Titan ships. We're the sharp edge of defense for the human influence in the galaxy. Out there beyond the reach of human space exploration, making sure things are safe, trying to change things if they're not."

"These Yautja came from there?"

"I don't think so. We'd have logged their ships leaving."

"But you still came."

"Your emergency call was passed through to us by another unit. You were lucky we were drifting back for a yearly resupply run, and we were closest to you. Otherwise…" Mains raised a hand and shrugged.

"They'd have killed us all," Niveau said.

"Probably not. There's evidence that if they attack a large population, they take captives."

"What for?"

Mains stood, groaning when his knees clicked. He'd been in space for too long, and running on zero grav for long periods in the *Ochse* to cut down on telltale power trails. "Beats me. Nothing good, you can bet on that."

"So you've got to get back to your post. Watching the habitat."

"Especially after this."

Niveau nodded. He didn't like it, but he understood, and Mains respected him for that.

"It'll be fine. Seventy days to the drophole in your *Apollo*, and your indies can stay awake to keep track of things. Oh, and what I just told you about the Yautja habitat we're watching? That's classified."

"Of course." Niveau stood and extended his hand. They shook. "Thanks."

"It's what we're here for." But Willis wasn't there any more. Neither was Reynolds. Mains saw their faces, Willis's stern smile that always seemed to hide something, Reynold's enthusiasm. For the first time since leading the VoidLarks out from the Excursionist base at Tyszka's Star, he would have to officiate at a funeral.

As he left the office, his comm implant chimed.

"L-T?" It was Faulkner, the signal coming from back on the *Ochse*.

"Yeah."

"I've picked up a sub-space signal from the 13th Excursionists. They're in full contact with Yautja on a deserted asteroid station, seventeen light years away along the Rim."

"The SpaceSurfers," Mains said.

"Yeah, Golden's unit. Shall I respond?"

Mains closed the door behind him and stood in the silent corridor. It was quiet, peaceful, the air treated and scented for comfort, and far, far away, old friends of his might be dying. He felt like he shouldn't be here.

"Acknowledge the signal, but we can't help."

"We need to get back on station," Faulkner said.

"Open channel," Mains said, and their communication was opened up to all VoidLarks.

It was time to move out.

Johnny Mains always thought that a deep space funeral was a strangely beautiful sight. An hour after lifting off from Southgate Station 12, he stood before his remaining crew and prepared to send two friends into the void.

Neither Willis nor Reynolds had any religious views, so the committal was short and sweet. A few words about each of them, some observations about their personalities and the brave way they'd both died, and an anecdote for each that brought a smile to grim faces. Then they all turned to watch the holo frame in their rec room, and Mains muttered his command to their ship's computer.

"Frodo, vent the bay."

A gentle hiss was all they heard, and then Reynolds and Willis were spat across their view of the void, both of them tumbling slowly from where the atmosphere had vented from the *Ochse*'s hold. It appeared that they traveled together, although it was inevitable that even a slight difference in trajectory would move them apart over time.

It was time that, for Mains, made this sight so enigmatic, even graceful. Gone from the world of the living, the two bodies now began their eternal journey through space. At every such funeral he had ever witnessed, it was always ensured that the coffin suits were fired away from Earth. Every moment of their journey was toward somewhere new and unknown, and whether or not they or their witnesses held any beliefs about soul, gods, or afterlife, this was a profound concept.

The dead had lost the ability to comprehend, but they could still commit to their avowed mission, and the purpose of any man or woman who decided to make their lives in the heavens—to explore, travel, and be a part of whatever else was out there.

"I always wonder if they'll be found," Cotronis said. Like everyone, she still wore her combat suit, and she had refused to wash the splash of Reynolds' blood from her bald scalp—not until after the funeral.

"Shouldn't be found," McVicar said. A big man, sometimes harsh, a man of few words, Mains knew that he and Reynolds had enjoyed a gentle romance. Uncomplicated companionship, casual sex. An Excursionist rarely displayed deeper feelings, on the surface at least, because of the proximity of their existence with the others. But who knew what hid beneath the surface?

"No, I mean... later." Cotronis brushed her hand over her stubbly scalp, pausing when she encountered the flaking blood. "Much later. A million years from now. Ten million. Maybe a billion years from now, when humans are dust, they'll still be tumbling through space. Way beyond whatever extremes the Human Sphere might have reached before we wiped ourselves out, or something we found wiped us out."

"Fucking hell, cheery bastard today aren't we, Corp?" Faulkner said. He was a short skinny guy, brusque, but with a sharp mind. He was a private, but Mains sometimes called him their resident scientist. Always good to have someone like him in a unit like this.

"It is cheery, though," Cotronis said. "That's how I want to go. Not blown up or burnt to death or eaten by who knows what? Out there, like that. Drifting away."

They all watched the screen. Mains liked the banter between his crew. But now the rec room felt horribly empty, and much bigger than before. Eight were now six, and the deaths would leave a hole that might never be filled.

"Until your ugly corpse gets in the way of a warping Titan ship and takes out five hundred people," Lieder said, and they all chuckled softly. Even McVicar. Lieder was ever the comedian, and she usually knew just when to drop a funny. Now, she'd defused the maudlin tension Mains felt building, and one he knew would return again and again in the foreseeable future. They'd all been Marines for a while, some of them a very long time. Most of them had lost friends before, but that never, ever made it easy to accept.

Lieder glanced back and offered him a sad smile. Mains nodded.

A gentle romance, he thought. He'd even whispered that to Lieder once, lying in her bed, the two of them still sticky with sweat and breathing hard. She'd laughed and said, *Didn't feel that gentle to me.*

"Let's get to it," he said. They were still watching the holo frame, even though the slowly tumbling coffin suits had shrunk to specks, and then disappeared completely. "Lieder, run the programs, set our course and let me know how long it'll be. Snowdon, full systems check on the *Ochse*. I hate landing her, shakes things up. Unshake anything that needs doing."

Lieder and Snowdon nodded, and Faulkner and Cotronis left the rec rooms to take up their stations.

"Suppose you want me to cook?" McVicar asked.

"Damn right. I'm hungry as hell."

The big man nodded. "I'll rustle up something. We need a treat."

The *Ochse* was one of the fastest ships in the Colonial Marines' arsenal. Specially developed for the Excursionist regiments, the Arrow-class assault and reconnaissance vessel was a product of centuries of spacecraft technological advancement, FTL-drive research, and sheer dogged persistence.

The breakthrough to faster-than-light travel had come hundreds of years before. Breaking through into FTL travel had been akin to the time when humans first left the surface of their planet, in that the technologies required were unique, dangerous, and slow to develop.

Some of the early wars in space had shoved development along apace.

The limits discovered beyond FTL—in sub-space planes where traditional laws of physics were usurped and replaced by a science far more complex, and some would say almost eldritch—had always been crippling, in both physical and monetary terms. Wars aside, Weyland-Yutani had the money. It had the resources. And it had the desire to succeed, aggressively pushing the envelope of the Human Sphere at every point in the Company's checkered history.

Once fallen, it had risen to prominence again and taken full control of the Colonial Marines, so that they were sometimes nicknamed the Corporate Marines. This made it not only the oldest and most powerful company in human history, but the most powerful entity, governments included. Since its troubled resurgence, its expenditure of time and money into experimental space-travel technology had multiplied a hundred times.

The Arrow class sat at the pinnacle of what was currently possible. While the Fiennes ships of the twenty-second century—great exploration vessels named after the first astronaut to venture beyond the Sol System—relied on light-travel technology, later ships such as the Titan drophole-builders could travel at small factors of FTL speed. Most Titan ships could reach five-times light speed. Some of the more powerful corporate vessels owned by the Company sometimes reached six or even seven-times.

Arrow ships could travel at fifteen-times the speed of light. The science involved was way beyond Mains, and even Faulkner suggested that there were probably only a handful of humans in the Sphere who even came close to understanding the concept and the mechanics. Fueled by refined and concentrated trimonite, it took several hundred tons of that ultra-rare mineral to provide fuel for a ship's average year's travel. The cost to build an Arrow ship was staggering. The cost of fueling it—the dangerous mining, transport, refining, and containment that went into production of the trimonite— was horrific.

There were more than three hundred Arrow ships currently

in service, patrolling beyond the furthest extent of a Human Sphere whose outer area was now something like three million square light years. At full speed it would take an Arrow more than two hundred years to circumnavigate the Sphere, during which time it would require almost a million tons of trimonite. Only just over half a million tons had ever been mined. It was postulated that there were almost limitless reserves buried on asteroids and planets, but the great irony was that ships, equipment, and people had to reach these places to mine it.

Humanity had still only ventured across one percent of the Milky Way galaxy. At unimaginable speeds, still the scales of cosmic travel were staggering.

That's where the dropholes came in. While FTL travel still entailed actual movement through space—albeit on planes and levels of existence beyond most people's ken—the dropholes worked on a very different basis. The science had been mooted since the late twentieth century, so long ago, but the reality and the ability to harness the science and put it to work hadn't occurred until a little over a century before. The dropholes weren't exactly holes, but more like the ends of an infinitely long, yet instantaneously traveled tube. They were folds in space, meaning that a ship could enter one end and emerge at the other at exactly the same moment.

To Mains, that sounded easy. But the dropholes needed to be built using methods way beyond his understanding involving particle accelerators, anti-matter generators, and other tech he wouldn't even recognize if it landed on him. The holes themselves were contained within vast circular structures, necessitating huge amounts of materials and years of construction.

Even after all this time, only about one in three drophole initiation attempts worked, and around one in fifty resulted in cataclysmic explosions, the first couple of which had taken out thousands of people and dozens of ships. Since then, the moment of implementation was performed remotely. Dropholes only worked one way. In one hole, out of the other, with no return journey. Matching holes were attuned to the same frequency, and the in-holes all required different activation codes. Thus, they provided rapid jumping points around the Sphere, but there were also huge distances to travel between locations, because two holes could not be created close together. As Titan ships pushed the Outer Rim of the Human Sphere ever further, so they paused to build new dropholes.

Over time, communities had built up around these ports. Some were official, manned research and maintenance stations commissioned by Weyland-Yutani and funded by the Company. Many more were unofficial, congregations of people, ships, and space stations, some of them charging for use of a hole, some protecting them.

The dropholes became the oases of space. They became home to roving travelers and explorers looking for a place to rest in the company of others—pirates and mercenaries, haulage vessels, and military convoys.

Though they used the dropholes, the Excursionists never hung around afterward. They preferred their own company.

* * *

Once resupplied from a W-Y Darkstar vessel, the *Ochse* powered up and headed back out. After all systems were set, Mains and the rest of the crew retired to their suspension pods while Frodo did all the work.

Mains didn't like being in suspension. The pods' concept was similar to cryo-pods in that they essentially paused their user's biological clock, holding them at a moment in time while vast distances could be traversed. One vital difference was that an Arrow's suspension pods had to buffer the users against physical and temporal forces so extreme that they were barely understood. There were stories, perhaps apocryphal, of the first test pilots who had edged past ten-times light speed, deciding not to immerse in their suspension pods until too late. At journey's end the two test pilots, still conscious and barely breathing, were raving, insane, and estimated to have a brain-age of over seventeen thousand years. Unable to move, unable to do anything for the seventeen real-time days of travel, they had lived one hundred and seventy centuries of nothing.

A cautionary tale which Mains didn't care to think about too much. But he still didn't like the pods. The sensation when they were flooded with gel was akin to drowning, and he'd never been able to breathe in the compound until he was almost passed out from holding his breath.

It was always a great relief, then, when the diamond-glass lid slid aside and he puked his guts up.

He leaned over the side of the pod and coughed, bringing up more of the gel from his gut and lungs. On contact with the air it dissolved to nothing, enabling his first couple of breaths to clear his lungs, but the part-digested remnants of his last meal before suspension remained. McVicar had cooked them a great jambalaya, and he watched chewed prawns and peppers shifting in and out of focus as he caught his breath.

"Hey, L-T, you really need to get another job."

Mains looked up, snot dribbling from his nose.

"Lieder, how are you always up and about first? Why do you always look so... fresh."

"Eww," his pilot said, pulling on her underwear. "Brown snot. That's not an image I'll sleep on."

"You'll sleep on whatever I fucking order you to."

"Yeah, yeah." She turned the other way. "Hey, Corp, my superior officer is making what I believe to be lewd and improper suggestions toward me!"

Cotronis was just slipping from her own pod. She was renowned as being the worst sleeper of them all, and the grumpiest upon waking.

"Eat me out, Lieder," she said.

Lieder laughed, Snowdon hurled, and the suspension bay echoed to the sounds of banter and puking, groaning and shuffling feet, and then the crew slowly getting dressed. None of it was forced, but the chatter was more ebullient than usual, and they all knew that they were making more noise to make up for the two of their comrades who were missing.

"Okay, let's get ourselves back up to speed," Mains said. "Disengage artificial grav. Systems check, weapons check, silent running. You know the drill."

"Please, no zero grav until I've finished here," Cotronis groaned, then puked.

Lieder leaned back against the wall.

"Bunch of pussies."

Ten minutes later, slowly spinning in the zero-G shower, Mains looked up when Lieder hauled herself in through the sealed entrance. She eyed him up and down, frowning.

"You're putting on weight."

"McVicar's cooking." He turned off the shower and passed his hand over the dryer, choosing medium heat. He deserved a bit of comfort. "What've you got?"

"Flight time was ninety-eight days, distance three point nine light years. We've wound down to sub-light speed and we're sixteen billion miles from the habitat. Frodo engaged our cloak seventeen minutes ago—we're an asteroid again. No sign we've been seen."

"And the SpaceSurfers?"

"The hunt took seven days. They neutralized the two Yautja, but lost their corporal. Golden took a spear through the shoulder and carried on fighting. Finished the Yautja one-on-one."

"Hard bastard."

"Strange there were two contacts at the same time, though."

"Yeah."

Mains nodded and started dressing. His flight suit had come adrift from the velcro wall fasteners and got wet. He cursed inwardly, then shook his head. A wet flight suit. It would dry in a few minutes. It wasn't as if he was dead.

"You okay, Johnny?" All the quips aside, Lieder's concern was obvious. The affection between them was deep, and try as he had to veer away from it, Mains found himself being drawn in. He thought Lieder did, too. It wasn't something either of them could discuss. The generally accepted rule— the *essential position*—was to have fun but keep your distance. But they'd progressed from energetic fucking to passionate lovemaking, and sometimes afterward they wrapped themselves in a silence so loaded, so heavy with unsaid things, that it felt suffocating.

"I'm fine," he said, pulling on his clothes. He pushed across the small shower room and bounced slowly from the wall.

"Sure?"

"I'm as fine as the rest of you," he amended, then he grabbed the wall and held himself steady, pushing softly so that he drifted toward Lieder. She remained where she was, halfway through the entrance skin, and he pressed his forehead against hers. A soft kiss, a silent moment.

"Clean your teeth, L-T," she said, smiling as she pushed back through the doorway.

Mains waited a moment before following her through.

The rest of the crew were on the flight deck. Lieder lowered herself into the pilot's seat, Faulkner sat at the main weapons array, the others were strapped into their relevant seats around the cramped area. The empty seats were painfully obvious.

"So what have we got, Frodo?" he asked.

The cool, welcoming voice of the ship's computer filled the flight deck.

"Nice to see you, L-T. There's no sign of any change in the Yautja habitat. Its course and orbit remain the same as before, I detect no drive trails in the vicinity, but until we get closer I won't be able to view the habitat itself."

"That's fine. What about chatter?"

"The usual Yautja communications. Sparse, short bursts. I'm running through the most up-to-date translation programs I have, but the dialects are barely recognizable. Only one anomaly I think you should know about, a repeating signal that feels out of place."

"What sort of signal?"

"The best I can make out, it sounds like a countdown."

"To what?"

"Sorry, L-T, I really can't tell. It's a complex self-repeating symbolic system I've never seen from them before."

"How do you know it's a countdown?"

"Just a hunch," the computer said.

"Thanks, Frodo. Is all this on the mainframe?"

"Of course."

Mains took his seat behind and to the left of Lieder. "Snowdon?"

"Already on it," she said. Snowdon was their self-professed Yautja expert. She'd been fascinated with the species since she was a kid, and claimed it was their martial society that encouraged her to sign up to the Colonial Marines. She not only kept up to date with intelligence, but spent some time forming theories and opinions of her own.

They ran silently for a while. Mains looked around the flight deck at his crew, his family, and his eyes lingered only for a moment on Reynolds' and Willis's seats. Their unscheduled excursion, the huge distances traveled for brief, shatteringly violent moments of combat, seemed to have energized them all.

The deck buzzed with excitement.

"Enough fucking around," he said. "Let's move in closer."

2

ISA PALANT

Love Grove Base, Research Station, LV-1529
May 2692 AD

Isa Palant needed the violence, the brutality, the fierce atmospherics, and violent electrical storms of LV-1529, to remind her of where she really was.

In truth, there was no need for her to be out here at all. Terraforming was a slow, dangerous process, and no planet wanted to accept its forced change. She could be safe and sound in Love Grove Base, enjoying the comfortable levels of life support, ensconced in her lab with her antique coffee machine, specially imported roasted coffee beans from Weaver's World, and a cot so that she could sleep with her work.

Her work was everything to her, as it had been to her parents. It took up every waking moment and most of her dreams, and that was precisely why it was good to get away.

"Bit of a bumpy ride coming up," Rogers said.

"I have every confidence in your driving skills."

"Me, too. It's this piece of shit rover I'm not sure about."

"It's held it together fine so far."

Knowing that wasn't quite true, Palant made sure her straps were secure, and she held the handle above her seat. They'd had to stop twice on the way out to the boundary, and Rogers had donned his protective suit both times to venture outside and strap up the loose exhaust. First time it was clogged with dust, second time it was split right open, and now it coughed and growled like an angry cat.

She'd wanted to help, but admitted ignorance when it came to anything mechanical. That just wasn't her field. Keith Rogers had been an engineer in the Colonial Marines and knew what he was doing. An indie now, he was a vital asset to Love Grove Base. Ostensibly there as part of their security force, he spent most of his time helping the base technicians keep the place running.

"Couple of miles to go," he said. "You want me to slow down?"

"You still trying to encourage me to park up somewhere quiet, Corporal Rogers?" she teased.

"Miss Palant, I knew from the beginning I had the wrong junk between my legs for you."

"Christ, you're beautifully subtle."

"I'm ex-military, as you keep reminding me. We thrive on subtlety."

Palant gave her deep, throaty laugh that drew so many people to her. She *enjoyed* laughing, did it as much as she could, and Rogers had proven to be an unexpected source of inspiration. She'd never have believed she could be such good friends with someone who was essentially a mercenary, but he had defied her expectations—humbled her in a way. A scientist, she welcomed every lesson, life lessons most of all. Her parents had made sure of that.

"Still, maybe a hand job…" he mumbled, and she leaned across the cab and punched him in the arm. "Ouch!"

"Big hard soldier."

"You're stronger than you look."

Palant noticed that he'd slowed the rover down. She smiled. He knew just how much she liked getting out here. It wasn't only to experience the true ruggedness of the place she had grown to call home, but also to clear her mind. She spent so much time at her work that she had to remove herself sometimes—not only from the lab, its samples, her computers and theories, but also the base itself. It flushed the accumulated debris away from her mind, and lent her a fresh perspective.

Still, every time she closed her eyes she saw the Yautja.

"Atmosphere processors," Rogers said.

"Where?" She peered through the windscreen. The self-cleaning perspex was working hard, smeared with droplets of filthy rain, scratched with years of impacts from dust-laden winds and heavier gravel thrown by the occasional twisters that leapt up in the vicinity of the base. She squinted, then between sweeps of the wiper arms she saw the first blinking lights high atop the westernmost of the three processing towers.

The design of atmosphere processors had hardly changed in the last century—vast pyramidal structures powered by nuclear-fusion reactors, their technology way beyond her understanding. Though a scientist, Palant always maintained that paleontology demanded an artist's mind. Some people saw the processors as beautiful things, but to her they were clumsy man-made edifices struggling against nature. Every gain they made was hard-won, and they weren't always successful. Nevertheless, recent analyses predicted that LV-1529 would be a Class 2 planet within fifteen years, and Class 1 in seven decades.

"Getting back to your monsters this afternoon?" Rogers asked.

"Yeah, why not. Got some ideas."

"What're you working on now?" He'd seen the samples in her lab, the bio-frozen remnants of Yautja gathered from various contacts made over the last decade. A hand, one finger missing, the tattered stump of its wrist cauterized by the laser-rifle blast that had blown it off. The lower jaw, tusks long and sharp, inner teeth loosened where a new set had started to push through, and the various samples of blood and bodily fluids. Sad things, he sometimes thought. Other times, scary.

"I'm trying to find out how their blood helps in wound repair and regeneration," she said. "It's something we only discovered recently with Eve."

"Ah, yeah, the only Yautja kept in captivity. Didn't it kill itself?"

"That's still debated. I believe it did. They found it dead in its cell, and I think it willed its hearts to stop beating." Palant so wished she'd had a chance to meet Eve—to talk, ask its real name. Attempting their language was another aim of her research, although the strand that had advanced the least. Company scientists had treated it more as a vivisection experiment than what it should have been—contact with an intelligent, highly advanced alien species.

"Originally I thought it might have been killed with nano-tech, and I spent a long time trying to look into that. Artificial tech first, then when I found no evidence of that I looked into bio-tech."

"Huh?"

"Naturally created nano-bots. W-Y have been researching it for years, without any real success. Essentially it takes tweaking genetics to create nano-bots from biological material already extant in a body, then programming those genes for specific tasks."

"Right," Rogers said. "I wonder what's for dinner."

She smiled, but knew he was joking. Rogers was brighter than he liked to let on, and they'd been friends long enough for him to understand what she talked about more than most. Sometimes she thought of inviting him to become her assistant, but she liked their relationship, and that kind of friendship required distance.

In her lab, she became far too intense.

"Thing is, after a long time looking into that, I started to think it was too basic. Old-fashioned thinking. I wasn't giving their biology the respect it deserved. I was looking more at tech than at an evolved natural ability. So now I've gone back to basics, comparing their blood to other creatures that can regenerate. Newts, starfish, flatworms. The axolotl, an amazing creature. Even mammals like deer, which can regrow their antlers, and some bats that can repair damaged wings."

"And the Company keep pumping resources at what you do?"

"Sure they do. BioWeapons and ArmoTech love me."

Rogers said nothing. They'd talked about this many times before, and he knew that her intentions were far more pure and honest. She was utterly fascinated with the Yautja, dreamed of making meaningful contact with them, and the best way to do that was to take advantage of the Company's ongoing desire to benefit from their various warlike technologies.

"Doesn't it bug you, playing the system to do what you want to do?" he asked at last. The Company paid his wages, too, and it was unusual to hear him vocalize what she knew he already thought.

"I don't see it like that," she said. "I just have wider horizons. It's still a great time for adventurers."

"You should get that on a T-shirt."

"They're really an amazing species," Palant said, ignoring his comment. As usual, when away from her lab, she was becoming anxious to return. Her life seemed to be one of contradictions. She valued this limited time away, then yearned to go back. She sought knowledge and dreamed of some sort of peaceful, mutually beneficial contact, yet worked for the Company whose stated aim was the furtherance of what it called the "science of war."

Her father had once explained it to her when she was still a dreamy teenager.

The Company are scared, he'd said. *We're pushing out into the galaxy, incredibly slowly, yet we already know we're far from alone. We've met other intelligent lifeforms, interacted, and made contact. Sometimes they're friendly, sometimes indifferent. On occasion, we've had to fight. There are the Yautja, who might have been visiting us for millennia, and the further we expand, the more they notice us. The Xenomorphs haunt the darker extremes of space. And there will inevitably be other, perhaps even more deadly civilizations. The further we go, the more we might discover, and the more we will be noticed.*

Weyland-Yutani know that, and they're doing the best they can to protect humanity against any threat. The problem is… that intention is easily corrupted. With so much at stake, and so many fortunes to be made, benevolent intentions can easily be drowned out.

She had never forgotten his words and the lesson they were meant to impart. Working for Weyland-Yutani now, she was more careful than ever to hold them close.

"Battening down the hatches," Rogers said. They were closing on Love Grove Base, and Isa could see windows and doorways covered with their heavy gray shields. Nestled in a small valley a mile from the nearest processor, it had been established by the facility builders almost fifty years ago, as a base from which they could construct and then maintain. After the processors' completion, the place had been adapted and expanded over the past twenty years by ArmoTech, the branch of Weyland-Yutani given to research into alien weapons and technology. Another example of their effectiveness at cost-cutting. Just one drophole away from the Outer Rim, it was regarded as an ideal place for Yautja research.

The base had been named by one of the foremen building the processor plants, a bittersweet take on his memories of better times and a kinder place. It was said his home had been Love Grove, a religious commune on Triton, Neptune's largest moon.

"Storm coming in," Palant said, and though the base was an ugly construction with very few nods to aesthetics, she was always pleased to see it. It was home, after all.

Palant's parents had been on their way here seventeen years before when they were killed. The report called it a freak accident. As their dropship descended from the orbiting military transport, two weather systems had clashed, resulting in violent electrical storms and two hundred miles-per-hour winds. The ship was tossed around the sky and flung to the ground like a toy, and all eighteen people on board had died. A great loss, but space was dangerous, everyone knew that.

Five years later Palant had followed her parents to Love Grove Base, landed safely, and had only been away a handful of times since.

Rogers guided the rover in between the buildings. The external doors slipped open, he maneuvered down into a subterranean garage, and the doors closed quickly behind them. Even though the atmosphere this close to the processors was breathable, the harsh weather conditions meant that sojourns outside were rare, and dangerous.

They parked, then Rogers wound down the rover's engine and set it in park.

"Drink this evening?" he asked.

"Sure. O'Malley's at eight?"

"It's a date." He always made that joke, ever since he'd first asked her out. Whatever he claimed, he *hadn't* known her preferences. Not then.

"Thanks for the ride. Did me good."

"Back to work, Yautja Woman!"

They parted ways in the garage area, and Palant made her way up into the base's main levels. Angela Svenlap met her in the central distribution area, holding a coffee clutched in both hands and leaning against the railings around the wide stairwell. Palant could see that she'd been waiting for her.

"Hey, Isa! Gerard Marshall signaled a transmission for you." She handed her the coffee.

"He did?"

"Only three times." Svenlap smiled. She looked tired and drawn, but had still come here to deliver her message—and who wouldn't? It wasn't every day that one of Weyland-Yutani's main executive officers, and one of the Thirteen, made a personal call to one of their employees.

"Okay, I'll call and accept."

"It's a two-way." Svenlap seemed excited, and smiled slightly at Isa's surprise.

"From Sol system?"

"Yeah. You know he never leaves. I've heard the Thirteen have been developing tech to conduct real-time conversations through sub-space."

"The energy that must take…"

"Guess he really wants to talk to you."

Palant lifted the cup in thanks and took a sip. Svenlap paused, as if debating whether to say more. Then she smiled again and wandered away, and Palant took a moment to breathe in the base's familiar, sterile atmosphere.

Marshall. He'd taken an interest in her research from the

start, and she'd never felt comfortable talking with him. She had never met him face to face, but seeing him in the holo frame always sent a shiver down her spine. He tried to present the attractive human face of the Company, but she knew some of his story. And it was ugly.

The coffee was scalding hot and bitter, not at all how Palant liked it, but Svenlap had gone to the trouble of bringing it, along with the message. She hadn't needed to. She was quiet, as unassuming as she was clever, her pale, sad face hiding a startling intellect.

Her area of interest was Yautja history, and so their research and analysis often benefitted from regular crossover. Much of the story Svenlap was building came from human history— ancient texts, more recent suspected contacts, and comparing known Yautja behavior—interactions with humans, and methods to historical situations. Palant found it fascinating, and while history also played a part in her research, she took much more of a hands-on approach.

Walking to her labs, she wondered why Marshall had been trying to contact her. He'd called three times. It must have been something urgent. Nevertheless, she was still relaxed from the twenty-hour trip with her friend, and her mindset was somewhat refreshed. She spent far too long immersed in research in one of the three rooms that made up her lab, breathing the same air, seeing the same sights, eating the same food. Sometimes, the weight of the nothingness all around them was suffocating. The irregular jaunts she made with Rogers usually enabled her to reset herself for the next bout of work. The base looked fresher after such trip, and her future seemed brighter.

She'd heard tales of people going mad in space. Data was unreliable, and probably distorted, but a good percentage of those who lived such a life suffered mental illness of some kind, ranging from slight personality disorders to suicidal tendencies. Evolution was struggling to keep up with humanity's progress. Palant's parents had often lamented about how people were designed to look at a green world with blue skies, and not this. Not inimical alien landscapes being tortured into shape by man-made technology. Not the shattering horror of infinity.

Outside the lab doors she breathed in the scent of cooling coffee, closed her eyes, and brushed her hand across the entry pad.

Inside, everything had changed.

"Fucking hell."

Palant rarely found the need to swear.

"Fucking, fucking hell."

In the main room, several heavy tables had been dragged together into the center, their scattered contents taken off and piled on a unit in the lab's far corner. Her initial thought was, *How dare they?* That accumulated debris consisted of a large part of her research for the past several months.

A tablet had been dropped on the floor, one corner dented, holo screen flickering with a trapped image. A stand of glass pipettes had tipped from the table and lay shattered. One of the lab's several safety drones had applied safety foam to the scattered glass, producing a clear, solidified bubble mass that was designed to isolate any dangerous or toxic elements let loose in a spill.

The pipettes had been empty. She had long wished for something to place in them.

It looked as if that wish had been granted.

The two Yautja corpses were still encased in their vacuum-packed coffin bags, a heavy white material stronger than steel hugging every contour of the bodies. Though they weren't visible, the nature of the bodies was obvious. Palant knew them so well.

One was taller than the other, almost as long as the nine-foot table it lay upon. Their bodies were broad, legs long, feet heavy and clawed. Both had arms crossed over their stomachs, but the one on the right seemed to be lacking something there. As for their heads, so broad and distinctive, one was bare, the long tusks tenting the tight material. The other seemed to still be wearing its helmet, though the shape was all wrong, with a deep depression in the left-hand side and a good portion of its mass missing.

They kept the helmet on to hold in what was left, she guessed.

She knew now why Marshall had been so keen to contact her. Palant could imagine him, smarmy and confident, breaking the secret to her face to face and enjoying the reaction she would try to control. She was glad she'd stolen the surprise from him.

Breathing hard, she entered the lab and closed the door behind her, sealing herself inside with these two majestic corpses.

She had seen plenty of body parts, studied data from other scientists, examined so much footage of Yautja attacks—most of it confused, much of it caught by Colonial Marines' combat-suit sensors—that she had even started to convince herself that she knew them well.

But she had never known them well. They were an enigma to her, and the more she studied and discovered, the more questions she had to ask herself. Now, perhaps some of those questions could be answered.

"Computer, what's the status of the bodies?" She had never felt the need to personalize her lab computer, not even granting it a name. Their relationship seemed to benefit from that.

"Afternoon, Isa. They've been out of stasis for just more than three hours. Decay rates—sample one, four percent; sample two, six percent."

"Too much," she said. "Prepare the pods." Her heart was beating fast, her senses alive. She thought she could smell decay in the lab, though that was impossible. She blinked and imagined one of the coffin bags moving. "Contact Central, tell them to send three technicians to help get them shifted. Are the pods functional?"

"Of course. I maintain them regularly and run daily tests. They'll be ready in seven minutes."

"Thanks." In one small room off the lab there were three stasis pods, two full-sized, one smaller, kept available for instances such as this. They were specially adapted to accommodate the Yautja physiology, and she had always dreamed of filling them.

What else do I need to do? Palant was breathing faster, tapping her left hand against her leg as she contemplated how much these corpses would feed her future. She closed her eyes and tried to breathe slower, imagining what her parents would say. It was nothing she could say aloud, not in a Company facility. They had always seen Weyland-Yutani as corrupt and morally bankrupt, and Palant had always felt a flush of shame at coming to work for them after her parents' deaths.

"But I can learn so much," she whispered, filling the lab with her hope.

"Sub-space comms incoming from Gerard Marshall, signal source Charon Station."

"Block it, I don't want to talk to—"

"Sorry. He's using his override." The mobile holo frame lifted from the far wall and drifted across the lab to her, and as it did so the space contained within blurred, flickered, and then changed.

Gerard Marshall smiled at her. He was visible from the shoulders up, leaning back in a chair with a fake background of waving grass, sunny skies, and flitting birds. Sub-space quirks distorted his image a little, flickering, giving him a ghostly echo to left and right that didn't quite mimic his own movements. She always found it strange talking to someone who was so far away. Almost five hundred light years, in this case. Somehow, the impossibility of it made the distances involved even more shocking.

"Isa Palant," he said, with what seemed like genuine affection. It made her skin crawl. "How are things on the edge of space?"

Isa waited for him to say more.

"You can answer," he said. "You know the Thirteen have been developing sub-space channels open for real-time conversation."

"Yes," Isa said. "Right. Things are…" She glanced past the frame at the two bodies, then smiled. "Well, you know how they are."

His three-dimensional image leaned closer, growing larger. "I hope you like them. Isn't it exciting? I tried talking to you earlier, I wanted to tell you all about them myself."

"I was off base," Palant said.

"Yes, well. You're back now." His replies were a little delayed, and they didn't match his image's movements. It was all very disconcerting.

She'd researched Marshall, as much as she could without being obviously and traceably intrusive. Though a senior executive at the Weyland-Yutani Corporation, he'd never left the Sol System, and he rarely traveled into environments without proper atmospheres—Earth, Titan, Mars, and the other system moons that were still being terraformed. She didn't know whether it was fear or need of comfort that made him an unwilling space traveler.

Now he was on Charon Station, the massive space habitat orbiting the home system at roughly the distance of Pluto's furthest orbit. It was known as the Colonial Marines' main control base and home for General Paul Bassett, the Marines' commander.

It was so strange, being able to have a real-time conversation over such a vast distance. Stranger still that the Thirteen kept such tech to themselves and a few close confidantes.

"They're quite spectacular," Palant said. She could hardly concentrate on the conversation. The bodies drew her attention.

"I hope you'll be able to—" The image flickered, his face ghosted, versions of him that seemed both younger and older.

Then it settled again. "—badly damaged? I was told not."

"I can't see yet, but they look quite complete. I can report to you later, after my initial examinations." It was a tacit request that he let her go, but Marshal wasn't yet finished.

"Please do. They were killed by a detachment of Excursionists on the Outer Rim. They'd attacked a medical research station, resulting in quite a few deaths. All very sad." He sighed, not sounding sad at all. "Isa, we've spoken before about what we expect of you. Now, more than ever, those expectations need to be fulfilled."

"Of course," she said.

"Of course." His smile grew thin. "I know your love of these things. I know that your intentions and desires are pure—but there has been a surge in attacks lately, across several sectors of the Outer Rim, and a few more deeper within the Sphere. Our prime concern, our number-one priority, is to understand as much as we can about Yautja weaponry and martial capabilities."

"Yes," she said.

"We're sending someone to work with you on this."

She raised her eyebrows, attention snapping back to Marshall.

"Milt McIlveen." More ghosting. One of his images seemed to sneer at the other. Isa wanted to look away, shut down the transmission, but she could not. "—a good man. As fascinated in them as you."

"But?"

"But…" That smile again, so two dimensional. "He has a true grasp of our requirements."

"So do I, Mr. Marshall."

"Yes. You do." He went to sign off, then paused. "Isa, I know you see me as a Company man. And I am, through and through. My aims are pure in this. Can you imagine what would happen if the Yautja launched a true attack?"

"They're not like that. Their society isn't built or structured that way. They're essentially loners, drawing together for special ceremonies, or mating, or perhaps other reasons we don't know about yet, but they're not conquerors. There's no scheming in what they do. There's an honesty to them."

"That honesty killed over twenty station staff and two Excursionists at Southgate Station 12," Marshall said. "And while I accept what you say, we can't second guess them. We don't know enough to do that. Keep your priorities in mind, that's all I'm saying. Your assistant will be there in seventeen days."

Palant smiled and nodded and kept smiling as Marshall's image faded away. The holo frame drifted back to its dock on the far wall, and the room seemed unnaturally silent.

"Help is here," the computer said. The doors opened behind her and three people stepped inside.

Palant crossed to the bodies and rested her hand on one of the coffin suits for the first time.

It was cold. Cold as space.

3

ANGELA SVENLAP

Love Grove Base, Research Station, LV-1529
May 2692 AD

Since the first signal had arrived a little over two years before, Angela Svenlap's life had been taking on meaning. Before that fateful moment, she had passed the days, months, and years with a mysterious hollowness inside. Highly intelligent, curious, eager to learn, she had long proven herself to be a forward-thinking and energetic person.

From her birthplace on Jupiter's moon Io, her journey out into the Human Sphere had taken years, because wherever she stopped she found something else to fascinate her. After a fateful meeting on Addison Prime, the focus of her curiosity had narrowed toward the Yautja. The old man had been a survivor of a Yautja attack on a Titan ship over fifty years earlier, and she had sat and interviewed him for days.

Since then, Svenlap had become an authority on Yautja

appearances throughout human history. The veracity of such reports dwindled the further back in time they went. For several hundred years before there were fairly reliable accounts, stored in free access quantum folds, storage streams, or even a few old hard discs she had come across or been sent by others who knew her interest. From before that, there were some books still in existence that recorded what *might* have been Yautja presences on Earth before interplanetary space travel.

Before that, only conjecture.

She liked investigating. It made her feel alive. But even while immersed in a new case, with every waking minute spent reading, cross-referencing, trying to match evidence with diverse and seemingly unconnected reportage and accounts, that hollowness within persisted.

Sometimes she tried to examine it. Assessing it from afar, the void averted its gaze. Looking directly inward at it made her depressed. It was as if she was uncertain who she was. As if the person she believed herself to be—the Angela Svenlap who had been building herself up around this dark hollow for the full fifty-seven years of her life—was merely a mannequin, constructed to camouflage something deeper and more shadowed.

Then that message—a few simple words that had brought meaning.

The Founders have not forgotten you.

Her life had changed in an instant. That change continued.

It was the older sightings she enjoyed researching most. She had one scanned photograph, several questionable testimonies, and a doctor's written report with much of its detail redacted. The photograph was black-and-white, out of focus, and hazed by battlefield smoke and chaos. The testimonies had been translated from their original Russian by a German soldier, and in turn translated again by an American academic several years after the end of World War Two. It had been a place of terror, a confused and hellish landscape, hardly the scene for trusted eyewitness accounts.

Finally, the doctor's report had been hacked to pieces by his superiors. It was this more than anything else that convinced Svenlap that she might have something.

She stared at the photo on the holo frame before her. After putting it through every focusing, adjustment, and clarification process she could think of—and allowing her computer to assess it with several approaches that hadn't even crossed her mind—she had returned the image to its original, seven-hundred-year-old form.

The shadow of a blasted building on the left. A street, piled with rubble and corpses and the blazing remains of a military vehicle of some kind. On the right, another ruined building, and framed in an open doorway, a figure. Too tall for the doorway, it seemed to be standing back and observing the chaos. Wide chest. Jutting jaw. The silhouette of a hairstyle quite unlike any worn by people of the time, men or women. In its lowered right hand, something that might have been a spear.

"Gotta be," she muttered for the dozenth time. Even though accounts provided hints, it was the photograph that gave her most faith. She had come to know the Yautja well, and was determined that this shadow would not haunt her. It was time to close the case.

"Confirmed Yautja sighting," she dictated, the computer recording every word. "Case study number three-three-nine. Location and time—Stalingrad, January 7th to the 11th, 1943. Number of kills…" She trailed off, thinking of those questionably translated accounts again, the heavily censored doctor's report. "Number of confirmed kills, twenty-eight, with more than a hundred more possibles." She paused again, then nodded.

The shadow in the photograph stared back, almost as if listening to her every word. It stood tall. Looked proud. She wondered what had happened to the alien—whether it had been killed and pulverized in that terrible battle, or escaped to hunt, stalk, and kill another day.

She was about to turn off the holo frame when a message arrival chimed in. Her heart stuttered. She gasped, half-stood, and reached for the frame, as if to pluck the message she so craved. Sweating like a phrail addict, she forced herself to sit back down and catch her breath. It had been almost ninety days since the last communication, and she'd begun to wonder if they had forgotten her again.

No, she thought. *They never forgot us. Never!*

"Message status?" she asked in a shaky voice.

"Private," her computer said. "Identifier, Beatrix Maloney. Duration, nineteen seconds. Broadcast source unknown."

"Play," Svenlap breathed.

The message played.

It kept playing, again and again, and as she remembered the words and their echoes they filled that empty place inside her, making it whole and heavy, a solid mass whose gravity drew her in and down, almost smothering the Svenlap she had become beneath the Svenlap she needed to be. Her thoughts belonged to this new person, and yet she felt herself more whole and complete than she ever had before.

The Founders have not forgotten you, and your patience is our power, your faith our strength. Build for us. Create for us.

It was inspiring stuff, and Svenlap grasped hold of the sense of belonging these words gave her. The final, more poetic sentence made her cry.

In the deep, in the dark, let light blossom to illuminate our way home.

"Home," she whispered as she rummaged, drifting from room to room in the deserted east wing of the base. It had been closed down several years ago after a particularly ferocious storm ripped out one wall and collapsed part of the flat roof, and the Love Grove Base management had decided that the remaining, solid areas of the sprawling building were plenty big enough for its current use. The atmosphere processors virtually ran themselves now, and these dozens of rooms built to house builders, engineers, and technicians were now redundant.

They had left so much behind.

"Home," Svenlap muttered again. She frowned, a little confused.

In one room, swirls of trimmed light-wire caught the glare of her flashlight and stored the light deep. She curled it around her hand, then tucked the ball into her bag. Across the room, on a dusty table, she found some semi-spherical objects, metallic containers the size of her hands which might once have been used to house laser charge pods. She pocketed two of these, as well as a scattering of bolts used to connect them tightly together.

Wind howled through the corridor as she moved toward the fallen eastern end of the wing. The walls ran with rivulets of moisture, and sand and grit had drifted, providing a strange internal landscape. Her flashlight cast shifting shadows across the ceiling.

The Founders have not forgotten you.

Alone in this deserted part of the base, breathing in an atmosphere heavy with dust and moisture and still not rich enough in oxygen to sustain her for more than a couple of hours, she felt watched and wanted, trusted and needed. Hers was a lofty mission.

There was only one instant when the old Svenlap peeked through. She staggered to a halt and thought through what she was doing. Her hands were scratched and cut from digging through old tools and hardware. The ghost of what she intended to build haunted her.

"Let light blossom," she said.

Shoving aside panels that had warped and fallen from the ceiling, she barged her way into one of the remotest rooms of the base. As far as she was aware, no one had been here for years, and the interior looked like part of the outside landscape. Open to the elements along one side, it had filled with sand, walls were down, furniture rusted and rotting over time in the acidic atmosphere.

In the far corner was the heavy door that led into a storage room. It was locked tight, but the hinges were decayed. Even using a steel bar, though, it took her half an hour of grunting and straining to prize the top hinge apart, then another twenty minutes to break open the bottom hinge. She paused for a rest and a drink, the water tasting rank as it swilled out her mouth and she swallowed dust she'd been breathing in. She feared what it might be doing to her insides, but at the same time, she knew that she didn't have long left to worry.

Groaning, sweating, her bleeding hands slipping again and again on the slick metal, Svenlap tugged the door far enough open to squeeze inside.

She used her flashlight again to find what she needed.

There was plenty there.

She had never been technically minded. She'd dabbled in engineering when she was younger, but drifted away when other interests took hold. Passions, like her obsession with Yautja history.

So now they had two dead Yautja on the base.

Scattered around the edges of her desk and discarded on the floor were the paraphernalia from her current work. Photographs, paper copies of scanned books, tactile objects that she found so much more beneficial than their electronic or holo equivalents.

Deep inside, Angela Svenlap knew that she should be beyond excited. She'd known about the bodies since before Palant returned from her off-base jaunt, and had barely been able to control her excitement. Later that day, she had intended to return to Palant's labs to see the bodies, perhaps have a really good look at them. They might be carrying trophies that could pin them down to a specific point in history. Imagine being able to locate some concrete piece of Yautja evidence from that Stalingrad battlefield!

But then the new message had arrived, and any enthusiasm for the Yautja flitted away. Now, in the center of her desk was the new focus of her attention.

The air stank of hot metal. Solder singed. Wires sparkled. It was an old-fashioned technology, but one which she suddenly understood more than she ever had before. She wasn't sure why.

The ideas rose from that dark place deep inside, now no longer dark—now bright and full of promise.

"Illuminate our way home," she whispered as she connected another wire. It looked a mess, but she knew it would work.

In a bag by her feet lay the stuff she'd brought from that destroyed room. Left over from the construction of the atmosphere processors, left behind when it never should have been, she had always known it was there, but had shown no interest. Why should she?

The old Angela Svenlap had no interest at all in explosives.

4

JOHNNY MAINS

Arrow-class vessel Ochse
Near Yautja Habitat designated UMF 12, beyond Outer Rim
July 2692 AD

For more than two centuries there had been a cold war between humanity and the Yautja. Occasional skirmishes were recorded, and sometimes the mysterious losses of remote vessels or communities were attributed to Yautja action.

In turn, there had been several cases of the alien ships being tracked and destroyed by Colonial Marines Spaceborne units when they strayed too close to human settlements. Thirty years before there had been a series of sporadic battles between Excursionists and a clan of particularly invasive Yautja across the southern Outer Rim, but that conflict had died out as quickly as it began, the enemy melting away into the void.

Captured tech was reverse engineered, incorporated into Excursionist craft and equipment, and then rapidly became outmoded. The Yautja, it seemed, didn't like their capabilities being turned against them, and they had an extremely advanced grasp of space travel, combat, and camouflage technologies.

They had never been declared an outright enemy, but they were far from friends.

Johnny Mains wasn't keen to move in closer to UMF 12—the Yautja habitat—for too long. The cloaking tech they were using was considered cutting edge, developed by the guys at ArmoTech who Colonial Marines affectionately called the Gadget Guys. It enabled ships to blend into the background, sometimes invisible to known scanning methods, sometimes disguised as an asteroid. Yet by its very definition, cutting edge had a short half-life. Cutting edge one day was outmoded the next, and Mains was constantly worried that the Yautja would see right through them.

"Frodo?" he asked.

"A little over three thousand miles," the ship's computer said.

"Almost close enough to see," Cotronis said. "McVicar, open a window!"

McVicar mumbled something coarse beneath his breath and continued monitoring the open communication channels.

"Anything, McVicar?" Mains asked.

"No, boss. Background stuff, but nothing new."

"You got translation filtering?"

"Of course." McVicar sounded put out, and Mains should have known the big man was on top of things. Of course he was. They all were—but Mains was nervous. He was already starting to doubt his idea of moving in much closer, but they were set on their course now.

From outside the *Ochse* would resemble a tumbling asteroid, and already their trajectory was taking them slowly away from UMF 12. They couldn't get too close and risk being taken out in a collision.

Faulkner was on weapons, and they were all powered up. The *Ochse* was heavily armed with laser cannons, a particle beam modulator, sub-space limiter, and micro-nukes. It also carried three drones that could be deployed and recovered, and Faulkner and Cotronis had fitted one of them with a cloaking device similar to the ship's. They were fully loaded and ready for a fight, but fighting was what Excursionist missions were tasked to avoid.

Lieder sat in her pilot's chair, although Frodo was controlling the *Ochse*'s very particular roll pattern, shifting longitudinally but keeping their forward cannons to bear toward the habitat. If something came at them—ship, missile, laser—they'd have a chance to retaliate before getting out of there.

Snowdon shifted her seat back and forth in front of a range of holo frames, gathering as much information as she could about the habitat. The massive craft really was close enough to see, and Snowdon was recording as much as possible. Mains could see that she was excited—but nervous, too. That was good. They all needed to stay on their toes.

"Snowdon, anything we should be concerned about?" He could have asked Frodo, but he preferred the human element.

"Looking much the same to me, L-T," she said. "No major change in the habitat's status since we were last here. There are a couple of new ships in orbit, but no sign that they're powering up. No significant drive trails. Same course and velocity as before."

"Just following the edge of the Human Sphere," Cotronis said.

"We've had border skirmishes before," Mains said.

"Yeah, but not with something this big. We have no idea how many of those bastards are living there."

"That's why they're just skimming," Snowdon offered. It was strange terminology, considering the fact that they were almost two light years beyond the notional Human Sphere— trillions of miles of mostly empty space. "Moving that thing into the Sphere would be an act of war."

"We should take it out," Cotronis said.

"And that *wouldn't* be war?" Mains asked. His corporal was experienced, dedicated, and intelligent, but sometimes her mouth was way ahead of her head.

"It's only the third time we've ever seen a habitat," Lieder said. "There's a lot we can learn from it. That why we're here."

"Right," Mains said.

"Right," Cotronis agreed, smiling. "I'll keep my nuclear wet dreams to myself."

"Want to take a look at what I've got?" Snowdon asked. "Our scans can't be too intrusive, but we're close enough for a couple of the holo cameras to have built up a pretty decent picture."

The flight deck went quiet, filled with a sense of anticipation. Until now none of them had actually viewed the Yautja habitat—not with their own eyes. Frodo had built up a huge set of data, including dimensions, composition, and as much intelligence about the structure's internal makeup as possible. But it was all data.

"Let's do it," Mains said.

Before their eyes, the viewing windows turned opaque and the components of a holo frame folded out of the ship's structure. They moved closer, edges touching, and then fogged up. Moments later it turned dark, spotted with stars. Snowdon slid her wheeled chair forward so that it was between Mains and Cotronis, then worked the small control tray in her lap.

Within the holo screen, the Yautja habitat appeared.

At first it was a long view. The habitat was visible as a whole, a little over six miles long, and from this perspective there was little detail to be seen. It looked like a long tube, wide in the middle and growing narrower toward each end. Towers and protrusions rose along its length, some of them taller than the main structure was thick. Mains guessed that some of those arms were almost a mile long. It gave UMF 12 the appearance of a strange, spined sea creature, spinning slowly around its long central axis.

"Aaaand closer..." Snowdon said.

The image grew, quickly becoming too large for the frame and zeroing in on the superstructure. They knew it was made from some sort of artificial material that resembled ultra-strong bone, and had long suspected that it was extruded by machines probably still active inside the habitat. Seeing the vessel's outer hull—or skin—close up only reinforced this image. The surface seemed smooth but uneven, pocked with random depressions and lined with staggered ridges. It was a pale gray color, almost off-white. Shadows might have been openings, or deeper depressions. Thin lines might have been cracks or fractures, or some sort of intentional hull markings on a massive scale.

As the habitat spun the view turned, and then blurred momentarily as one of the tall arms swept past.

"Are those arms docking towers of some sort?" Mains asked.

"That's the best guess," Snowdon said. "There are signs of ships docked along some of them, but there are also hollows in the hull that might be hangars. It's difficult to tell."

"You said there were a couple of ships orbiting?"

"There are. Too far away to see in any detail."

"It's huge," Lieder said, awed. Over the last few decades W-Y had started building space habitats, vast structures possessing space drives but intended for orbit around moons or planets. Some of them were even larger than UMF 12, but they were bulky vessels, with little grace or finesse. This Yautja habitat had a smoothness, a startling beauty that Mains knew had a lot to do with its provenance. This was an alien vessel. For all they knew it was older than civilized humankind.

"Keep gathering information," Mains said. He was getting twitchy—they should have never come so close. In all their time here, he didn't believe that they had done anything to alert the Yautja to their presence. He had no wish to change that now. This was a silent mission, not an active one.

Brief diversions, such as the fight at Southgate Station 12, might once have invigorated him, but no more. Losing good people only depressed him, and he'd long ago decided that he would rather watch than fight.

"L-T, we've got incoming comms from Tyszka's Star," McVicar said. Two hundred light years in from the Outer Rim, Tyszka's Star was the hub at which all Excursionist units were pulled together and trained, and from which every Arrow ship was launched. Communications from there were rare, and opening up receivers for a sub-space signal could cause a flare of Bannon radiation.

If someone was looking in the right direction at the right time, it could give away a ship's location...

"More attacks?" Lieder asked.

"Maybe. Give us a bit of a nudge."

"You sure, Johnny?" Lieder raised her eyebrows, and Mains looked around the deck at the others. Faulkner and Snowdon glanced at each other. Cotronis frowned.

"Of course he's sure," McVicar said. "Further away we are, the less chance of them seeing us."

"You know what happens," Mains said. "They see a splash and they'll be on to us, but there's no way we can ignore comms from Tyszka."

"I'll shove us along a bit." Lieder ran some telemetry, calculated a burn, then gave them five seconds. She didn't check anything with Frodo, and Mains liked her confidence. He also knew that if anything she did might be a risk, the computer would intercede.

A little less than an hour later, McVicar opened sub-space comms and narrowed to specified Excursionist channel levels. The message from Tyszka arrived, and he fed the signal into the bridge's system. The voice that greeted them belonged to General Wendy Hetfield herself.

"All units, be aware that Yautja activity over the past ninety days has increased and expanded hugely from the previous several years. The 5th, 9th, 13th, 17th, and 23rd Excursionists have all been involved in contacts, and the 11th is missing in the Holgate system. Each contact so far has involved no more than three Yautja individuals.

"There are also reports of at least seven Yautja ships being sighted within the Sphere by other military and civilian observers. If seven are seen, there might actually be seventy. Be aware, remain alert, keep channels open. For those units currently surveilling Yautja craft, any launch toward or into the Human Sphere is to be taken as predatory and hostile, and all necessary action should be taken.

"You have twelve hours to absorb this information before you respond."

The familiar low whine of sub-space white noise replaced Hetfield's voice as the transmission ended. It was the sound of infinity, and it always gave Mains the chills. It sounded like indifference.

"And I thought we were the only ones at the party," Lieder said.

"Seems not," Mains said. Sometimes a year went by without any Excursionist unit engaging with Yautja, but now there had been at least five contacts within ninety days, with an entire unit missing. There could be many reasons for the 11th being quiet, but with everything else going on, their silence wasn't comforting.

"You want me to slow us down again?" Lieder asked, one eyebrow raised.

"Leave us drifting for now," Mains said, "but stay sharp. Nothing might happen here."

"Or everything might," McVicar said, his laconic voice giving his pronouncement weight.

"The first thing that needs to happen is dinner," Cotronis said.

McVicar rolled his eyes.

"Hey," Faulkner said. "You know you're the best cook."

They drifted further away from the habitat, but they were still closer than they had been for some time, and all the *Ochse*'s observation systems worked flat out keeping watch. They didn't need to be on the bridge for that to work, and Frodo would alert the crew to any anomalies immediately. But Lieder had learned her skills flying atmosphere skimmers on Ganymede, and Mains knew that she liked the impression of being in control. Though she very rarely flew or steered the *Ochse* on manual, she still liked to call it her bird.

"You're sure?" he asked. She remained in her pilot's seat, one foot up on the bank of controls before her, seat reclined.

"Someone's got to stay in charge while you bastards eat."

"I'll bring your food up to you."

"Thanks."

Her voice sounded strange. Not weak, but distracted.

"You okay?"

"Yeah. No. Just thinking about Willis and Reynolds, and

those other units must have lost people. Wonder what we're getting into."

"That's why we're out here. Why we have to keep a close watch on that." He nodded to the holo screen, even though it was now clear.

"Guess I always thought it would be an easy mission."

"Drifting around beyond the boundaries of human exploration?"

"Yeah. Well." She smiled at him, almost said something, turned away. Mains wanted to hold onto the moment. Their closeness was something they both struggled with—they rarely spoke of it, but knew it was there. Sometimes he thought of it as love, but set against the vast, withering reality of deep space, love seemed such a vacuous, pointless concept.

It was a depressing idea.

He watched Lieder for a moment as she tapped her foot to some internal beat, then left the bridge and made his way down to the rec room.

They ate together, discussed the transmission from Tyszka, and the air was heavy with tension. A sense of nervous anticipation filled the room. They quipped and swore. The food was good. They had spent a long time cooped up together in this ship, and although there were individual cabins with their own bathrooms, a hydroponic room where they grew fresh food, a gym, a hold where the drones and a small shuttle were parked, and various other spaces where it was easy to retreat to when solitude was desired, this room was the beating heart of the ship.

There were VR games, a huge library of books on the

reading terminals, comfortable chairs and even a small bar. They'd personalized the space and made it their own, the VoidLark's home away from home. Nevertheless, it was each other's company that made it work.

The ship felt larger than ever with the deaths of Reynolds and Willis, and that loss had brought home the seriousness and danger inherent in their mission. Things had changed.

Frodo's soft chime startled him awake. For a few seconds Mains gasped and looked around, trying to place himself, feeling lost.

"Lights," he said, and a gentle glow grew from the panels around his room.

"Wassit?" Lieder said. She opened one eye and looked at him. "You look like shit."

"Frodo," Mains said. He sat up in bed. Checked the time. Tugged on his underwear, threw Lieder hers. Slapped his cheeks a couple of times to bring himself awake. It had been fifteen days since the signal from Tyszka's Star, and he'd almost allowed himself to relax.

"Sorry to trouble you all," the computer said. Mains knew that Frodo was addressing the whole crew. "Four ships have just departed their docks on UMF 12, and seem to be preparing to leave."

"Flight deck, everyone," Mains said, although he knew he didn't need to. "Frodo, turn on the shipwide grav."

Dressing quickly, he and Lieder dashed from his room and almost collided with Faulkner. Together they passed through the rec room and up to the flight deck, efficient and fast, and three minutes after Frodo's warning the whole crew were at their stations.

"Mark them up," Mains said. McVicar engaged the big screen display. Initially it showed an expanse of nothing, but he zeroed in on the habitat, and four data bubbles marked where the ships were shifting slowly away from the vast mass. They were almost thirty million miles from the habitat now, drifting on station between it and the Human Sphere, but the *Ochse* could get there in less than an hour.

"What's our status?" he asked.

"Still cloaked," Lieder said. "Engines at ninety-seven percent charge. All drive systems green."

"Weapons?"

"All systems green," Faulkner said.

Mains's heart was beating fast, but his actions and reactions were smooth and assured. He glanced around the bridge and saw that confidence echoed in the faces of his crew. They were trained, efficient, experienced. That's why they were Excursionists.

Leading my people into battle again, he thought, and there was a sudden pang in his chest at the danger they were facing.

"Be careful, guys," he said. Lieder glanced at him but he stared only ahead. As he watched, one of the Yautja ships peeled away from the habitat and powered toward the edge of the screen.

"Designated Bastard One," McVicar said. "Bearing zero one-four-one."

"Toward the Sphere," Mains said, but McVicar was too busy to reply.

"Bastard Two, zero one-five-eight. Bastard Three, zero one-four-nine. Bastard Four, zero two-one-six." The display view pulled back to show the moving objects in relation to the habitat, each red speck now marked with its designation, as well as a data bubble showing relative velocity, shifting bearings, and other data.

"Bastard Four's coming right at us," Cotronis said. "Check our cloaking system again."

"Still looks active," Lieder said. "Frodo?"

"The *Ochse*'s cloaking device is fully functioning," the computer said.

"Plot exact course," Mains said.

"Zero two-one-four," McVicar said. "Shifted slightly. Current comparative velocities put us within seven thousand miles of each other."

"Too close," Cotronis said. "L-T, they've seen us."

"That's not certain, but if we decloak they will for sure. Timescales?"

"Their accelerations are variable," McVicar said.

"Classic Yautja distraction techniques," Snowdon said. "They're on a battle footing."

"You're sure?" Mains asked.

"They're not just going for a picnic."

"McVicar, prepare to open a sub-space channel to Tyszka's Star, record a message to send. Tell them what's happening, and that we're engaging."

There was no reaction. Everyone knew what had to be done, and they were already preparing.

"Faulkner, give me a best-case class one strategy here."

Mains was the L-T, but Faulkner was the weapons guy. With distances and trajectories involved, he'd be able to plan the best method of assault. A class one was an action in which their survival was of paramount importance. A class two was a suicide assault.

"Working on it."

"At current acceleration, how long until Bastard Four is at its closest to us?"

"Just over seventeen minutes."

"Suit up, people," Mains said. There was a flurry of movement as the crew grabbed the combat suits always stored behind their seats and pulled them on. Magnetic clasps clicked, air hissed as life-support systems were tested, comms crackled and whispered. As Mains pulled on his own suit, wrapping himself in protective and aggressive tech, Cotronis stood by him. They helped each other secure and check their suits.

"Tough odds," she said.

"We always knew it would be if something happened."

"Maybe we should assault the habitat itself."

He'd thought of that. As far as he knew, they were the only ones tracking a habitat such as this. Other Excursionist units spent months playing cat and mouse with Yautja ships, occasionally ending the chase with a brief, violent combat, more often than not losing touch. The *Ochse* had been on station for over a year. They were in a strong position, but attacking the habitat would vastly reduce the chances of their survival.

They might not even get close.

"I'd rather take out these four ships, then hang back. If

they send more, we keeping fighting—but hopefully they'll get the message."

"Something's going on, Johnny. Across the Rim."

"We've seen no signs that they're gearing up for war."

"I didn't say war."

"It's what you were thinking." Mains shook his head. "We take out a few ships and it's tit for tat, always has been with the Yautja. If we burn their habitat, that's an act of war. We have no idea what the death toll would be, because we don't really know how many live there. But you know these freaks. Ask Snowdon. No one knows how long they live, and it's all pride and honor with them. If you ask me, that's just another cause for hunting and killing, but if we destroy something like this, they'll come after something bigger. Escalation. Our job out here is to prevent war, not cause one."

"Yeah, okay, but we have to consider that the habitat's a target, if the situation calls for it." She turned away, but Mains grabbed her arm. The others were looking. Even Frodo seemed silent and expectant.

"We're in combat now," Mains said to them all. "Let's stay frosty."

Suited up with all personal systems in ready mode, weapons ready in slings beside their seats, they took their places. Mains walked among them, saying nothing but watching them work in a loaded silence. They held together like one oiled machine, only this one was missing two parts.

"L-T," Faulkner said after a few minutes. "I've got a combat solution."

"Let's hear it."

* * *

"On my mark," Mains said. "Three... two... one... *hit it*."

Frodo was ready. All systems had been programmed, and they'd gone over the action profile three times. Now all they had to do was sit in their seats and monitor events.

The *Ochse*'s cloak was disengaged. At the same time the subspace channel was opened and their message fired through to Tyszka's Star. A second later their thrusters fired, throwing the ship into an acceleration that would have turned its occupants into wet smears had the hull not been shielded.

The Yautja ship designated Bastard Four showed the first signs of reacting, but Faulkner's combat solution was already in play. Brought to bear on very precise trajectories, the *Ochse*'s front laser cannons let loose a staggered series of shots that perforated the space around the enemy ship. Seconds later it bloomed into a cloud of gas and debris, and disappeared from the scanner.

"Bastard Four down," Faulkner announced. "Drone One launched." With a disconcerting thud, one of the ship's drones dropped from the hold's open bay doors and then streaked away from them, ion engine blasting at full thrust as its onboard weapon systems hunkered ready.

"Status of the other three ships?" Mains asked. He could see the screen, but knew that McVicar would be analyzing even the slightest changes in bearing or velocity.

"Bastards One and Two maintaining their original courses," McVicar said. "Three is swinging around and coming for us. Largest of the four."

"Have they seen the drone?"

"Doesn't look like it."

"L-T, three more ships are leaving the habitat," Snowdon said.

"Faulkner?"

"Frodo, Drone Two."

Another thud and the second drone left the ship.

"Bastard Three's down," Faulkner said. "Drone Two is heading for One and Two."

Mains had already seen the green arrow wink out on the screen.

"They got it?"

"Yes. Hold on." Faulkner's fingers danced across his control panels. "Frodo?"

"Ready."

"Micro-nukes away. Particle modulator firing up."

"Let's not aim that thing anywhere near the habitat," Mains said.

"L-T!" Cotronis said, but he sent a stern glance her way.

"We've had this discussion. We're not here to start a war, Corporal."

"But maybe they are!"

"Second wave of Yautja ships are splitting up, courses staggered," Snowdon said. "They're coming for us."

"Sure they are," Mains said. "Okay, evasive action."

"The modulator?" Faulkner asked.

"Only if we get a shot that doesn't put the habitat at risk." He'd seen a particle modulator at work before. An immense weapon, but with a spread of effects that were difficult to control, it required a sustained, focused shot to work properly. Not ideal when they were already taking evasive action.

"Bastards One and Two have spiraled up to light speed and vanished," McVicar said.

"Bearing?" Mains asked.

"As before."

"Removed themselves from the fight," Lieder said.

"Or taken it elsewhere," Cotronis said.

"The micro-nukes have been taken out by Yautja countermeasure," Snowdon said. "Sir, we need to make a decision here."

"Fight or flight," Lieder said.

"We don't run from a fight we started," Mains said. "Lieder, swing us around so that we've got a clear field of fire on Bastards Five, Six, and Seven."

Lieder's fingers danced across her controls and Frodo twisted their ship. Mains felt the movements, an unsettling sense of leaving the ghost of himself behind. It was always disconcerting, but something they were all trained for. It didn't prevent him from wanting to puke.

"Five and Six have fired," Faulkner said, but even as he spoke Frodo had launched their countermeasures. Light bloomed on the screen as explosions grew and faded a hundred miles behind them.

"L-T, I've got a—" Faulkner began.

"Bastard One uncloaking!" Snowdon shouted. "Fifteen miles to starboard, laser cannons—"

The ship jumped. Atmosphere vented. The gravity system flicked off, making them sickeningly weightless. Someone screamed. Mains was pressed back in his seat as protective restraints locked down across his body, and just before a shield of hardening foam closed around him, he saw a combat suit bouncing from the bulkhead above him. Sliced neatly in two, it trailed strings of viscera.

Blood flowed, spiraled, and splashed.

5

LUCY-ANNE

Swartwood Station 3, orbiting Weaver's World
July 2692 AD

"Of course you can have chocolate, Honey, but only after school."

"Promise, Mommy?"

"I promise."

Lucy-Anne pouted. "Do you have to go to work?"

Her mother smiled and tickled her, reducing Lucy-Anne to the usual squirming, giggling mess. The girl tried to run away, darting across their cabin and expecting her mother to follow, grab her back, tickle her some more—but her mother had been acting strange lately. Distracted, not sleeping very well. She looked tired, and sometimes Lucy-Anne crept from her sleeping cubby and saw her sitting in the middle of a darkened cabin, hand resting on the comms control as if expecting it to speak to her.

The only person who spoke to them regularly was Daddy, and Daddy was away.

Though only eight, Lucy-Anne already recognized the future that was laid out for her. She'd only seen her father six times in the last four years, and the joy of seeing him in his Colonial Marines uniform had dulled. Now her mommy was training to do the same, and the time would soon come when the schooling wing of Swartwood Station would become Lucy-Anne's home.

She knew that when the time came, she would also don the uniform. She wasn't quite sure what she felt about that. She liked the warm feel of her daddy's combat suit, the way it closed around her, and all the things she could see, hear, and do inside. Its computer even seemed to know her name.

She would still rather they were all home together.

"Mommy?" Her mommy was looking at her in a weird way. Head to one side, eyes wide and wet, right hand fisted and tapping at her thigh as if to a tune only one of them could hear.

"You're a good girl."

"I know," Lucy-Anne said.

"Chocolate after school."

"Okay."

Her mommy was quiet for a moment longer, and Lucy-Anne thought she was going to cry. But then she blinked a few times, turned her head as if listening, and smiled.

"So can you walk yourself to school today? Mommy's got something to do."

"Can I go across the walkway?"

"Sure you can."

"Yay!" Lucy-Anne loved the walkway. It made her feel like she was flying. "Love you, Mommy!"

Her mother came close and hugged her tighter than she ever had before, but she didn't speak.

Lucy-Anne was known among many of the residents of Swartwood Station 3. It was her bright pink dungarees that set her apart. Most girls her age were already dressing in combat fatigues matching their parents', but Lucy-Anne had always loved pink.

People smiled and nodded to her as she left the accommodation wing, a few exchanged brief pleasantries, and soon she was halfway to the station's hub and ready to cross the walkway. Swartwood Station 3 consisted of a large hub and four huge pods, unofficially called Mark, Matthew, Luke, and John. Lucy-Anne didn't know where the names came from, but she liked that her school was in Luke. It was a nice place, brightly decorated and run by teachers who everyone liked.

Mark was the accommodation pod, Matthew the training center, and John was the hangar, where ships came and went. The Hub was the main control center of the space station. There were almost two thousand people on board, and a third of those were kids. She liked having so many children to play with. From the moment she headed out on the walkway, she forgot that one day soon her parents would leave her here alone.

That was the main reason she liked the walkway between Mark and Luke. Not only did it feel like flying, but it helped her to forget.

Six hundred and fifty yards long, the tunnel was made almost entirely of diamonite-impregnated glass. Wide enough for several people to pass each other, it gave an all-round view that never got old. Usually when she came this way, alone, she ended up being late for school, and sometimes she got into trouble for that. That was why she normally had to go all the way to the hub and back up the main arm to Luke. It wasn't very often mommy let her come this way. And she'd been promised chocolate after school.

Maybe she's missing Daddy, Lucy-Anne thought. *Like me.*

She stood and stared.

Beneath her, visible through the clear floor, was the hub of Swartwood Station, the whole structure spinning in its orbit to provide artificial gravity. So she looked up and out, through the glass ceiling at the endless space beyond. She never tired of looking, and didn't understand how anyone could. She was staring at forever. Anything could be out there. If space really was infinite, her daddy had told her—and scientists, he said, still couldn't agree exactly on that fact—then somewhere out there was a square planet. In infinity, anything was possible.

Somewhere out there was another her.

Lucy-Anne still wasn't sure whether she liked that idea, but she enjoyed staring, and thinking that if she could expand the direction she was staring, just enough, she might see an alien somewhere far, far away who was looking right back at her. She wondered what that alien was thinking, and whether it was thinking about her.

She wondered all the time.

As she watched, the glowing arc of Weaver's World slowly

swung into view. It was an amazing place that mommy told her was called a Goldilocks planet because it was already somewhere people could live. They'd been down there a few times together, and once with Daddy, all three of them taking a trip north from the space elevator station on the equator and enjoying twenty days on safari. The main island of Weaver's World was called Ellia, and it was home to an amazing array of flora and fauna. Lucy-Anne had worried that humans being there would get in the way of the planet's nature, but her mother had told her she shouldn't worry about that.

They'd watched a herd of cat-sized lizards hunting massive elephantish creatures. They'd seen a cloud of sparkling bats forming complex shapes and patterns over a deep ravine at dusk. Eight-winged butterflies had sung to her, and for dinner they'd eaten fruit that tasted of coconut and chocolate.

The thought of chocolate stirred her from her reverie, and a tall Marine passing by chuckled.

"You'll be late for school, Lucy-Anne!" he said.

"I just can't help looking at—"

Something punched her feet. Her vision blurred, stars smeared, and the visible shoulder of Weaver's World pulsed as if the planet had taken a deep breath.

"Oh my God!" the Marine shouted, and Lucy-Anne looked down between her feet, through the glass floor, at what was happening below. As she saw, the noise came—a boom, thumping her ears; a roar, like water boiling; a crackling, crumpling sound. The hub was birthing fire, great shattered swathes of its superstructure shoved out into space on boiling plumes of flame and debris. The fire quickly retreated as air was drawn out, and then other objects followed. A deck of seating from the large conference center. People, spinning and colliding with wreckage. Some of them were burning as they emerged. Some of them were coming apart, limbs cartwheeling away from the station, colliding with the arms and pods, disappearing into the void.

"Mommy!" Lucy-Anne screamed. She looked at the tall Marine for help, but he was already running back along the walkway toward the accommodation pod.

A huge chunk of the hub powered into the leg connecting it with Luke, crumpling the metal like paper and ripping it aside. The chunk ricocheted up and away from the station, the leg tearing and parting, and the mass of Luke itself started to rip free of the walkway.

Lucy-Anne fell to her knees, stood again, and followed the Marine back toward Mark. Mommy would be there. Mommy with her sad eyes and far-away look, sitting awake at night listening to things Lucy-Anne couldn't hear. Bringing stuff home she did not recognize. Making things she didn't know.

"Mommy!"

Mark exploded. She saw its entire supporting arm fracture, and the air pressure inside the accommodation pod split its hull apart. Sparkling flames soon guttered out in the vacuum of space, and a flood of bodies spewed out from one rupture carried in a cloud of escaping atmosphere, impacting each other, grasping on, glistening frostily as air turned to ice around them.

Mommy! she tried to scream again, but her voice was swallowed by terror.

She ran. The Marine was ahead of her, sprinting, but already everything felt wrong. Lucy-Anne's stomach dropped, she felt suddenly lighter. A deafening whistling sound filled her head.

All around her, outside the clear walkway, the darkness of space was filled with glimmering, spinning, horrific debris.

Just as the Marine reached the doorway leading into Mark, the whole walkway before him erupted. He disappeared. The glass walls sang as they were ripped apart, and still trying to shout for her mother, Lucy-Anne was grabbed by an invisible hand and tugged toward infinity.

6

GERARD MARSHALL

Charon Station, Sol System
July 2692 AD

General Paul Bassett, commanding officer of the entirety of the Colonial Marine forces, including all Spaceborne, Terrestrial, and Excursionist units, was a prick.

Gerard Marshall had long thought this, since before they'd met face to face, and now that he was on Charon Station—the General's command center—they had met many, many times, giving Marshall cause to consider and revise his initial assessment.

The General was a *complete* prick.

Like now. Being summoned to his rooms by a combat droid, instead of the General finding time to call him personally. *General Paul Bassett requests your attendance in his command suite at eleven hundred hours for a...* A quick holo message from the great man himself would have sufficed. It wasn't as if they had different agendas. There should have been agreement between them, a common ground. Instead, this clash of personalities that seemed to grow every time they met.

Marshall tried to analyze it dispassionately, and he'd come to the conclusion that they simply rubbed each other up the wrong way. That wouldn't have been a problem if they were just two plebs or grunts bickering their way through the day, but when one of them was a general in charge of quarter of a million troops, and the other was one of the Thirteen, the Weyland-Yutani company board, there was so much more at stake.

Neither of them could let their egos get in the way of what they were here for, and Marshall feared that being summoned to the command suite could only mean more bad news.

Charon Station was huge. Orbiting the Sol System every thirty years at almost four billion miles from the sun, it had been the Colonial Marines' main command base for almost sixty years. In that time it had been expanded and upgraded to such an extent that it was now more of a complex of interconnected space stations than one single structure. Seven individual vessels housed barracks, hangars, storage holds, communications, offices, and other essential needs that went to serve as a permanent home for more than seven hundred staff, as well as a rotating garrison of a thousand Marines along with their weapons, equipment, and craft.

Almost forty years earlier, a whole section of Charon Station had been destroyed by an asteroid impact, with the loss of four hundred lives. It was a huge blow to the Colonial Marines, and it came at a time when skirmishes had broken out across the Human Sphere between the Colonials and several rogue military units seeking independence. When the catastrophe occurred, doubt and paranoia had bitten in hard, but all evidence had always pointed to a freak accident. Since then, sweeper ships were stationed several thousand miles ahead of the station's orbit, destroying any space debris that was considered even a vague threat to the station.

Gerard Marshall had been here for more than twelve weeks, and he hated the place. He hated being anywhere that involved breathing conditioned, artificially manufactured air, walking with the aid of faux gravity, eating food processed from bacteria and bugs and insects, and where a slight accident could result in him being sucked into the cold vacuum of a painful demise. As one of the Thirteen, he knew far too much about what could go wrong in space. He had covered up enough disasters, after all. He'd even initiated a few.

It was starting to look like he'd be here for a long time more. He hated the idea of that, but he could also not contain his excitement. As chief officer of the Thirteen, covering alien technology and weaponry acquisition, and director of ArmoTech, recent events meant that this was an exciting time to be alive.

The Thirteen wanted him close to Bassett. In all the military, the General was the man they trusted most. Yet complete trust wasn't something that the Thirteen allowed, and so Marshall was here to observe, oversee, and if it became necessary, to intervene.

Bassett's rooms were at the center of the command pod, one of the smaller sections of Charon Station, yet also the most heavily defended. A Sleek-class destroyer was docked permanently against the pod, crewed around the clock and ready to launch within thirty seconds, if the need arose. The pod itself was triple-constructed, possessed cloaking technology the equal to the Arrow-class ships used by Excursionists, and if the need arose it could break away and become its own individual spacecraft.

The first time Marshall had crossed one of the 450-yard-long connecting bridges to the command pod, Bassett had taken pleasure in telling him that each bridge was equipped with a series of explosive rings that could split it in half in milliseconds. Bad enough that the bridges were completely transparent.

Yes, Basset really was a prize prick.

"Who goes there?" The big Marine standing at the end of the bridge brought his nano-rifle to bear.

"Really?" Marshall asked.

"Second warning, Mr. Marshall."

"You just told me my name."

The Marine took a step back into a shooting stance, the nano-rifle's control panel casting a faint blue glow onto his faceplate. Marshall could only make out his eyes behind the visor, all other facial features hidden. He never liked the threatening impersonality of combat suits, but supposed that was one of their more subtle weapons.

"Third warning."

Marshall sighed. "Gerard Marshall, seventh chair of the Weyland-Yutani Thirteen, ID code seven-one-gamma-three-november."

The marine stood to attention again, and Marshall heard

the distant whisper of his combat computer confirming the identity of the man standing before him.

"Thank you, Sir. General Bassett is expecting you. You can find him in the VR suite of his control room."

"Right." Marshall walked past the marine toward the doorway, which faded open, then he paused. "Don't you ever...?" The marine turned to look down at Marshall, faceplate giving nothing away. The combat suit was silent. The rifle still glowed, and Marshall wondered what setting it was kept on. He'd seen such rifles fired before in demonstrations, had witnessed their firepower. Immense, and horrific.

"Never mind," he said. "Carry on."

The door grew dark and solid again behind him, a containment field more impregnable than three-inch steel, and he was in the command pod.

As he moved through the command pod, several other marines watched him pass them by, then a female marine minus her combat helmet nodded and accompanied him along an elevated walkway that skirted the main control globe. The room was huge, fifty yards across, bustling, filled with holo frames, computer terminal points, and people drifting back and forth on air chairs. It never failed to send a shiver down his spine. This was the beating heart of the Company's military machine, and an uncomfortable truth beat through this place with every pulse.

The Marines were the only reason that W-Y had once again become the power it was today.

No organization could reach such a wide-ranging ubiquitousness without a powerful force behind them.

"You'll know where to find him," the marine said, and she handed Marshall a pair of swimming briefs.

"Really?" he asked.

The woman smiled. He was glad. Any sign of humanity among these people comforted him.

Maybe she was an android.

Marshall took the briefs and stepped through into the VR control room staging area. It was empty, apart from a small pile of neatly folded military clothing, a pair of boots, and a set of glasses. Bassett was one of the few people Marshall knew who eschewed corrective surgery for his defective eyesight. Perhaps because the glasses made him distinctive.

Marshall stripped and pulled on the briefs, feeling self-conscious of his sagging stomach and weak limbs. If he'd spent a long time in space he might at least have been able to blame his weakness on muscle and bone degeneration. Yet there were treatments to deal with that, and exercises, and everyone knew he preferred the sensation of solid ground beneath his feet. He had a great mind, but his physical laziness was apparent.

Bassett's rooms behind the control globe were mostly functional and sparse, but the VR suite itself was a huge indulgence, an extravagance the General enjoyed courtesy of the Company. Marshall had been in there several times before, and he found it disconcerting. This time, he had no idea what to expect.

Pushing through the darkened air lock and emerging into the suite, the scene took his breath away.

An ocean stretched out before him. The light blue sky,

endless above the azure waters, was streaked with high clouds caught in some invisible airstream. Waves broke against the sandy beach. Waters foamed, bubbles slid across the smoothed sand, crabs scuttled into cover, retreating from the blazing sun.

Marshall stood in the shadows of overhanging palm trees and he took a few quick steps forward, groaning when he felt the sunlight on his skin. There was nothing like it. Life-support systems, air conditioning, direct heating panels set in his rooms, none of them could match the honest feel of true sunlight.

"Beautiful, isn't it?" Bassett said. He was sitting in a beach chair close to where the waves reached, the chair's feet and his own sunk in the sand. Almost seventy years old, he was one of the fittest men Marshall had ever seen. Toned and tall, his torso a relief map of knotted muscle, his limbs strong and lean, he carried no spare ounce of fat, and performed no unnecessary movements. He looked as though he'd been born with the claw scar that split his nose and right cheek. From a bug hunt, he'd said the first time Marshall had asked him about it. Like his poor eyesight, he chose not to have corrective surgery to remove the gruesome battle wound.

The most surprising thing about the scene was that Bassett was crying.

"Where are we?" Marshall asked. He had no wish to mention the tears.

"Weaver's World," Bassett said. "Eastern shores of Ellia, its largest continent. Just on the equator. It's an hour 'til sunset, and soon you'll see one of the three moons manifest out over the sea. It's eclipsed up to now by one of the other moons. Quite a beautiful sight. I've sat here and watched it three times today."

"Is everything all right?"

Bassett looked away from Marshall, out across the sea. Trees rustled behind them, the breeze reaching down and lifting Marshall's hair. *If I close my eyes, it's real,* he thought, but he was afraid to do so. He didn't like these VR suites. They were a lie, and in a few minutes he'd have to step out onto a deck again, the freezing indifference of space all around. Space only wanted him dead.

Bassett whispered some command and the imagery faded quickly away, replaced by something else. The transition was disconcerting and dizzying, and Marshall staggered a few steps to his right. Sand between his toes, then cool metal, and then the silky swish of grass.

He gasped and took in a couple of quick breaths. The beachy scent was replaced with the perfume of wild flowers, and the hint of heat or burning. The landscape was wide and lush, a flowing grassy plain giving rise to impossibly tall trees in the distance. To his left was a range of peaks so high he couldn't see their summits, hidden in the haze of distance. To the right, the plains gave way to rolling hills, and beyond them were the unmistakable stacks of atmosphere processors. Marshall squinted, trying to see through the haze.

The processors looked strange.

"Gonzalez Six," Bassett said. He was standing now, still in his swimming shorts. There were other scars on his body that Marshall had not seen before. He wondered whether they were from the same bug hunt. "Formerly LV-204. One of the first worlds successfully terraformed, although to be fair it was already almost there. The processors…" He pointed at them, mountainous constructs in the distance. "They were decommissioned and abandoned almost a century ago. Apparently they're home to a species of beetle now. Billions of them."

"General, why did you call me here?"

"I'm not a sentimental man," the soldier said. He issued a command and the noise faded away to nothing, leaving them standing in an incredible, aromatic, utterly silent landscape. "I can't afford to be. Sentimentality gets in the way of duty. But then, you wouldn't understand that."

"I wouldn't?"

"You don't have it in you to be sentimental." There was no judgement there, only a statement of fact. Marshall started to object, but realized that he couldn't. Unlike many Company people he worked with, he prided himself on his honesty.

"I lost my son today," the General said. "We vacationed as a family on Weaver's World once, spent three months traveling up the eastern coast of Ellia by hovercraft. When he was older, he and I went on a hunting trip to Gonzalez Six. We didn't catch anything."

"I'm sorry," Marshall said, but at the same time he thought, *What has this got to do with me?*

"Close down," Bassett said, and the VR suite wound itself down. From an uncanny representation of a world over a hundred light years away, to a metal cube lined with tech and buzzing with leftover energy, all in the space of a few seconds.

"What happened?" Marshall asked.

"Murder," the General said. He seemed to have gathered

himself now, wiping openly at his eyes and then standing tall, staring Marshall in the eye. "Mass murder, in fact. Come through to my office. I'll show you."

The image in the holo frame wasn't very clear. It had been taken from seventy miles out, by a ship on its final approach to Swartwood Station 3. But it was clear enough.

As the huge space station came apart in a glow of shimmering debris, Marshall realized that he was holding his breath. The footage ended, the frame clouded to its neutral form, and General Bassett slumped down in his large leather seat.

"Who would do something like this?" Marshall asked. "Red Four?" He had personal experience of the anti W-Y terrorist group. One of his ex-subordinates was now one of the leading Four of the organization's name, a ratty, devious man whose dislike of expansionism and big business had led him to others of the same ilk, and from there to radicalization.

"They don't have the capability—not any more—and much as I hate those fuckers, I really don't think they'd attempt something so... grotesque."

"Probably not," Marshall agreed. He glanced at the General, hesitant to verbalize his next thought. "Accident?" he asked softly.

"Not according to a blast signature recorded by three ships within a thousand mile radius. It was a small device, probably plasma based, but planted in a position that indicates a good structural knowledge of the station. These things are built to withstand blasts, and airlock doors should have ensured the survival of as many staff as possible. But... whoever did it, they knew what they were doing."

"How many?" Marshall asked.

"One thousand, nine hundred and thirty." Bassett shrugged. "Give or take a couple of ship's crews."

"Fucking hell."

"My son, Harry, had been based there for six months. He was a flight trainer. Two of the others survived, they were out on flights, but he was off-duty, probably asleep. Six hundred children."

Marshall sat heavily into a sofa. "I'm sorry, Paul."

The General seemed surprised at the use of his given name, and he nodded once.

"So what is this?" Marshall asked.

"We're still investigating. I've issued a level one alert to all Colonial Marines, as well as support staff and organizations. I suggest you advise the Thirteen to do the same for Weyland-Yutani."

"Of course. You don't think this is anything to do with...?"

"Yautja?" Bassett didn't scoff, as Marshall had been expecting. Instead he tapped his fingers on his desk, tracing the deep groove across his nose with his other hand. "We've had more attacks from them in the last three months than the past three years combined. Something's happening with them, and we have people trying to work out what. I know you do, too. Isa Palant?"

"She's one of our best, yes," Marshall said, "and I've sent someone from my own staff to aid her research."

"Yautja are weird. Slave to tradition and history, which

112

I suppose is natural given the age they can reach. Maybe there's a religious aspect to their increased attacks, a species anniversary of some kind. Something in their calendar that suggests they have to take more skulls, win more trophy hunts. I hate the bastard things, and I have good cause, but the increased attacks are mostly across the Outer Rim. They've never tried anything like this. I honestly don't think they would. Where's the honor in murdering two thousand innocents at a distance, with a bomb?"

"No honor," Marshall said, cringing inwardly. Bassett hadn't needed his question answered.

"We need to remain vigilant," Bassett said. "We'll track down those responsible, but in the meantime our priority is to ensure that this doesn't happen again."

"Of course," Marshall said. "Will you be…?"

"Compassionate leave?" Bassett said, laughing without humor "My ex-wife will arrange a memorial. I won't be there. I have quarter of a million children, Marshall."

Marshall nodded and stood, stepping forward and holding out his hand. The General surprised him by shaking it.

As he left Bassett's rooms and passed back through the huge control globe, Marshall paused on the walkway and looked with new eyes. In one holo frame halfway across the globe, the exploding Smartwood Station 3 appeared again, slowed down to a tenth of its true speed while two people observed the footage, probing with thin laser filaments, changing and dissecting the image and viewing the data.

Elsewhere, a group of Marines huddled around a comms point, listening intently. Closer to where he stood, a frame floated above two seated Marines, the image within showing a sweating, agitated soldier imparting information while shadows darted back and forth behind him. There were flames. He was bleeding.

The female marine who'd brought him here appeared at the end of the walkway, closing the distance quickly.

"This way," she said.

"Just a minute." Marshall knew that Colonial Marines kept their business close, but she knew who he was, and she would never attempt to hurry him on.

There was a buzz throughout the globe that he'd not noticed before, a sort of restrained energy pulsing for release. People walked smartly to and fro. Holo frames showed desperate faces, desolate scenes, or blankness. In the center of the vast room glowed a clear image, five yards across. A representation of the Human Sphere, thousands of points of white light glimmering, and here and there red lights bloomed. Perhaps he was looking at a map of Yautja contact, and if so there were more than he had expected.

Marshall realized with a cool rush that the Colonial Marines were already on a war footing.

"What happens now?" he whispered, not realizing that the marine had sidled up to him.

"Now we do what we're trained for," she said. "Come on, Sir. I'll show you back to the bridge."

Marshall followed her from the control globe, leaving behind those red flaring lights and urgent sub-space communications from scores or hundreds of light years away. He had a report to make to the Thirteen. Along with

Xenomorphs, the Yautja were a species whose secrets had long eluded Weyland-Yutani.

And war was often profitable.

7

LILIYA

Testimony

When I was young—in age, not appearance, because I've always looked this way—I worked with a small group of scientists chasing comets. There were three they were targeting, two of which were back in the Sol System for the first time in centuries. They had landed probes on them decades before, but those had long since run out of power.

The scientists wanted to retrieve the three probes in order to download all experimental data they had been unable to transmit. They were good people, as independent as anyone can be involved in deep space travel and exploration. They took me along because of my ability to work in hostile environments. They knew I was different, and they never let that go.

"We're looking for the origins of life in the universe," one of them said to me one day. "Comets might carry the blueprints. Knowing where we come from, that would be a profound moment—but then, I don't suppose that worries you that much. You already know where *you* came from."

He didn't say it in a cruel way. It was matter-of-fact. But it struck home with me. My age approximated my appearance about then, and already I was starting to question.

When I was adrift in that escape pod after leaving the *Evelyn-Tew*, waiting to be picked up by Wordsworth and his Founders, with all that time on my own, my questions turned to deep musings. As the years passed by, and then the decades, before they finally came for me, I found myself sleeping and dreaming of where I had come from and what I was supposed to do.

Androids were never meant to dream.

It's difficult to comprehend spending that amount of time alone. I was adrift for almost forty years. Wordsworth had told me it would be months at most, but he encountered problems, so they left me. They knew that I had left the system, traveling perpendicular to the orbital plane and venturing into deserted space, and the Founders believed that was the safest place for me. It was highly unlikely that I'd be found at random. They were right.

Forty years, alone in an escape pod too small to move around in. No viewing portals. No navigational system. Once I launched from *Evelyn-Tew* and programmed a fuel burn, I was set on my course.

I had to close down most of my systems, but my consciousness remained—sometimes awake, sometimes absorbed in what approximated sleep. Dreaming. I lived every day of those forty years alone.

That gave me plenty of time to think.

I was confident that I'd done the right thing. Though I had caused many lives to be lost, I always considered the Founders' philosophies to be admirable. To begin with, they were pure in intent and outlook, and that was something I respected so much. Even forty years later, when an older, wiser Wordsworth and his people finally found and retrieved me, there was an ebullience about them, a confidence and excitement about what they were doing and where they were going. I was caught up in that, then as before.

Wordsworth himself nursed me back to health. After so long, many of my systems had failed, and much of my biological self had petrified. He donated his own cells and blood to help me and then…

I'm getting ahead of myself.

First, I need to tell you about the Founders. You might have heard about them, but probably not. They were one obscure religion among many, and when they disappeared it was probably assumed that Wordsworth and his followers had died, or lost themselves between the stars that existed within the Human Sphere. Many people had done so before, and some of them managed to set up their own independent communities and live out their lives on remote space stations, abandoned bases, on planets or moons, or constantly moving on captured Titan ships or other transports.

Yet that assumption gives no credit to Wordsworth's ambitions and drive, nor his abilities. He was a genius, and everything he stood for and achieved should be respected.

The Founders saw themselves as pilgrims, seeking religious and philosophical freedom from the taint of the Human Sphere. They were a collective of much older groups once persecuted by Weyland-Yutani, as well as other corporations and organizations now faded into history. They were all working at the fringes of their fields, the edge of understanding, and sometimes the boundaries of acceptability.

They were persecuted because they strived to bring themselves closer to God by almost *becoming* gods. They were comprised of scientists, forward thinkers, those disillusioned with humanity, and those who believed that its true purpose was to progress as far and fast as it could.

As part of this they were experimenting with longevity— and succeeding. They had also developed a much more effective faster-than-light drive and kept it to themselves, viewing it as their potential means of escape. They did not believe that they had to share their great discoveries with everyone else. Looked down upon by the wider community, they became introverted. Some would say rightly so.

I would agree.

Much like the Pilgrim Fathers of Earth's ancient history, they were seeking a new, free world, believing that they could establish a utopia away from the sphere of human influence. Thus they chose to flee—not just persecution, but the confines of humanity's influence.

Using their newly developed FTL drive they left the Human Sphere far behind, and were the first humans to explore far beyond.

That was why I was taken with them, and why I did what I did. The advanced Xenomorph research I stole from the *Evelyn-Tew* was vital to the Founders' future. They knew there were dangers out there, things unknown and perhaps unknowable. Legend had it Weyland himself had gone searching, and no one knew what became of him. The Founders required the means to confront these dangers as well as they could.

The idea of harnessing such beasts, weaponizing them, *controlling* them, was one defense against the unknown. As well as against the beasts themselves.

I still don't believe I was an afterthought. I simply think that Wordsworth assumed I was safest where I was, drifting alone until all preparations were made and the Founders were ready to depart. I was *vital* to them. These current events illustrate that—in ways more terrible, more tragic, than I could ever have imagined.

For that, my guilt runs even deeper.

8

LILIYA

Beyond the Human Sphere
July 2692 AD

"In the deep, in the dark, let light blossom to illuminate our way home."

The messages had been designed to instill hope. Two years before, even as she had sent the first of them as instructed by Beatrix Maloney herself, Liliya had grasped onto the notion that this was all for the good.

The messages said so.

Sent on a sub-space frequency that could only be known to descendants of those left behind over two centuries before, they spoke of a great return, a welcoming into a brave new world, and they seeded a promise that had originally been left behind. *We will come back for you.*

Now, they *were* coming back, but Liliya knew that it wasn't hope they brought. Halfway through sending the final message, suspicions aroused, she discovered that the messages communicated far more than mere words.

"You were never forgotten," she said. The room she stood in was circular, warm, comfortable, grown rather than built. Just another part of the incredible technology the Founders had discovered out among the stars, and which the Rage were now carrying back in their starships. "You were always fresh in our minds, while we traveled and explored, while we discovered and developed. In the centuries since we left we have grown, and now that return is at hand, our growth will be your future."

Liliya had a script but did not need it. The messages were memorized the first time Beatrix recited them to her, and the lies were clearer than ever as she spoke them aloud. Her words were recorded into the transmission bubble, alive in the air before her, loaded and ready to send.

There was something else in the transmission bubble that her words could not have put there. An infestation, like a smear on the air. Perhaps Beatrix assumed she would never see it, and if Liliya hadn't been so suspicious, so jaded by all that was happening and what she suspected would happen in the near future, maybe she wouldn't have seen it.

Her senses were more open and alert than ever before, looking for deception, and her mind was so much greater than it had ever been. Beatrix had seen to that, almost without realizing it. More than three hundred years old, Liliya might well be the oldest synthetic in the galaxy. In her unnaturally long existence, she had learned so much.

"For now, our return is your secret, and it must remain so," she said, her words coalescing and dancing, merging with the errant message in the transmission bubble, readying to be sent.

How did I not notice this before? she thought. *If it was there all those other times, how could I not see it?* Maybe she hadn't been looking with enough suspicion, and with such corrupted thoughts.

Everything that should have been right had gone wrong.

"Listen to these words. Revel in them. They are your prayer."

Her speech finished, Liliya stepped back to the edge of the room and whispered, "Store." The transmission bubble shrank down to nothing, and then the unit at the center of the chamber issued a soft red glow. The message was ready.

Liliya paused.

What else was in there?

Her orders were to dictate the message, and then send it immediately, and like every other time, she almost did just that.

Almost.

But in her three centuries, she had also become cranky. She had her own mind, her own desires, and following orders was something she only did if she saw fit. She always gave the *impression* that she was doing as instructed, but sometimes she paused, took a breath, and analyzed her actions.

Even after so long, she was still becoming human.

She accessed the ship's Brain and assessed where Beatrix was right now. Close, and moving toward her. But not *too* close.

Liliya crossed the room and pressed her hand against the glowing unit. She closed her eyes and retreated into her own mind, that old computerized consciousness that now merged with the even more complex element that she liked to call her *soul*. She probed deep, listening to the speech she had just spoken.

Deeper, and there was something else there, arcane and confusing. At first she thought the message was corrupted, and that perhaps the alien technology the Rage had adopted was intruding into their reality once more.

But then she analyzed what she found, and realized that this was in fact a very human subversion.

She gasped and stepped back, wiping her hand on her trousers. Biological programming! Alien technology, far beyond the comprehension of any of them. Too dangerous, too unknown to be used—but Beatrix Maloney was using it anyway.

"Stupid," Liliya said. Biological programming was the building and programming of nano-devices crafted from existing living matter. The prompt-coding could be applied in many ways—directly, intravenously, by airborne contagion...

Or by suggestion.

Buried beneath the surface message of hope her transmission carried was a command. Liliya did her best to understand it, and her suspicions of what to expect probably helped. Combined with her spoken message, the covert transmission would initiate a process of nano-construction, control, and eventual destruction.

"All lies," she said, and then she heard the familiar sound of Beatrix Maloney's approach. The gentle hum of her platform drifting through the air and then, as she grew closer, the gurgle and swish of her suspension system.

"Liliya?" she called even before she entered the room. "Have you finished?"

"No," Liliya said, "and I won't."

Beatrix entered. Her platform floated through the doorway and hovered, holding the thin, ancient woman two feet above the floor. Propped in a sitting position, torso and limbs suspended in the clear gel containment suit, she presented a pathetic image, but Liliya knew that she was anything but pathetic. With strength came power, and Beatrix had plenty of both.

"Won't?"

"Beatrix," Liliya said sadly, shaking her head.

"You've known all along," the old woman said. "Since Wordsworth died and I took over, you've always known what my final aim would be."

"I've always known that returning was your plan," Liliya responded. "Of course, but not like this. What message are you sending? What are you asking people to do? I never expected our return to be so *aggressive*."

"And why not?" Maloney countered. "They drove us away in the first place. Banished us to deep space—to the cold, the dangers."

"The Founders fled of their own accord!"

"Do you really think that, Liliya?"

"I *know* that. I was there."

"And so was I. While you were floating in your escape pod for decades, I saw what it was like for the Founders, two centuries ago. Persecuted. Vilified for their beliefs. Driven out, and now we're taking back what should always have been ours."

"Wordsworth would have never done it like this."

"Wordsworth is dead!" Maloney spat, her suspension fluid bubbling as if in reaction to her mood. "And he was weak."

"If what you say is true, we should return in peace. Share what we've found… all that knowledge, that technology."

Beatrix laughed, a surprisingly light, airy sound from someone so old, so strange.

"You think they'll welcome us with open arms?"

"Why not? We'll be bringing technology and advances the likes of which they can't dream."

"They'll steal it from us. All of it—you know that as well as me. *Better* than me. You were there when it all began, and if it weren't for you—"

"Don't say that. Don't pretend I'm responsible."

"I'm not pretending, Liliya. If it weren't for you, we wouldn't have *them*!"

Them, Liliya thought bitterly. *I can't accept that I made them.*

"Send the message, Liliya."

"And what will happen?"

"It will smooth our return." The old woman smiled, a wrinkled grimace that split her face.

"It'll corrupt those who hear it. You *know* it will build biologically based nano-bots to reprogram their minds. What will it make them do? What destruction will it cause?"

Beatrix floated closer, and Liliya stepped between her and the unit. The room felt suddenly much smaller, as if the walls had grown inward. This old woman, this one-time friend, now meant her harm. Liliya could see that in her eyes. She could see madness there, too, had recognized that for some time. In her foolishness she'd believed that she might be able to temper it.

"What's the point in finding utopia if you can't take it home?" Beatrix said.

"You call this utopia?" Liliya laughed, shoving against the floating platform and sending Beatrix clattering against the wall. They both froze. Liliya had never struck out at her before.

"Liliya—"

"I won't allow it," Liliya said. "I can't!"

"You'll do as I tell you."

"No," she said. "I'm not cowed by you, Beatrix. I'm not a machine, like your followers."

Maloney sneered, but then seemed to see something in Liliya's expression that gave her doubt.

"Guards," she whispered.

Liliya could have fought. She might even have been able to take down the two Rage troopers and cancel the sub-space broadcast, but she couldn't halt it forever, and right then a new idea was already blooming. In truth, it had been there since Wordsworth's murder by this woman's hand.

Liliya allowed herself to be pulled aside and watched as Beatrix drifted forward, reached out with her gel-supported arm, and sent the message.

"We'll be there soon," the Rage leader said to Liliya. "Make up your mind."

I already have, Liliya thought.

It was time to steal, and flee again.

9

ISA PALANT

Love Grove Base, Research Station, LV-1529
July 2692 AD

"So is he as much of a prick as you'd feared?"

"I can't help liking him." Isa shrugged and took another swig from Rogers's hip flask. She imported coffee beans, he brought in single malt. As he sometimes said, they were made for each other. "He's a Company man through and through, but he's as excited about the Yautja as I am."

"Weird," Rogers said, seat reclined, feet on the rover's steering column. "I can just picture the two of you, alone in that lab. Those dead things there, naked. Your dilated pupils, those surgical gloves…"

"Shit, Rogers, is there anything on your mind other than sex?"

"Only occasionally," he said. He frowned, staring through the windscreen at the storm raging outside. The rover rocked slightly where it was parked.

Palant took another swig, then passed the hip flask back to her friend. He saluted her and drank—kept looking at her and smiling, and she knew that he'd missed her. It took a trip away from the base to make her realize that she'd missed him, too. Almost fifty days had passed since the two dead Yautja had been delivered, and she had worked every day since, sometimes fourteen hours each day.

Milt McIlveen had arrived twelve days after Marshall's communication with her, and had worked with her ever since. Her entire existence had become focused on the bodies. For a while, she forgot where she was.

It had taken a lot of persuading from Rogers to get her out here again, but now she was so glad that she'd relented.

"You look pale," he said. "Tired and overworked."

"Aren't we all?"

"Why do you think I pull this duty as much as I can?"

"Oh, yes, aren't we supposed to be patrolling the boundary?"

"Nothing to patrol it against."

"There's always something," Palant said, and she heard her father's voice again, telling her that space would never truly be known to humanity. That they were trespassing there.

"So what do you think happened to Svenlap?"

"It's weird," Palant said. "I saw her the day before she disappeared. Last time you and I were out here together, the day the dead Yautja arrived. She seemed fine then, if a little tired, and she loved her job, was as passionate about their history and society as I am about their physiology and tech. Then, nothing. Her rooms were ransacked, but there's no sign of where she went, or why."

"Yeah, weird."

"I'm still hoping she'll be found. It's been a long time, but Love Grove is a big place, and there are lots of sections that have been shut off for a while. Since the processor construction was finished, in fact."

"Those sections have been searched," Rogers said. Isa knew that. He and the other indies had done much of the searching, with nothing to report apart from empty rooms and failing structures.

"Still, she might be hiding."

"No," he said, "she's gone." He took another drink and passed it back to her. Isa could feel the warm glow permeating her torso, the gentle tiredness settling over her. She didn't want to get drunk because she had so much work still to do, yet sitting out here with Rogers, isolated in the rover, getting drunk seemed like a good idea. Isa had many colleagues, but he felt like a true friend. Warmth in the coldness of space.

"What do you mean?"

He waved at the windscreen. They couldn't see much, because today's storm was harsher than most. Sand scoured the transparent surface, grit rasped against the rover's hull. Its exhaust had been fixed, but the chassis still creaked and groaned in complaint.

"Out there… Wandered out, got lost, died. Doubt there's much left of her now."

"I don't believe that," Palant said, even though it had always been a possibility. She'd spent some time considering whether it could have happened, and she didn't like where her imagination took her. Angela would have likely suffocated from the low oxygen levels before anything else killed her—the cold, thirst, the violent storms.

"Seen it before," Rogers said. "Space madness. Sometimes people start dwelling on where we are and how far away everything else is. The scale and scope of things get inside your head, the pressure of nothing, and your mind goes *pop*."

"'Pop?' That a scientific term?"

He smiled sadly. "We should be getting back." He started the rover, and the growl of its motor was a friendly sound.

Palant watched from her window as they moved across the desolate landscape, imagining Svenlap lying out there somewhere, almost buried in dust. It would be a sad end for a clever woman, but space madness was a very real condition. Sometimes it got to her, too—the mere contemplation of the insignificance of things. It occasionally made her jealous of the few who still clung onto old religions, but mostly she saw through their belief to the cold fears underneath.

Everyone had their way of handling things.

It took twenty minutes to crawl back to Love Grove Base, and in that time Palant's mind went from the missing scientist to the work that still awaited her back in her labs. She'd left McIlveen toiling there, and hoped that by now he might have retired for the night. It was true, she couldn't help liking him, but she liked working on her own more.

"O'Malley's?" Rogers asked. Isa hadn't been for some time, and she'd feared that he would suggest it. Though she had been determined to turn him down, she nodded and smiled. Maybe the single malt had chilled her more than she'd realized, but right then a glass of the indies' potent brew and a game of air pool felt like the best idea ever.

"I don't think I could do this without you," she said. The statement surprised her, though the words' honesty did not. It wasn't like her to open herself up like this. She thought of it as one of her faults, being closed in and introverted, and she supposed it went with her work. Such an obsession, such focus, removed her from the world.

"Pussy," Rogers said.

"You wish." She smiled, he laughed, and the rover hit a rock and jolted them both against their restraints. "I so fucking wish you'd learn to drive properly."

"You want a go, Yautja-girl?"

"You ask me now, when we're back."

"Sit on my lap and I'll let you park."

The banter continued as they approached the ramp leading down to the subterranean garages. Isa loved being out with her friend, loved even more returning to the base. The desolate wasteland of LV-1529 frightened her, and some time back she'd pushed a proposal to name the planet. Nobody really wanted to. The terraformers who had built the processors fifty years before hadn't bothered, so why should a bunch of scientists and indies? Rogers had mocked her. A name would make the planet seem somehow tamer?

Really?

"Open the doors please, navigator."

"Yes, Sir. Right away, Sir." Isa flipped the switch that sent a signal to open the garage doors, and Rogers drove quickly down toward the ramp. Isa winced. Every time she expected the rising ramp to scrape across the top of the rover, and every time Rogers timed it perfectly.

Inside, the screaming winds and abrasive, grit-laden atmosphere disappeared, replaced with the comforting drone of the rover's engine. Lights flickered on in the cavernous space, shadows danced.

One of them moved.

"What's that?" Palant asked.

"What?"

"Over by the fuel tanks. There, again!" She pointed. The shadow flitted between two of the larger fuel tanks, then appeared again beyond, slinking along the base of a wall toward one of the doors that led up into the single-level base.

Rogers sounded the rover's siren. A brief, shattering horn, it echoed within the garage space, amplified and repeating.

"Svenlap," he said.

"You're sure?" Palant squinted, leaned to the side to get a better view through the dust-smeared windscreen. He was right, it was Svenlap, but she was a wretched wraith of the woman she had been. "What the hell…"

"She's let herself go," Rogers said quietly. "Come on. She looks scared, we'll take it easy."

He cut the engine and the rover's glaring headlamps died out, leaving the garage bathed in the softer ceiling and wall lights.

The woman had reached a door. Svenlap tugged at the handle, but it would not open. Personal ID tags were needed to open most electronic doors throughout the complex, and everyone wore them on a small bracelet almost without thinking. Svenlap must have lost hers—but more than that, she must have forgotten that it was even required.

Palant jumped from the cab. A gust of wind struck her right side, carrying dust and sand that stung the exposed skin on her arm and face. She gasped, squinted, and glanced that way. The rover was still within the heavy garage door's sensor zone, and the door was only halfway closed.

"Angela," she called, facing forward again. She took a few steps forward, leaving the rover ticking and creaking behind her as it cooled down. Svenlap turned and crouched, her stance so animalistic that Palant caught her breath and stopped walking.

"Lost it," Rogers said from just behind her. "And what was she doing by the fuel tanks?"

"Hiding," Palant whispered.

"Better places to hide." Rogers jogged over toward the tanks, and Isa let him go. Her focus was on the woman.

"Angela, it's me, Isa. Everything's okay. You're safe, there's nothing to worry about, so why don't we all—"

Svenlap ran. Considering her physical condition, her speed was surprising, and she ran with a spidery gait that dragged her shadow scampering behind her. Isa glanced across at Rogers, then gave chase. Svenlap was heading for the far corner of the garage, where another doorway led to an unused staircase leading up into the ruined sector of the base.

"Svenlap!" Rogers called.

Palant turned and saw him running toward her. He looked very serious, and his side weapon was drawn. As he drew alongside her he slowed, but did not stop. "She's been doing something," he said, passing her. Palant ran after him.

As Rogers approached, Svenlap changed direction,

disappearing behind the rover and out into the blasting storm.

"Wait!" Rogers shouted.

"Rogers, what is it?" Isa said. She was keeping up with him, but her lungs were burning and her legs aching. She should have paid more attention to her fitness. She should pay more attention to everything, and not let her work consume her. Rogers had been trying to tell her that for months, sometimes to her face, and more often with subtle suggestion.

"She's planted something by the fuel tanks," he said. "A device. I can't see exactly what. And she's been missing for some time."

They passed out from the safety of the garage and into the storm. Rogers tried shouting something into the comms band on his wrist, but she didn't know whether he was successful. Her senses were battered—blasting wind abrading her skin, ears clogged with grit, eyes stinging, sand grinding between her teeth and the taste of sulphur on her tongue. She attempted to keep up with him, but he soon drew ahead of her, and past him she could just make out Svenlap's shadow sprinting directly away from the base.

Then Svenlap stopped.

"Put it down!" she heard Rogers shouting. "Svenlap, slowly, put it down, and we can talk and—"

Svenlap's voice cut in, surprisingly loud in the storm, as if carried by the airborne grit.

"I will illuminate their way."

Rogers shouted something else. Isa never knew what it was, because a booming blast erupted behind her, the landscape glared alight as if by a lightning strike, and a hot fist smashed into her back, lifted and carried her forward, melting her into the air.

Something solid flipped past her and struck Rogers, and it was strange, she couldn't quite understand what happened, but where he had been one now he was two, a small part of him bouncing across the hard ground, the larger part falling flat.

Beyond, Svenlap was spreadeagled on her back with flames rising from her hair.

Palant struck the ground hard. Light gave way to dark and everything went away.

Get up, it's only a graze, she heard her father say. He was looking down at her, smiling his kindly smile and holding out his hand, but behind the smile was the impatience that had always been there. He loved his wife and daughter, Isa was certain of that, but he loved his work more.

But it hurts, she thought. *My back hurts, and my head, and my legs where they were scraped across the ground when the explosion…*

Her father vanished into smoke, and his final whispered words were roars of flame, the pained squeals of crumpling metal structures, the dull thump of more distant detonations.

Palant was lying on her side, left arm trapped beneath her. She rolled onto her back, clenched both fists, tensed and turned her feet, ready for agony but relieved when there was only intense discomfort. Cuts and lacerations, but no broken bones, at least.

"Rogers," she whispered, words stolen by the destruction. The sky was on fire.

Almost a mile away, the first of the processor towers seemed to be alight, but it was only the dull, damp metal framing reflecting flames from closer by. She had never seen the towers so clearly, even during days when the storms were reduced to blustery gusts and showers. It was almost beautiful.

Closer, more horrific, so confusing that it took her a while to understand, and longer still to believe, Love Grove Base was burning.

Someone shouted, voice rising into a scream. It sounded agonized, but quickly broke into a high, staccato laugh.

Palant sat up, rolled onto her side, stood. Her knees were shredded and bleeding, filled with grit and stinging. Her gloveless hands were similarly slashed, but she could work her fingers, and closing her eyes she tried to balance herself, get her bearings so that—

Rogers!

The scream had not come from him, she was sure.

Palant opened her eyes again and turned around, looking away from the burning base. Her shadow was cast before her, long and twitchy, and within its lengthy grasp stood Svenlap. The hair was burnt from her scalp, one eye swollen, blackened and closed. Her mouth hung open and emitted a continuous laugh, rising and falling as she drew air into scorched lungs, again and again.

"What have you done?" Palant tried to shout, but she had no voice.

Between her and the still-smoking Svenlap, Rogers lay on the ground. His head was gone, sheared off by the flying debris, and Isa stepped forward and started looking for it.

It's over here somewhere, I saw it come off and bounce away and if I can only… Her thoughts trailed off and she sobbed once, loud and shuddering. Her lungs ached. She drew in a big breath and coughed, then shouted.

"What have you done?"

Svenlap drew a gun from her jacket pocket. It was a squat, ugly thing, and Isa recognized it as an indie sidearm. A laser pistol. Rogers had let her fire his once, and she'd sliced a rock in two at one hundred paces.

She had nowhere to run.

The weapon was not intended for her.

With a loud hiss and a flare of white light, Svenlap pressed the barrel beneath her chin and laser-blasted her head into a red mist.

Palant turned away and crouched down, and when she lifted her head again she saw what had become of her home.

Distant screams punctured the air. Tortured metal or dying people, she did not know.

The place where the subterranean garage had been was now a volcanic pit of boiling flame, smoke, and intermittent explosions, the building structure slumped down all around as if sucked into the fiery hollow. The fires reached further afield, wavering fingers reaching for the sky and being flitted away by the strong winds. Flames spread. Other explosions might have occurred, or perhaps the conflagration had spread rapidly, flowing with the spilled and burning fuel from the tanks.

Shock was waiting to take her down, but buffering her against that was the knowledge that so many people would need her help. If anyone else had survived.

She stood and skirted around to the south of the base. It was all single story, with a few areas like the garage buried deeper in the ground, and escape should have been easy. Yet the further she went without seeing anyone else, the more terrified she became. There were almost a hundred people on the base, mostly scientists from the ArmoTech division and indies that they'd hired themselves when the Company suggested that a Colonial Marine presence would not be required. A few kids lived there, too, belonging to researchers who couldn't bear to be away from their families. In the beginning Palant had resented their presence, but then as the children grew older, she'd started to look at them with a gentle yearning.

Now, she felt so alone. Heat radiated from the burning base and aggravated the burns on her exposed skin, but her back faced the desolate landscape of LV-1529, the world they had never bothered naming. It was cold.

"Anyone!" she shouted. Her voice was weak against the blasting wind, the growling flames. Fires danced across the base, whipped by the storm. The stink of melting plastics and hot metals reached her, and something else.

Cooking meat.

She thought of the dead Yautja in her labs, and a rush of panic grabbed her. Then she felt ashamed when she remembered Rogers dropping down, his head bouncing away. Her research was stored in local data clouds and her personal quantum storage fold, but Rogers was gone forever.

Him and many more.

"Anyone!" she shouted again, and from somewhere a voice replied.

Palant ran, skirting around the edges of the base. She clambered over rocks, stepped across a rough track cut into the land by repeated rover missions, and circled toward the east wing. This part of the base was dilapidated and unused, and it appeared that Svenlap had not felt the need to plant any devices here. From one facade tumbled long ago, a line of people staggered out into the inimical landscape.

Isa ran to them, recognizing a few indies and some of the base support staff. As she approached a sense of panic gripped her, because she didn't know who she was looking for. *My only friend is dead*, she thought, and although that was not quite true—because she mixed socially with most people on the base—Rogers's loss bit in deep.

The people were confused, some injured, but the indies were reacting well to the crisis, making sure they all stayed together and moved away from the blazing buildings. A dull explosion thumped through the ground, and a swirling tower of flame and smoke rose above the north wing. This was the largest part of the expanded base, and home to Palant's labs.

"Isa!" someone shouted. Milt McIlveen approached, and she surprised herself when tears threatened. He was a Company man, yes, but they'd grown friendly in the short time they had been working together. He had his orders, but he was very open about them. Now he looked lost and terrified. As he stood before her, blinking rapidly, she wiped her eyes and took him into her embrace.

"What happened?" he asked, his cheek against hers.

"Sabotage," she said. "Come on. We've got to get away until the fire's out, then see what's left."

"Life support is gone," he said. "I heard someone say that as we came out."

Fear stroked Palant's heart.

"Control's gone, too," McIlveen continued, "and the main comms center, and no one knows about the landing pad."

"Don't worry about all that right now," Palant said. "Let's think about today. Tomorrow can look after itself."

One of the indie sergeants approached her. "Rogers?" he asked.

"He's dead," Palant said. "It was Svenlap. We found her in the garage. She must have been living rough, building and planting devices, and when we chased her outside she detonated the bombs."

Her words caught the attention of the other survivors.

"Let's move away from here," the sergeant said. "Everyone in twos, hold each other's hands, follow in a line!"

"Where to?" Palant asked.

"For now, the processors," he said. "It's too dangerous to stay here. Automated firefighting systems are down. Life support's fucked, and once these flames die down it'll hit zero pretty damn quick out here. Love Grove Base is finished."

"There's nowhere we can survive long-term beneath the processor towers," she said.

"I'm not thinking long-term," the sergeant said. "Just until tomorrow. You all get to the processors, me and my team will stay here and look for survivors."

Palant looked around. There were maybe fifteen people

there, half of them indies. There must have been more survivors. There had to be.

"I'm staying, too."

"Isa—"

"I'm staying, Sergeant!"

"Me, too," McIlveen said, and Palant felt a rush of affection for him. He was shocked, terrified, but he didn't want to run.

As it turned out, *nobody* wanted to run.

They looked for survivors. As the flames raged, fanned by the winds and fed by fuel inside the base—oxygen tanks, chemical storage rooms, food stores—the survivors were split into teams and led on a series of search-and-rescue missions.

Palant and McIlveen were on one team, along with the indie sergeant and a couple of the base's technical and support staff. The techies carried key cards to every door, and knew override codes for almost every area of the base, so they took the lead, but much of the sprawling structure was already destroyed by explosions and the resulting firestorm. Although five teams searched for a long time, they found very few people to rescue.

They saw lots of bodies. Some of them they dragged outside. Others they could not drag.

At the back of Palant's mind was the possibility of finding her way to her labs, but it soon became clear that the whole north wing was an inferno, roof collapsed and purple flames roaring from its heart where the fire had found a chemical store. They donned face-masks, but could not draw too close. The flames rose into an indigo glow that was shredded by the wind.

* * *

After several hours they regrouped beyond the ruined east wing. There were twenty people, including two kids who had both lost their parents. Everyone was wide-eyed and shocked—even the indies.

Some of them had been in bed when the first explosion engulfed the garage fuel tanks. Others had been working, a young couple had been drinking in the rec room, and one of the children was still wearing a VR suit. Everything had changed in the blink of an eye, and now that their artificial environment of false safety was gone, the cool indifference of their surroundings was starting to freeze their bones. The cold set the rictus of loss in their expressions.

Three survivors were badly burned. The indies gave them all a heavy dose of phrail to block the pain, and they sat huddled together sheltered from the wind behind a rock, wounds covered with bio-gel, goggles failing to hide their fear.

"Processor?" Palant asked.

"It's our safest bet for now," the sergeant said. His name was Sharp. There were rumors he'd once killed four men in a knife fight, back when he was a kid. He'd been burned during a rescue, the dark skin of his cheek and jaw now glowing with bio-gel.

"What about the landing pad?" The landing pad was north of the first processor, just over a mile from the base and out of sight in a shallow valley.

"Can't get any signal from there," Sharp said. "Only McMahon had time to get her combat suit on, and it's registering nothing. That's a problem for later. Once we get to the network beneath the processor, I'll send two of my people to see what's there."

"You think she might have blown the *Pegasus*?"

Sharp shrugged. "Depends on what her reasons were."

To Palant, the idea of Svenlap meaning them harm was indecipherable.

"If the *Pegasus* has gone?"

"Then we'll have to arrange a rescue."

"With no comms room?"

He held her arm, and she realized her voice had been rising. For some reason the other survivors were looking to her. Perhaps because she had been here longer than anyone else, or maybe because she was the senior scientist here. "Yautja Woman," some of them called her behind her back, echoing Rogers' nickname for her, though not always with affection.

"There's always a way," he said.

Palant nodded, and even managed a smile.

As they walked away from the burning base and toward the foot of the nearest atmosphere processor, helping the wounded and each other, the storm came in harder than ever. Rogers's body was likely already buried beneath the dust.

1 0

JOHNNY MAINS

Arrow-class vessel Ochse
Near Yautja Habitat designated UMF 12, beyond Outer Rim
July 2692 AD

They were going to crash, and they were going to die. But not without a fight.

Frodo had successfully sealed the hull breach and settled the *Ochse*'s atmosphere imbalance, and three seconds later the protective foam layers the ship had sprayed around each surviving VoidLark had melted away. The ship was a mess.

The Yautja vessel, Bastard One, had straddled the hull with a spray-burst of laser fire, and the *Ochse* shuddered and shook as Frodo tried to settle their spin. Parts of McVicar's body drifted around the cabin, bumping from bulkheads and control units. Faulkner brushed his torso aside and spat a gob of blood away. His eyes remained focused on his combat screens.

"Bastard One down!" he said. "Mini-nuke got through."

"Thank fuck for that," Cotronis said.

"Status," Mains asked. Frodo answered, having already assessed all systems, both functional and damaged.

"Weapons fully online, life support seventy-seven percent, but I can hold that steady for a while. Hull breached in seventeen places. I've sealed them all but there's still venting from somewhere. Attempting to locate. The drive shielding is damaged. Reactor compromised."

Oh, fuck, Mains thought. "Repairable?" he asked.

"Possibly, but remote systems in the engine compartment are smashed," Frodo said. "Sorry."

"I'll go," Cotronis said.

"Sara—"

"L-T, I'm the most qualified, and I'm all suited up. No problem." She was already unstrapped and pulling herself across the flight deck, knocking McVicar's drifting body aside. The air was speckled with bubbles of his blood and fluids, colliding and growing, splashing against objects and people. None of them could bear to mention the loss just yet. They were in combat, and introspection was a waste of time and effort.

Mains glanced over at McVicar's comms station. A laser blast had punched through the unit and sliced the chair in two. If there was anything salvageable there, it would have to wait until later.

"There's only one thing we can do," Lieder said.

"The habitat," Snowdon said.

Mains was glad they were all thinking it already. "You're about to get your opportunity to meet these fuckers that fascinate you so much, Snowdon," he said.

"I'd really rather not."

"Lieder, plot me a course. Faulkner, enemy status?"

"Bastards Five, Six, and Seven standing off."

"Waiting for the kill?" Snowdon asked.

"Frodo, what do we look like?"

"The *Ochse* is venting radiation from the reactor breach," the computer said. "Bulkhead three is shielding the reactor from the rest of the ship, but the repaired hull breaches in the engine room are not shielded."

"So to them it looks like we're dead."

"That's possible, Johnny," Frodo replied.

Cotronis was at the flight-deck door, sealing her collar and enabling all her suit systems.

"Sara," Mains said. "Be careful in there. One nick in that suit and you're dead."

"No problem," she said, as if it didn't really matter—and perhaps it didn't. They were contemplating crash-landing their stricken ship on a Yautja habitat.

Hell of a way to go.

Cotronis left the flight deck, and Faulkner caught their attention.

"Bastards Five, Six, and Seven are closing, distance less than twenty miles."

"PBM ready?" Mains asked.

"Affirmative. If we fire in… seventeen seconds, field of fire will avoid the habitat."

"Initiate," he said. "Keep ready with a cancel command."

"Got it."

A countdown appeared on all their main screens, also

reflected on their suit systems. They went quiet, checking statuses, monitoring their drift and spin. Lieder gave Mains the thumbs up, confirming that she'd calculated a successful approach.

Mains could only wonder about a landing. It was highly probable that the habitat had defensive systems that would blast them into a cloud of particles before they even knew what was coming. That, or more Yautja ships would swing out to finish them off. With the drive reactor damaged, any quick maneuvers might cause a catastrophic overload.

They didn't have much fight left in them, but they might have one last surprise.

Three… two… one…

The ship hummed.

"PMB fired," Faulkner said. "Bastards Five and Six are down. Seven has swung around and is heading back toward the habitat. Slowly. It's venting atmosphere and radiation, and all ship's systems appear to be offline."

"Finish the fucker off," Lieder said.

"No," Mains said. "Let it go. It's not a danger to us right now."

"The reactor leak is worsening," Frodo cut in. "It's very uncertain, but we could experience full breach within fifteen minutes."

"Let's ram them," Lieder said. "Full engine burn and we'll hit…" She checked her instruments. "…point-oh-oh-three light speed. Five hundred miles per second, break their habitat in two. Burn them."

"Cotronis?" Mains asked.

"I'm close to the engine-room bulkhead," she said through their suit comms.

"You heard what Frodo said. Get out of there."

A hiss, a clanking noise as something damaged struggled to work. Then Cotronis spoke again.

"I've accessed the engine room. It's fucked, but I'll do what I can, Johnny. You do what you have to. Get us down onto that thing."

Mains frowned and looked at Faulkner, Lieder, and Snowdon. They all understood the risk Cotronis was taking.

"With the radiation levels present I don't think—" Frodo began, but Mains cut the computer off.

"We know!" he shouted. "Faulkner, all weapons systems offline, but don't move your hand an inch from the ready button. Lieder, you had an approach?"

"Affirmative."

"Program it. Let me know."

Mains closed his eyes for a moment and breathed deeply. He assessed the situation, analyzed their decisions, looking forward not back. The *Ochse* vibrated around them, and warning lights flickered on screens across his captain's display. Their trusty ship was in its death throes, and that did not bode well for them. Nevertheless, he was happy with what they had done, and their future course. The most vital aspect was that they had sent a warning to Tyszka's Star.

Whatever came next was about survival.

"Johnny?" It was Cotronis. She'd been his corporal for six years, a strong and capable second in command. He couldn't say that he really knew her—wasn't sure anyone did—but she was a good soldier, and a good person.

"Sara?"

"Manual repair is screwed, it's really smashed up in here and all circuits are fried, but I think I can wind down the emergency containment by hand."

"What are the levels?" he asked.

"I'm getting a pretty good suntan."

Lieder switched to a private channel. "Johnny, her combat suit isn't graded much higher than level three."

"I know," he said. He switched back to all channels. "Sara, you know the risks. Get the hell out of there the second you can. If you can give us ten minutes' grace, we can land."

"Right," she said. "Better weapon up." She cut comms, and Mains imagined her in the damaged, steaming, smoke-filled engine room, standing six feet from a leaking reactor that would be cooking her slowly from the inside out, even with her combat suit.

"You heard the Corporal," he said. "Weapon up. Lieder, initiate our approach. And give us a full-screen view."

He plucked his own weapons from their clasps around his seat and packed them on and in his combat suit. The laser sidearm clipped to his right thigh, plasma grenades hung around his belt, and his com-rifle slipped into a holster across his shoulders.

The compact rifle had been developed especially for Excursionists. It carried a charge pack and magazine, and was programmable to fire plasma bursts, laser sprays, micro-dot solid munitions, and nano-ordinance that exploded, shredded, or expanded according to programming. It could lay down a withering field of fire, or act as a sniping weapon over a distance of two miles. Its on-board systems were linked to the combat-suit computer, and in the hands of an experienced user the com-rifle was a formidable weapon.

The micron-thin suits themselves were at the cutting edge of military tech. Fireproof, self-sustaining, fully loaded with med-packs, resistant to Xenomorph blood (to a degree), fully flexing yet acting as armor when required, and incorporating the latest in retro-engineered Yautja invisibility technology, they were designed and fitted to individual wearers. They acted as exoskeletons, life support, and strength enhancement according to the situation.

Mains also packed a mini-drone in each shoulder pad, each one capable of acting independently and traveling up to fifteen miles from his suit. They could relay back information, build a three-dimensional map of a battlefield, and launch remote attacks. The fine, clear helmet layer hugged his facial contours and fed information directly to his eye, forming a virtual display that overlaid any information he required across whatever his surroundings might be.

Securing his suit and weaponry, he sent a thought prompt to his suit's onboard computer and it fired up all systems, running diagnostics and reporting full function.

If the time came, he was ready for a fight.

On each of their console screens, a three-dimensional image appeared of their local region of space. UMF 12 was in the bottom right of the image, and in the top left was the green arrow indicating their own ship. Their approach began. Mains looked for the red squares of Yautja ships, but although several more had launched from the habitat, they were heading away. Into the Human Sphere.

Could this be a war? he wondered. Perhaps Lieder was right in her suicide scenario. Maybe they really should launch everything they had at the habitat, then ram it with their last dregs of energy and life. Yet nothing was certain. Finding out more should be his priority, but he'd never believed that the surveilling of the habitat would actually include landing on it.

"Lieder, you got a place to land?"

"I've chosen a spot on the outer surface, close to the heavy central third."

"Faulkner, eyes on their weapons. If something activates, see if you can take it out before it fires."

"Way ahead of you, L-T."

"Sara?"

"We're good," she said, voice strained, "but it won't last. Frodo?"

"Core is already in overload," the computer said. "Full containment breach any time after approximately twelve minutes from now."

"Hit it, Lieder."

Lieder touched her panel and the *Ochse* shook, as if shivering at the fate toward which its crew was directing it. On Mains's console screen, the little green arrow approached the white mass of the habitat.

"We're about to make history," he said. "First humans to land on a Yautja habitat."

"And live to tell the tale," Faulkner said.

"Don't get ahead of yourself, Faulkner," Lieder said.

In all his time as a Colonial Marine and then an Excursionist, Johnny had never been so close to death.

He was pleased that he felt afraid.

They had been tracking the habitat for a long time, but in reality they knew very little about it. They'd discovered more in the past hour—seeing at least a score of Yautja ships launched, destroying several, and now drifting in toward the habitat surface for a landing—than in the past twelve months combined.

"Landing in three minutes," Lieder said. Her voice was tense. They all were. Frodo was poised to initiate countermeasures the instant any surface weapons fired at them, but so far their approach seemed to have been ignored.

Mains was under no illusion that they were going unnoticed.

"Two more ships launched," Faulkner said. "As it stands, no threat to us."

"Track them." Mains was worried. And confused. They'd fought a space battle and now, fatally damaged, they were attempting to land on an enemy vessel, yet the enemy seemed unconcerned. If the situation was reversed, he would have destroyed their ship the moment it was disabled, negating any further potential for aggression. He knew the Yautja were different, and perhaps that was it. Maybe they didn't want to blast a ship that was adrift. Perhaps that went against whatever weird code of honor they had.

"Approaching selected landing zone," Lieder said, then she added, "Shit me, will you look at that."

They were all looking. They each had the same view on their main console screen, captured by cameras at the *Ochse*'s nose. Even Cotronis, now isolated in the ship's weapons hold, could view it on her combat-suit display.

"I've been to some pretty fucking desolate places in my time," Faulkner said, "but this beats them all."

The surface of the habitat resembled the sand-packed expanse of a wide, pale beach. Even though it was vast, because of its cylindrical nature the horizon was close. It was scattered with low-level mounds, and here and there were dark lines that might have been deep crevasses. There were also the tall protuberances, sprouting from the habitat like giant tusks and pushing far out into space. Instruments showed that the largest of them was almost three miles high, and as Mains watched, the ship dipped down beneath its furthest reach.

"Launch dock for ships," Lieder said. "Look, see that one ahead?"

As the *Ochse* slowed to match the habitat's speed, ahead of them they saw one of the spine-like structures heavy with several sleek, silvery fruits of diverse shape and size. Yautja ships.

"Get us down quick," Mains said. "Sara, you okay?"

"Fucking dandy." She didn't sound dandy. Frodo had already told Mains how much radiation Cotronis had been exposed to, and even with the combat suit it would be the end of her. The only uncertainty was how long it would take her to die. If they could get some anti-radiation shots into her, perhaps she could live for another few weeks.

Perhaps, but they were hardly in the best of scenarios for treating someone so critically ill.

"L-T, something weird on long-range scanners," Faulkner said. "A ship cycling out of FTL."

"Distance?"

"Uncertain."

"Why?"

"It's a weird signal, Johnny. Sensors and scanners are confused, but it's closing quickly."

"Yautja ship?" Snowdon asked.

"Doesn't matter," Lieder said. "We're landing in fifteen seconds. Surface gravity is point eight standard. No atmosphere to speak of."

"No sign of aggression from the habitat," Faulkner said.

"They're waiting," Snowdon said. "Let us land, then they'll hunt us."

"Delightful," Mains said. "Snowdon, send a message to Tyszka's Star, tell them our status and position, report the launch of seven more Yautja ships."

"Ready to go."

"Frodo?"

"You'll have time to get clear and find cover before the reactor goes critical. There's an entry to the interior half a mile across the surface. I'll send coordinates to your suits, and I'll drift the ship off to reduce the chances of the blast catching you."

"Thanks. Give us as much time as you can." He frowned. The ship's computer would be dead within a few minutes, and he felt like he should say something else, but it wasn't like a synthetic mind. Not AI. He'd never perceived any sense of personality from the machine.

Lieder glanced across at him, as did Snowdon. Perhaps they were thinking the same thing.

"It's really all right," Frodo said, surprising them all. Mains held his breath, expecting it to continue, but there was no more.

"That other ship?"

"It's gone," Faulkner said. "Cloaked, maybe, but vanished."

"Okay, guys, let's get to the ramp." They left their stations for the last time, Lieder remaining behind longer than the others to confirm that the landing sequence was continuing according to plan. Moments later she was with them at the entrance to the flight deck.

"Snowdon, come with me to grab Sara. You two, lower the ramp. One minute."

Mains and Snowdon diverted to the weapons hold. Cotronis was leaning against the wall, a defender cradled in her arms. A heavy weapon, it was hardly the sort of gun to take with them on the run, but its firepower might be useful.

"Sara, we'll—"

"Let's just go," she said. She led the way through the hold and down to the docking ramp. Lieder and Faulkner were already there.

Mains knew that there was no need to tell his VoidLarks to activate their suits.

Instead, he said, "Let's make history."

With no time to vent the ship comfortably, the ramp dropped and a storm of air burst out around him. Standing solid, braced against the pressure at his back, Mains winced, then started down the still-lowering ramp. In a moment he was closed in a world of complete silence, and staggering scope.

The suit's clear-skin helmet was held half an inch from his skin around his mouth and nose. It closely followed his head's contour, so there was nothing to obscure his view of the amazing, daunting new world onto which they had stepped.

"Let's hustle," he said, voice muffled and dead. The location of the closest entry down into the habitat was projected onto his view. As they ran, Snowdon taking lead, Lieder bringing up their rear, Mains tried to take everything in.

The endless span of space enveloped them. Even though there was a comfortable gravity, he felt as if with every step he'd lift from the ground and be drawn into the darkness. It was cold, and vast, and it bled his heat and hope and his sense of self. He couldn't help glancing up, training be damned. He was only human, and humans really shouldn't be exposed like this, he mused, touching the ground with their feet and open space with their heads. No atmosphere meant utter silence, and every breath, every creak of his aging joints, felt like something only he could hear.

"I think I just shit myself," Faulkner said.

"Keep it down," Mains said, but not too harshly. "And stay sharp. Check your suit status." He sent an order to his own computer, and the suit flashed a rapid series of green lights into his view.

"Frodo, how long do we have?" he asked.

"Five minutes, maybe less," the ship's computer said. "I'm

trying to lift off again, but the ship's not behaving. I'd run quickly, if I were you."

Mains pulled to one side and glanced back. The *Ochse* looked so out of place clinging to this vast vessel, a sleek and beautiful craft now marred by the scars of battle. It had made a perfect landing, but this might be the ship's final moments.

Lieder slowed, but he waved her on.

"I've got the rear," he said.

"Yeah, I remember." She tried to smile as she ran past, but there was a tension to her features that distorted her smile.

He followed, checked movement sensors, saw nothing. Way ahead of them was one of the docking arms, rising high from the habitat's surface and reflecting weak starlight from several ships hanging toward its summit. The sight was quite beautiful, but if the craft were manned, the Yautja on board might be watching them even now, running like ants across the surface of their home. They might be preparing weapons, and in a flash barely perceived, the VoidLarks might end.

"Ten o'clock," Snowdon said, just as a red light flashed in Mains's view.

"Two of them," Lieder confirmed.

Two Yautja were standing watching them. A hundred yards apart, they were both wearing their battle helmets and holding long-bladed weapons. They were too far away to make out in detail.

"Split up, but keep running," Mains said. "We haven't got time for this."

The Yautja to the left broke into a run, heading opposite in an effort to flank them. Mains sent an order to his suit, drew his com-rifle, and fired a nano-bot charge. The bots arrowed toward the Yautja, and as it cloaked and flickered from view they dispersed into a wide cloud and ignited. The Yautja appeared again, cloak malfunctioning, going to its knees in a fading bloom of a thousand small explosions. Mains's suit told him that it was still alive, but wounded.

That would do for now. They had to keep running.

Snowdon had engaged the other Yautja and winged it with a laser blast. It cloaked and dodged, then several blazing shots arced in at them from its shoulder blaster. Snowdon's suit hardened and deflected one impact, but it sent her sprawling across the gray ground.

Faulkner launched one of his mini-drones. The fist-sized black object darted high and then dived at the Yautja, firing its laser and scoring several lines across the ground.

While it was targeting and fighting the drone, Faulkner hit it with a skillful laser shot.

"Keep running!" Mains said. "Snowdon?"

"I'm good." She was up and running again, panting hard.

"Frodo?"

"Sorry, Johnny. The *Ochse* thinks this is a good place to meet its end."

"Thanks, Frodo," he said. It was as much of a goodbye as he could muster.

"Good luck," their ship's computer replied. "Keep up this speed and I calculate you'll get to the access with seventeen seconds to spare. There's a tunnel to the left, but go right, then drop down the shaft. That'll be your best chance."

A couple of minutes later they reached a gentle hump in the

smooth flat ground, around the other side of which was a dark opening. Snowdon paused, panting, hesitant.

"No choice," Mains said. "Sara?"

Cotronis hadn't spoken since leaving the ship. Still clasping the defender she staggered and fell.

Faulkner scooped her up and slumped her over his shoulder.

Mains went first, com-rifle at the ready. It was dark, but their suit lights flickered on and illuminated the way. A tunnel began to their left, smooth and sloping gently away. An atmosphere field hazed the air a few yards along, indicating that the habitat's interior had an atmosphere. No use if it didn't suit humans, though. To their right, an open shaft headed down, too deep for their lights to penetrate all the way.

They each pulled a filament from their belts, slapped its glue bulb against the wall, and jumped.

In Mains's view, the countdown hit four. It went no lower.

As the world erupted and he fell, his last thought was, *I wish I could have seen inside.*

1 1

LILIYA

Testimony

The first hundred years was a true voyage of discovery.

The Founders had commissioned three ships, called *Hamlet*, *Othello*, and *Macbeth*. When they were delivered the ships were taken to an independent port close to the edge of the Sphere, a place of smugglers, pirates, and mercenaries. This was almost three hundred years ago, around 2400, and the Sphere was a much smaller place then. After the secret FTL drives were retrofitted, the Founders gathered, boarded the ships, and took a drophole to the very edge of known space.

I can still remember that moment well. Wordsworth and I stood on the bridge of the *Othello*, along with a dozen other leading members of the Founders. Beatrix Maloney was there, a different woman back then. More honest, more open and optimistic. There was no great ceremony. After the three ships had moved away from the drophole and its attendant space station, we launched into outer space.

We weren't the first, of course. The Fiennes ships had already been gone for a long time, vast craft filled with thousands of colonists in cryo-sleep, on a one-way trip toward somewhere that *might* be habitable. In a way, their journey was more terrifying than ours, because these brave people had no inkling of whether or not they would ever wake up.

Some of them know now. They've woken into nightmare. But I'll tell you more about that later. The history of what we were attempting is important to fully understand the dreadful present. Perhaps there will be lessons... or maybe humanity can never learn.

We slept for three years, and traveled one-hundred-and-fifty trillion miles. I was given the option of staying awake. As an artificial human I had no real need of sleep, and Wordsworth liked the idea of me patrolling the *Othello*, communicating with the AIs on board *Hamlet* and *Macbeth*, ensuring that everything was as it should be. Everything was automated, of course. There was nothing I could really do, but although his aims and intentions were grand, Wordsworth was human, and like any human he liked a sense of control over and above the machines he was using.

But I had spent too long awake and alone in the *Evelyn-Tew*'s escape pod, and Wordsworth understood that. So I slept with them, a thousand Founders on each ship settling into a thousand days' cryo-sleep while the craft took us far beyond the Human Sphere of influence.

There's a myth about artificial humans that enter cryo-sleep. It's said that we invade nearby sleepers' dreams. I've never understood the origins of that story, nor the barely veiled fear of us that it displays. Humans made us, after all. Humans made *me*, with their hands and their flesh-cloning methods, and I have long come to accept that. I can confirm that the myth is a lie. First, no human dreams in hyper-sleep, so the story is ridiculous. If a human *did* dream, they would die, because that would mean their body was experiencing temporal anomalies while in the cryo-pod. Growing older. Three years of growing older with no food, drink, or outside influence… it's well documented how faulty cryo-pods quickly destroy a human mind and body.

It's a lie also because I inhabit only my own dreams, which I am not meant to have. I cannot sleep in any way that a human would recognize, and even in cryo-suspension my mind exists on lower planes than it is easy to understand. It's not as… awful as sitting awake in that escape pod, but it *is* very different.

I can't recall my dreams from that time. That troubled me to begin with, because I have total recall, and forgetting something meant that I was not functioning to my full capacity. However, I soon came to relish the fact that those dreams were hazy, at best. It made me feel more human.

I shared these thoughts with Wordsworth, later, when things were going bad, and he embraced me and called me daughter.

After three years, the computers began waking us up.

Hamlet was gone. *Othello's* computer could not tell us what had happened, and *Macbeth's* AI had no record or recollection of the *Hamlet* ever having existed. The vagaries of FTL travel at work. We never did discover what happened to the ship's thousand sleeping souls.

With the Founders reduced to two thousand in number, we began our journey in earnest. We were beyond any human reach now, past even where the very earliest Fiennes ships, with their basic light-speed drives, might have reached. We were in deepest, darkest space, and traveling among stars that would look very different back home.

Free from interference, Wordsworth and the Founders continued with their experiments. In one of *Othello*'s three holds, preparations were made to begin using some of the research I had stolen from the *Evelyn-Tew*. All we needed were samples, and that was what drove our next thirty years of travel.

Always heading away from the Human Sphere, we explored, curiosity taking us to some amazing places. A small moon where silica deposits swayed and pulsed like living things. A gas giant where we found drifting masses the size of continents, self-warming, sparking electrical charges beyond measure, which might have been a form of life beyond our comprehension. A star system where seven planets shared roughly the same orbit, along with a cloud of billions of asteroids that might once have been sister worlds.

We took dropships down to a dozen planets and moons. Wordsworth said we were looking for somewhere to live, and I believed that—we all did, but we were also looking for something else. Samples on which we could use that stolen research, to develop something deadly—a weapon to protect us through all our travels.

On one planet we found a derelict spaceship. It was very old, and much of it had decayed beyond recognition in the planet's acidic atmosphere. We remained there for thirty days, but discovered nothing of any use or interest. No bodies, no sign of the beings that had crewed the ship, no technology that any of us could even begin to understand. It was a strange feeling leaving that wreck behind. For most of humanity, such a find would have been something to celebrate, a turning point in our history and understanding of the universe.

For us, it was one more step into the unknown.

All the while, the Founders continued the experiments that had attracted persecution from within the Human Sphere. I understood some of it, but not all. Genetic sampling, quantum quantification, multiverse balancing, quark replacement therapy. Cutting edge theories, brought to life in the labs contained in the holds of the *Othello* and *Macbeth*. Many of the Founders indulged in these experiments, while others found their roles in maintaining and running the ships themselves. It was a peaceful time. I'm not sure how to convey the feeling better than that. No one was forced into any particular role. The ship's AIs ran themselves, to an extent, but there were still tasks to be carried out. Otherwise our continued existence would have been unsustainable.

On *Othello*, a vast green pod was created where plants and foodstuffs were grown, and a group of people took that upon themselves. Another group experimented in creating a reliable and non-mechanical artificial gravity. It was as if the seed of a flourishing community had boarded those ships decades before, and in blooming, the flower it produced was close to perfection.

For a while, Wordsworth and the Founders existed in something approaching the utopia they had left the Human Sphere to seek.

As time went on, their genetic research, dabbling in longevity, became more serious. Wordsworth was an old man then, almost a hundred years old, and an air of desperation hung around him. Illnesses were dealt with quickly, and in the space of four years he had a heart-and-lung transplant, bone-marrow transplant, four cancers removed, and a brain rejuvenation.

He was dying, and he surprised me by being terrified.

"It's not that there's nothing beyond death," he told me one day. I was in his cabin. We'd taken to drinking ship-brewed whiskey together in the evenings, although my internals meant that the alcohol was bled instantly from my system. It made him quiet and contemplative. Maudlin, even. "It's not that at all. I want to go on, Liliya, and see what else there is to see. Can you understand that? The Founders followed me out here because we were looking for a kind of freedom, and somewhere to call home."

I told him we already had that.

"Freedom, yes," he said. "In a sense, but I'll never call a spaceship home." He shook his head. "You wouldn't understand."

That hurt me, but I let it go. I still looked exactly as I had seventy years before, when he first sent me to the *Evelyn-Tew*.

One day we fell into orbit around a star, following the orbital path of its third planet, and Wordsworth found what he wanted. Down on the planet there were seas of a jelly-like substance. It was analyzed and found to have remarkable properties. Rejuvenation. Medical applications for whole libraries full of illnesses. Even, when adapted over time, the reversal of aging.

They should have spent longer testing it, of course, but

some of the original Founders had already died, and although there were births on both ships, and our population of two thousand was stable, the originals who were still alive were growing very old. Almost all of them wanted to pursue the aim they had started with, and so they created a medicine from the gel. Brought up vast quantities of it, built vats in the holds, and produced a daily dose that would hopefully help them to live longer.

Against all odds, and despite my stark misgivings, it actually worked—for a time. For long enough to find the place we called "Midsummer." At first we thought it was a small moon, but then it became clear that it was artificial. An alien space habitat, perhaps five million years old. Long dead, or so we thought, but deep beneath the surface, in places I wish we had not ventured, we found something else.

They were asleep, and should have been left that way.

But Wordsworth woke them up.

1 2

LILIYA

Beyond the Human Sphere
July 2692 AD

Macbeth was a much different ship from the one that fled the Human Sphere two hundred years before. Faster, larger, changed beyond recognition, it would have taken Liliya a standard day to walk from bow to stern—and she knew every inch of it, including where to hide.

She had broken away from the guards as they were taking her toward a secure cell. Shipborn, they still held her in awe, an old woman who did not show her years, an artificial person who could not be told apart from any other human. With all the things they had discovered on Midsummer, Liliya thought she would have been regarded as relatively normal. Yet still she was considered extraordinary, and such a wonder closer to home was more powerful than one found in the depths of space.

The man and woman were so afraid of her that they almost didn't fight when she broke her bindings. Almost. She put them down as gently as she could, and then she fled. Down through the bowels of the *Macbeth*'s accommodation levels, past the dining and recreation rooms, she made her way through the transformed vessel like a virus through a giant's veins.

On Midsummer they had discovered incredible technologies, many of them so advanced that machine and biology were difficult to tell apart. After a long time spent studying and analyzing, it had become clear that the habitat itself was still growing, new areas extruded from huge slug-like creatures they had found deep beneath the giant, spherical habitat's outer crust.

One of those creatures had been brought on board *Macbeth*, and it wandered the ship at will, unhindered and unfettered. Unknowable, untouchable by any means of communication they had tried, it had quickly begun to expand and improve upon the ship's structure and design. It built not only structural and solid portions of the ship, but controls, electronics, and other more arcane tech whose uses were even now still being learned. Over a century it had remade the ship from the inside out, extruding material from its various appendages and forming, molding, refining, and hardening it in place.

They still did not know whether it was truly a creature or a machine. It resembled a large slug but had mechanical parts. It fed and excreted, but also had a constantly recharging power source. Whatever it was, wherever it came from, its reason for being was to build.

The modern *Macbeth* looked more like it had been grown, instead of built, and it was faster and more efficient than ever. Liliya moved through these strange spaces now—once corridors and vestibules and doorways, now tunnels and valves, hollows and atriums. Taking the creature on board had been a risk with which she had not agreed, but by then Wordsworth was dead and Beatrix Maloney was in charge.

The whole dynamic of the Founders had changed.

No longer Founders… they had become the Rage.

Her suspicions had been building for some time. Maloney's insistence that they return to the Human Sphere, her renaming of their dwindling, troubled civilization, and now the messages they had been sending with covert meanings, all pointed toward something Liliya hated even considering. Maloney had virtually admitted herself that this could not be a peaceful return.

Like a web cast through the interior of the *Macbeth*, feeding along its tunnels and hidden places, Liliya's reach had spread and expanded more than anyone knew. She had kept quiet the scope of her influence and knowledge. Being friendly with one person did not mean she had to tell another. Having a hand in one man's research did not preclude her from stealing from a woman's gathering knowledge. In the center of the web Liliya, the spider, watched and waited, spied and shivered as the picture grew of what was happening, where, and why.

She knew that the violence had already commenced. Still beyond the Human Sphere, attacks had been launched on another species. Trials, Maloney and her Inner Sanctum had called them. Mock assaults, testing the weapons at their disposal before the real attack began and the true purpose of the Rage would be revealed.

The insidious message Maloney had asked her to send had been the last straw. Liliya should have rebelled years ago, fought against everything she saw happening and knew might happen in the coming months and years, but loyalty ran deep, and her commitment to the Founders and the philosophy upon which they were based was implanted way down in her artificial memory.

She had long ago moved beyond the simple matter of programming. Her years in the escape pod had both damaged her and made her more... human. She had become her own agent, as much an individual as any other person, with goals and aims, likes and dislikes, but a steadily building sense of dread about the Rage and what they planned had shadowed her existence for years.

It was time to slip out from beneath those shadows.

The irony of what she planned was not lost on her. Almost three hundred years ago, she had stolen the prized research from a special ship, doomed it and its occupants, and launched herself into space. The difference this time was that she fully intended to be the captain of her own destiny. She would steal as before, and leave the ship from which she stole. But she had a destination in mind.

The Rage was going home.

Liliya had to reach there faster.

Maloney and her Founders would know of her escape soon enough. Floating in their support structures, enveloped in the rejuvenating gel, their old minds would come together in agreement—Liliya would have to be stopped.

She's known me for forever, Liliya thought, remembering again and again how she had shoved Beatrix Maloney across the room and into the wall. Such aggression was unheard of, committed against a friend and ally, and it had set her synapses sparking in confusion, but she wasn't sure Maloney *was* still a friend. Perhaps she never had been.

Heading toward the rear of the ship, she passed one of the original Founders, Erika Simons, submerged in her gel tank aboard the robotic walking support structure she favored. Her eyes looked swollen through the magnifying gel, all body movement slow as the contraption took her wherever she commanded. She looked at Liliya, corners of her mouth turning up in something resembling a smile. Her skin was a pasty white, hair a startled sculpture in the thick fluid, her wasted, naked body shriveled and sickly. The gel kept her alive and functioning, and Liliya knew not to let appearances deceive. Simons might be more than three hundred years old, but her mind was as sharp as a knife.

Liliya smiled as they passed by in the narrow tunnel, watching for any sign that Erika knew of her escape. There were no indications, at least outwardly. The woman's walker carried her away, insect-like and almost totally silent.

Liliya hurried on.

She passed a couple of shipborn going about their duties, and soon she was in a tunnel that curved around the swollen belly of the ship's hold. She knew what was contained in there—it was no secret, because the Rage all bore the same intention. Every child, man, and woman, whether they were ten years old or three hundred. Pregnant with violence and death, the hold was a place that Liliya had no wish to visit, ever again.

Maybe I can stop it all now, she thought. The idea struck her, feeling as hard as a punch, and she paused, blinking in the weak light and trying to imagine what that might entail. Destruction on a grand scale. Murder, when every instinct within her—every thought, movement, or inclination derived from her original programming, expanded and mused upon over the decades and centuries since—told her that murder was a bad thing.

I could sabotage the support network in there. I could blast open the hull, vent everything to hyperspace. One simple act, and the whole ship would be torn apart, become a smear across time and space, and then nothing. No sign that we had ever existed. Nothing left of me.

She wasn't sure what made her forge ahead with her original plan. She tried to tell herself that it was her base synthetic programming and the tenets laid down in her original, ancient synapse circuits, but she also thought it might be because she was more human than many of the people on the *Macbeth*, and in that humanity she had discovered fear.

Fear of death, and the nothing that would follow.

She passed the hold. It was vast and it took some time, but behind it she knew there was a place she had to visit before attempting to flee. As soon as her escape was announced around the ship, nowhere would be safe.

The laboratory was one of several on the *Macbeth*, but this one was closest to the hold and the things it contained. It was a large, low-ceilinged room, the floor level but walls and ceiling textured and lined like the insides of a living thing. Another place created almost completely by the creature they had found on Midsummer.

She paused and looked around. So much of what had been achieved in here had been seeded by what she had stolen from the *Evelyn-Tew*, research that had been the catalyst for the monstrosities the *Macbeth* now bore back toward the Human Sphere. Discoveries on that alien habitat, Midsummer, had contributed, true, but the information she had carried had started it all. It had given the Founders—and later, Beatrix Maloney and the Rage—the abilities that made them what they were today.

Unbeatable, perhaps.

Monstrous, for sure.

As Liliya crossed the lab toward the cool storage hollows in the wall, a voice halted her in her tracks.

"Come to steal, Liliya?" It was Erika Simons. She must have learned of Liliya's transgression and returned quickly to the lab. Her construct skittered from the shadows at the rear of the room, carrying the shriveled woman in her tank of gel. Her words were flat and monotone, an electrical facsimile of what her true voice had once been, driven purely by thought patterns. Grotesquely, her mouth still moved when she spoke, the mysterious clear substance distorting and bubbling.

"Not to steal," Liliya said.

"Then what?" Two more shapes moved behind Erika. One was a shipborn, weak and strange-looking from the decades of in-breeding. Not even the technology they had found on

Midsummer could expand their limited gene pool.

The other figure was one of the generals. The generals were combat androids, designed and built specifically by the Rage elders to control their monstrous troops, and programmed with every scrap of military history, tactics, and strategy the Rage could acquire. From early human history, through the technological revolution and three World Wars, and into the territorial conflicts that had marked the first centuries of space exploration and colonization, the droids knew it all.

This one liked to call himself Napoleon.

In some ways they were more advanced than Liliya. They carried nano-technology originally discovered on Midsummer and modified to link them symbiotically to their armies. They could control two thousand troops with a thought. Yet in other ways, they were so much less than her.

Built for war, their aesthetics had become an afterthought. They were humanoid but not human, with blank faces and haunting, empty expressions. Their eyes were white with black pupils. The blood in their veins was the clear gel, a lubricant rather than a life-giver. Liliya found them unsettling, and had never felt of the same ilk.

Napoleon stared at her, one hand resting on his sidearm. That was another technology they had taken from Midsummer— his weapon could punch a hole through the *Macbeth*, if he signaled it to do so.

"What are you doing here?" Erika asked again, but her questioning was a stalling tactic, and she didn't wait for an answer.

The shipborn came first, darting around the aged woman and drawing a stun baton from her belt. She looked afraid but determined, keen to prove herself to the elder.

Liliya had to think and act quickly. If the baton struck her she would be paralyzed for an instant, long enough for Napoleon to grasp and crush her into submission. But this situation was completely alien to her. Violence had not been a part of her life—not even with everything the Founders and then the Rage had been through. Losing their sister ships, exploring new worlds, combating system failures and potential disasters, discovering Midsummer, and eventually being forced to leave that artificial world because it could never be a home to them.

Liliya was not built to fight.

The woman swung the baton, feinted, and then kicked out, intending to trip her and land the baton on her neck.

Liliya grasped the shipborn's foot in both hands and twisted. The woman grunted, half-turned in the air, and hit the deck face first. The baton bounced from her hand, and Liliya caught it in mid-air. Pausing only for a second, she brought it down hard on the woman's lower back.

The charge surged, the woman's legs spasmed, and she vomited, staring across the floor and blinking rapidly as tears and blood flowed from her eyes. Though it wasn't designed to kill, this had been an unlucky hit. The blinking lessened, and Liliya's internals ran cold as she watched the woman die.

Even as she felt a rush of sorrow over what she had done, Napoleon came at her. He kept his sidearm holstered.

"Liliya, come quietly," Erika pleaded. Even with the monotone, there was no trace of evil in her voice, only sadness—but Liliya knew what she and the others wanted to do, and she had to keep that at the forefront of her mind. No backing down, not now. No letting weakness take hold.

She slumped, feigning capitulation, and then lashed out with the stun baton. It caught Napoleon between the eyes, pulping the bridge of his nose. The impact sent clear gel splashing, and the charge pulsed into his eyes and burst them across his cheeks.

He whined a little, stepped back, and pulled his weapon.

Ten times her equal in a fight, he was built for war, yet he had made a foolish mistake in underestimating her. He would not do so again, and she would have no second chance.

She leapt across the lab and circled behind Erika. Her construct clattered its legs as the elder turned it, twisting in her gel bubble to follow Liliya's progress. She was faster. She grabbed one of the construct's rear legs and pressed in close, her face a hand's width from Erika's, with only gel and the bubble's soft outer layer between them.

"On the floor!" she shouted at Napoleon, but the baton's charge must have done more than melt his eyes and burst his nose. It must have fried some of his wet circuits, even damaged some of the hardware that shielded his central brain stem.

"No!" he shouted, pivoting, ignoring her command, and zeroing his aim on her shout. Then he fired.

Instinct dropped Liliya to the floor behind the elder. A blast, a wet thud, a splash, and she was showered with warm gel, metal shards, and then a heavier, redder chunk of meat. She shoved herself backward, away from what Erika had become, but not soon enough.

The dead elder slumped from her platform upon the crippled construct, her limp body landing across Liliya's legs.

Her head was open, her brain exposed, flowing, merging with the gel that even now pulsed and flowed as it tried in vain to nurse and heal.

"Now it's done," Liliya said, shaking her head. "Now it's done." Something broke inside her with an audible snap. It was an electrical click as something shorted, a quantum hiccup, thoughts colliding, and she felt herself being torn in every direction.

Erika, exposed to the air for the first time in decades, twitched and clasped at the floor. Her wet mouth opened and closed, bubbles popping as her lungs attempted to process air. Her left eyelid flickered, but she was already dead, and everything Liliya witnessed of the elder was merely memory.

Napoleon froze in his shooting stance. His head turned seventy degrees to the left, then back, and that movement repeated again and again. She didn't know whether it was a result of the baton damage, or a reaction inspired by what he had done and who he had killed. Liliya *did* know that each general was built with a self-destruct facility that could tear the *Macbeth* apart.

Slowly, quietly, she pushed herself backward, shoving Erika's paper-light corpse from her left leg with her right foot. Napoleon continued in his strange movement. His shooting hand was dipping slowly, the weapon aiming at the floor, then at his feet. His head turned, back and forth. His left eye dripped fluid onto his pale blue uniform.

She crawled across the lab, then when she was behind a table she stood. Moving quickly, she reached into one of the cold-storage recesses and opened the skin-like door.

Inside sat row upon row of applicators. They resembled small handguns. Set on her course now, she didn't even pause before plucking one out, pressing it to the side of her neck, and pressing the trigger.

A hiss, a click.

As of that moment, Liliya carried the nano-creation the Rage had made their own. As yet inactive, it still made her feel different.

She felt *loaded*.

Out in the hallways and shadowy routes leading beneath the *Macbeth*'s amazing engine room, Liliya sharpened her senses and hid away every time she heard what might be footsteps. But no one approached. She heard the whisper of an alert passing through the ship, and knew that the generals and shipborn security force would be aware of what she had done.

They would blame her, she knew. Erika was one of the ninety-eight elders still left from the original Founders. The loss would be mourned, and avenged.

She felt sad. Damaged. She had killed a woman, and her core programming was corrupted by that act. Glitches caused periods of blankness as she moved toward the ship's hangar. Dark spots appeared in her vision, and then explosions of light. She didn't know what was happening. Control slipped, and a thought she had never entertained before came from nowhere and surprised her. *I could simply shut down.*

Shocked, angry, she drove the idea from her mind, but she

had to be away. She didn't have long left. They would catch her and punish her, and then take their battle back to where she had come from, so long ago. A battle that would be partly fed by what she had stolen.

She pressed a hand to the red spot on her neck.

I've stolen it back, she thought. *I am a thief. I'm a thief of hope, and now I have to keep hold of it.*

Eighteen minutes later, Liliya slipped from the *Macbeth* in an assault ship and dropped into a parallel hyperspace plane. Seconds later she was ten million miles away, and ready to accelerate even faster.

Beatrix Maloney would not let her escape so easily.

She would send an army to bring her back.

1 3

GERARD MARSHALL

Charon Station, Sol System
July 2692 AD

As usual when he woke up, Gerard Marshall felt sick.

When he was awake he could handle the constant movement to which space travel seemed to subject his stomach, even though everyone told him it wasn't even possible to detect it. The artificial gravity felt like the real thing, they asserted— there were vibration dampers, and the whole of Charon Station was equipped with static sinks and displacement buffers.

He knew all that, yet didn't believe a word of it. Awake, keeping his vomit reflex under control was a case of mind over matter, and something he'd become very good at. Asleep, however, the dreams took over, the nightmares about floating naked in space. Freezing. Suffocating as infinity sucked the life from him.

He sat up on his cot and took several deep breaths, blinking away the ice across his eyes and the sight of nothing staring back at him. It helped to look down at his toes. Glancing around his cabin helped even more, because he had pictures of his kids across one wall, even a couple of his ex-wife. She'd been beautiful.

Probably still is, he supposed, but he didn't like to think of her screwing a fucking tug pilot.

He could have had both of them killed.

Marshall smiled at the thought. It was ridiculous, and yet the anger the idea courted helped to settle his stomach. Wherever she was now, he quite hoped she was happy. She'd been a lovely woman when they had met, and deep down he knew that her loveliness persisted, despite her having been married to him. And she was a much better parent than he had ever been to their two beautiful children.

The tug pilot, though...

He hoped the bastard was hit by a meteorite.

"Somebody take me home," he muttered, and as if in response his holo frame glowed blue and drifted from the wall, forming in mid-air. The words JAMES BARCLAY pulsed in the frame, and Marshall caught his breath. One of the Thirteen, Barclay was one of the few people he'd ever met who truly spooked him.

"What the hell does *he* want?" he muttered.

The frame's color deepened and a continuous chime began. The call was urgent. Barclay *really* wanted to speak to him.

Marshall smoothed his hair, went to answer, then at the last second realized that he was still naked.

He tried to laugh as he quickly dressed, but the prospect of talking to Barclay troubled him too much. The man was only thirty years old, the youngest of the Thirteen by far, and he had already died three times. Once when he was born and his umbilical strangled him. Again when he was seventeen and his father, a Weyland-Yutani executive, went mad on Mars and shot six members of his own family. Finally when he was twenty-six, and the ship on which he was traveling struck a piece of space debris that turned out to be the remnants of a 20th-century deep space probe.

Each time, rapid medical intervention and the best treatment money could buy had brought him back. Most people called him lucky. Gerard Marshall thought he was cursed and unnatural, and he had given up researching just how Barclay had been brought back to life that third time. Everyone else on the ship had died, and he had been adrift in a space suit for seventeen days.

Dressed, hair smoothed again, Marshall answered the call.

"Gerard, about time," Barclay said, even as his image fizzled into existence.

"I was asleep," Marshall said.

"The Thirteen don't sleep. They just close their eyes and rest."

And they don't die, Marshall thought. *Spooky bastard.* He smiled and nodded, and started to utter some welcoming pleasantries, but Barclay spoke first.

"We've lost contact with Milt McIlveen," he said. "The scientist you sent to oversee Isa Palant's work."

"You were in touch with him?" Marshall replied, surprise loosening his tongue. The Thirteen were all equal, but most of them looked to Barclay as de facto leader. His personality invited that, as did his weird history.

"Of course," came the response. "Your business is essential to all of the Thirteen, Gerard. It's *all* of our business. Isn't that always the case?"

Marshall frowned and shook his head.

"What do you mean, lost touch?"

"McIlveen was giving me daily updates concerning his research. Four days have now passed without contact. I've checked with other sources, and in that time there's been no contact with Love Grove Base. With what's been happening elsewhere, I think we should be concerned."

"I think so, too," Marshall agreed. Southgate Station 12 hadn't been the only target of sabotage. There had been at least seventeen other attacks throughout the Human Sphere, all of them targeting Colonial Marine or Company assets. A Spaceborne frigate had been badly damaged on its patrol through the Addison Prime system, the attacker a member of the ship's crew. It was adrift, its few survivors still awaiting rescue. Elsewhere, three orbiting staging posts had been destroyed, nineteen light years apart and yet in an almost perfectly synchronized attack, with the loss of more than eight hundred Marines and support crew.

Moon bases, asteroid stations, and even a training colony on Whitman's World, the attacks had been unexpected in every case. However, they hadn't always been successful— the assailant on New London had been intercepted before she could deliver her explosive payload, the resulting explosion killing only her and flattening a forest of trees. Nevertheless, the incidents had seeded a sense of suspicion and fear across the Sphere.

"Doesn't Section Seven have anything to go on?" Marshall asked. Section Seven were a special force of ex-Marines reporting exclusively to Weyland-Yutani's Thirteen, brought together almost a century before to track and combat any terrorist organizations or activity against the Company. Renowned for their dedication and brutality, their reputation alone often was enough to quell a potential uprising or covert campaign.

"They've been following this since the attack on Southgate Station 12," Barclay said. He shrugged, and it was strange to see such uncertainty in his expression. "They can't find any link, and I'm certain this is no known organization."

"Something new, then," Marshall said.

"And just at the time when Yautja activity is increasing at an alarming rate."

"Yes, I've been following the attacks."

"Of course you have," Barclay said. "Did you see the final message from the VoidLarks?"

"I did. Johnny Mains is one of the best Excursionist leaders we have. Don't write him off yet."

"We can't afford complacency."

"I'm not complacent," Marshall said. "An attack on Love Grove Base is pointless, from a military standpoint, but Isa and McIlveen were in possession of two complete Yautja specimens. That was no secret."

"No secret to the Yautja, too, perhaps."

"You think they're instigating these attacks? With human collaborators?"

Barclay pressed his lips together and leaned forward, as if to bring himself closer than the several billions of miles between them.

"We've always underestimated them," he said. "You know that as well as I do. They're so... *other*, that we've never really come close to understanding them. No real societal structure we can perceive. No politics, and only hints at some form of religion. For them, everything is the hunt. They're born hunting, live stalking, and die for the kill—but maybe there's more to them than we believe."

"General Bassett is on a war footing."

"Yes, I know. Marshall, we need to move ahead of them. Being one step behind means we'll lose in whatever is to come. Whatever Palant and McIlveen might have found out from those specimens, we need to know. Retrieve what you can of their research, but if you believe there's even a shred missing, get some people out there." He paused, then added, "You have assets?"

"Of course," Marshall said, genuinely aggrieved.

"Of course." Barclay smiled. "We have our differences, Gerard. I know you think I'm something of a freak, but believe me, my priority is yours. I want to persist and survive as long as possible. I've died three times, and I've seen nothing—*nothing*—beyond what I have here."

Marshall didn't know what to say, so he merely nodded.

"Keep me informed," Barclay said. His image vanished abruptly, and the holo frame parted and floated back to its dock on the wall.

Marshall took in a deep breath, relaxed, closed his eyes.

Then he accessed his personal quantum fold and searched for any research Palant and McIlveen had uploaded. There was plenty… but not enough. Nothing he saw surprised him, and little there was new.

It'll be in her head, he thought. *That's where Isa keeps her most valuable ideas, and I know she'll keep the best bits to herself. McIlveen won't have been able to plumb that.*

He checked further, in other places where Palant might have stored some of her discoveries, yet he already knew what had to be done—for his own peace of mind, and that of the Thirteen. For Palant, too, if there was even the slightest chance that she was still alive.

It was time to call Halley.

1 4

AKOKO HALLEY

Charon Station, Sol System
July 2692 AD

Major Akoko Halley of the 39th Spaceborne, the DevilDogs—
the youngest general in the Colonial Marines at the tender
age of thirty-two—was earning her nickname of "Snow
Dog" more than ever today.

Deeply proud of her African heritage, she'd never taken
offense, because she knew that "Snow" referred to her
personality. Cool with everyone, ice-cold under pressure, but
brilliant, too, hence her early command of the 39th Spaceborne,
one of the oldest, most respected, and most battle-hardened
units in all the Colonial Marines.

If she had taken offense, her troops would have dropped
the nickname instantly. Snow Dog she might be, but they
loved her.

It was the first time in seven years that she'd returned to

the outer edge of the Sol System, hoping to head in-system for some R & R. She'd even considered returning to Earth, and it would have been the first time since she was eight years old, when she'd left for the Kuiper belt with her parents. They were dead now, but she had promised them both that she would return to Africa one day, make a pilgrimage to their home town and maybe even see the house where she was born. It was a promise she'd dwelled on for more than two decades, eager to keep because she prided herself on keeping her word, but not keen to carry out because…

Well, Earth. It was nothing like home.

The only place that felt like home was out here, with her troops.

"Three hours, I told you!" she shouted at Sergeant Major Mikey Huyck. "Not three days!"

"They'll be ready, Major."

"Doesn't look like it." Flight deck C of the *Charon* was awash with Marines and their kit. The four docked frigates were loaded with provisions, weaponed-up and ready to go, but the Marines themselves milled, too relaxed and chill to be ready to fly to war. Though there was nothing official yet, that's what they had to assume was coming. They were heading for Addison Prime, partly to rescue survivors from the frigate damaged by an unknown saboteur, but also to stage a series of drophole jumps further out toward the Outer Rim.

There was talk of a Yautja incursion, and Halley had come up against one of those bastards before. She respected their strength, combat prowess, and skill at killing, but the idea of them launching a concerted, organized assault against the Human Sphere…

It was chilling, and didn't feel right to her—but she was here to follow orders, and General Bassett had been very clear.

"We will be ready," Huyck said, quieter. Halley nodded and offered him a twitch that might have been a smile. She knew they would, and he knew that she knew. Her DevilDogs had yet to let her down.

She walked among her troops, exchanging words here and there, inspecting kit and uniforms, fending off a few ribald jokes. Some of the male troops enjoyed having a good-looking female major, but they knew exactly where to draw the line. Few had ever ventured beyond it. One who had, Private Gove, carried a broken nose for his pains.

The comms strap on her wrist buzzed, and an image and name appeared. Gerard Marshall? She caught her breath, and her blood ran cold. She hadn't spoken to him in over three years, and she'd have been happy if they never conversed again. Yet she'd always known that she would hear from him. Aware that he was now on Charon Station, it had become an inevitability. People like him put value on knowledge, the more damning the better. He could hold a sword over her neck any time he wished, and people like him always wanted something.

The injury had occurred in one of her first simulated combat drops. A pulled disc in her back, excruciating pain, and an instant prescription for phrail. Trouble was, she was one of the point-seven percent of the population that still found phrail addictive, and she'd kept her addiction quiet. By the time it had her in its grasp, to not keep it quiet—and to lose any chance she might have of acquiring the drug—was unthinkable.

Every waking moment revolved around where she could get her next fix, and her career had rapidly veered to the edge of a quick, long drop. Addicts were ejected from Colonial Marines training faster than those who were merely unfit, averse to space travel, or morally against anyone or anything that needed killing.

The man who saved her was in Gerard Marshall's employ, and Marshall was the sort of man who kept such information tucked neatly away. Never waved around or gloated over, yet it was always there. She couldn't even call it blackmail, because Marshall had never mentioned the addiction directly to her—but she knew. That was enough to place her permanently in his shadow. He could destroy her at any moment, and she had to assume that if a situation ever called for it, he wouldn't hesitate.

She tapped the strap.

"Marshall," she said. "I'm pretty busy right now."

"Not too busy to see me, I hope?"

"See you?"

"I have something for you to do for me. A mission. I'm on Pod 7, level fourteen. Someone will meet you at the elevator."

"But I'm getting ready for—"

"I'll have it cleared with General Bassett before you arrive."

"Marshall, I really can't just drop everything." She knew she was pushing it.

"Major, this is connected to your preparations. The bulk of your DevilDogs can carry out a salvage operation without you, but there's something more important I need you to do.

Come over, and we'll talk about it."

Halley turned aside so that Marshall couldn't see her face. Anger burned behind her eyes, but fear, too, at the memories his face and voice had encouraged to surface. She hated any hint of her addiction, and the path to ruin it had once promised.

Huyck caught her eye across the flight deck. *What?* he mouthed. She shook her head and looked down at her comms strap once more.

"I'm leaving on this mission in less than an hour," she said. "I can spare you ten minutes."

"I'll have coffee ready."

Halley signed off without replying, then strode across the flight deck. Her presence sent an invisible shockwave of activity and diligence ahead of her, and by the time she reached the bank of elevators the troops were hustling toward the boarding ramps.

Her strap chimed again. Huyck.

"Sir?"

"Carry on, Mikey. Marshall wants to see me."

"The guy from the Thirteen? What does he want?"

"Says he's got something for me to do. Dunno. Make sure the troops hustle, and I'll be back as soon as I can." She broke the connection and caught Huyck's eye across the deck, nodding once before entering one of the elevators. She muttered the location, then swayed slightly as the elevator began its journey.

I don't owe him anything, she thought. *I'm the strong one here. Me.*

She stood straight and tall as the elevator deposited her at the shuttle deck.

* * *

Fifteen minutes later she was standing in front of a desk in Gerard Marshall's room, having declined the invitation to sit, struggling to find a way to refuse the mission he had laid out for her.

"I'm not Special Forces, Marshall," she said. "Not an Excursionist, or an Injection Ops specialist. I'm a major and I have almost seven thousand troops under my command. You want me to go and rescue a scientist who's almost certainly dead?"

"There's no guarantee that she's dead. And the research is the priority."

"Oh, right, let's not confuse the Company's moralities here."

Marshall raised an eyebrow.

"Everything we do is for the good of humanity."

Halley snorted. She hated speaking to people like Marshall. A civilian, he held no authority over her—there was no need for her to stand to attention or call him "Sir." But there was no denying the fact that he was one of the Thirteen. Whether that made him one of the thirteen most powerful people across the breadth and depth of the Human Sphere could be debated, but he was certainly up there.

"It's important!" he said firmly, his voice rising. "If you intend to fly off to war with your troops, Isa Palant and what she's discovered might make that war shorter and less costly."

"But why me?" she asked.

"Because I trust you."

"Because you can make me go." She stared at him, not daring to break her gaze.

"I want someone I can trust," he persisted.

"And you can trust me because?"

"What are you trying to have me say, Major?"

"We both know what you hold over me." She murmured, chilled, angry, and scared. She hated the fact that this situation was getting out of hand. He hadn't said or insinuated a thing—it was all in her head. Maybe that was why he was such a good politician. He could make everyone else blame themselves.

"I can't order you to do this," he said. "I'm not military, but I've already cleared it with General Bassett. He's agreed with you taking his Bolt-class ship, and it's being readied right now. Not as fast as the Excursionist ships, but pretty close. I've had someone calculate flight details, including drophole coordinates and flight times, and they've already been communicated to the ship's computer. Forty-eight days to reach LV-1529, including three drops. Not an easy trip, not gentle on your body or mind. So pick a small, reliable crew. Make this mission a priority. It's not about whether or not I can make you go, or whatever it is I might or might not have on you, Halley. This is important. Get past your own problems and think on a bigger scale."

"Is that what you're doing? You and the Thirteen?"

"Always," he said. He leaned back in his chair to look up at her, in charge in every way.

There was nothing left to say. Halley nodded and turned to leave his plush cabin.

"Halley?" he said. "Check in with me every standard day."

"No problem." She left without looking at him again, and outside she marched along the corridor, displaying no emotion, no reaction. She knew he'd be watching.

For years, she'd known that he'd been watching.

"Special mission? Who does he think we are, Excursionists?"

Halley shrugged. "I received confirmation from General Bassett on my way back here."

"What ship do we take?" Huyck asked.

"He's given us the *Pixie*."

"You're joking."

"Do I look like a comedian?" Halley gave him her sternest look—it wasn't hard—and Huyck burst out laughing.

"Find something amusing, Sergeant Major?"

He wiped his eyes, shook his head.

"Mikey, we'll need to get a crew together. You, me, four others. Good people. I'm thinking Nassise to pilot, Bestwick for comms."

"Sprenkel and Gove?"

She nodded and smiled. "Yeah, good. We all know Gove likes me. Gather them up, tell them to get their kit and meet us in Hangar 6 in…" She looked at her wrist strap. "One hour."

Huyck threw a casual salute and jogged away across the flight deck. She watched him go, then scanned the area.

This was what Halley loved—here, in front of her now. The bustle of thousands of Marines preparing for departure, the sound of transports trundling the last bits of equipment toward their ships, excited banter, mutterings of *Snow Dog* as they saw her watching them, a sea of uniforms across the flight deck, faces she knew and many she would get to know on their forthcoming mission. This was what she had been trained for, and she could not live without it.

Young though she was, she saw every one of these Colonial Marines as her child, and cared about him or her as much as she ever would her own.

Small covert missions were the stuff of bar room whispers and mess room rumors. That wasn't her.

It seemed her orders had changed.

She'd asked General Bassett why she had to do what Marshall asked, of course. His reply, though shocking her, had put an end to her objections.

"We're all Company people now."

1 5

JOHNNY MAINS

Yautja Habitat designated UMF 12, beyond Outer Rim
July 2692 AD

Johnny Mains was playing in a forest just down the road from their house, across a field and stream and in a place where signs of an old war were sometimes still visible. It was autumn, leaves were falling, undergrowth fading back. The fall exposed a rusted metal hulk that his father had once told him had been an attack drone.

There was little left to identify its use now, let alone which side it had been on. Paint had flaked and given way to rust. Pieces had been torn off as souvenirs, others had fallen away over time. Maybe it was a hundred years old. Johnny didn't care, because as a kid anything like this was magical. A key to the past, a tactile thing upon which he could lay his hand and feel the echoing vibration of a battle long-since won and lost.

I'm going to be a soldier, he decided, one hand on the fallen thing, the other shading his eyes against low autumn sunlight dappling through denuded trees. *Just like dad*.

His father had left several years before, and Johnny hardly remembered him, just the image of a hulking shadow and the smell of sweat, alcohol, and aftershave. His mother told Johnny that he was never coming back, but he lived in hope. Even a dead thing like this old drone held living echoes.

"Johnny," someone said, a voice deep in his ear. "Come back." Mains looked around, frowning, listening for his mother's voice calling him in. There was no way he could hear her from here, their home was more than a mile away across fields and a road, past the stream, and—

"Johnny!" Someone slapped his face and he jerked awake. The autumn trees vanished, the pleasant coolness against his skin, and Lieder and Snowdon were staring down at him.

"L-T!" Snowdon said. "We've got to hustle. Three incoming."

Mains sat up, groaning, looking around. Snowdon and Lieder squatted in front of him, Faulkner hunkered down a few steps away with the defender. Cotronis was leaning against a rough wall of the cavern-like structure, chin on her chest. She might have been dead. The cables that had arrested their falls hung like loose webbing, disconnected now from their suits.

The ground shook. Dust fell and grit pattered across his face mask. A roar rumbled around them, unending.

"Everyone okay?" Mains asked. At the same time he

checked his suit's computer to assess his own condition, anything worth noting flicking up in his view. Bruising to the left shoulder and upper arm, sprained ligaments in his left knee, an impact wound to his head that would result in bruising. His suit had taken the brunt of the impact, but there was no helping his own body taking a beating from such a fall. The cables had arrested their descent, but it seemed that the *Ochse*'s detonation had sent them tumbling.

"Bumps and bruises." Lieder said. "The Corp's not so hot."

"I'm fine!" Cotronis snapped. "Carried the defender, didn't I?" She lifted her head and smiled at him through pale lips.

Mains was glad to hear her sounding like her old self, even if she didn't look it.

"Openings to outside have atmosphere shields," Lieder said, "but the air in here's only about fifteen percent oxygen, with some heavy trace elements. Breathable, but not for more than a few minutes."

"Everyone's suits functioning?"

"We're good."

Mains's combat view came to life and he saw the approaching danger. It looked like three Yautja, converging on their position from three different directions. The closest was an estimated four minutes away, so they had time to prepare, but no time to answer the many questions that still assaulted his dizzied brain.

How bad was the damage to UMF 12 from the *Ochse*'s detonation? What was the layout of the huge habitat's interior? How many Yautja were on board? Where had their ships been going, and why? The suits were equipped with communications channels and failsafes, but not to the extent of having sub-space broadcasters. They could talk to each other anywhere on the habitat, but for now they were cut off from the rest of humanity. Any message they sent with their basic suit transmitters would take years to even reach the Outer Rim.

"Okay guys, we go offensive," he said. "Too early to dig in—we have no idea of our surroundings or what's going on elsewhere. I see no signs of the enemy beyond these three, so once we've dealt with them we'll recce and see just how much shit we're in."

As Mains stood, the ground shook beneath his feet. Immediate surroundings gave the impression of being on a planet, not an artificial vessel. The walls and floor were some kind of dark rock, no straight edges or right angles. Moisture dripped from everywhere and ran in glistening rivulets through channels eroded into the ground. The air was heavy and warm, humid to the point of saturation, and it was only their suits' climate control keeping them comfortable. Even so, his face mask clouded slightly with each exhalation, misting away in seconds.

It was hot out there.

"Faulkner, Lieder, you get thirty yards ahead, camo up and wait. Cotronis, you'll have to settle down here. Snowdon, ten yards the other way with me."

"I want to be—" Cotronis began.

"Corporal, if those things get past any one of us, you'll be here to stop them attacking the other's flank." Mains's tone brooked no argument, and he didn't have time for discussion.

In minutes the first of three Yautja would be upon them. Back on Southgate Station 12, with a full complement and battle plans drawn up, they'd lost Willis and Reynolds against just two of these hunter killers. Now, shaken up and weakened, and on the enemy's home turf, the odds were stacked much higher against them.

"You got it, Johnny," Cotronis said.

"Okay," Mains said. "Suit lights off, everyone on infrared. Camo up." His suit obeyed his thought prompt, switching his view and initiating its cloaking shield. Reverse-engineered from captured Yautja technology, their cloaking devices were clunky and threaded through every part of their suits, but worth every gram of weight. As he and Snowdon headed off along the uneven tunnel, she started flickering from view. He made sure his suit sensors were attuned to the devices' specific frequencies so that he could still make out the shadow-shape of every one of his unit. To outside eyes, however, they would be faded into the dark, damp, stony background.

"Here," Snowdon said as the tunnel opened up ahead of them. The ceiling was high, the concave floor sloping down several yards beneath them, and Mains saw at least six other tunnels feeding into the area. There was some tech on the far wall, but he couldn't quite make it out. His suit scanned it, but was no wiser. Yautja technology seemed to advance quickly and change rapidly, and it also differed drastically from place to place, as if developing independently. For every new discovery, a dozen more questions arose.

That was why Mains couldn't put total trust in the cloaking tech. It was of Yautja origin, taken apart and bastardized by the Company's ArmoTech division, copied by people in labs who would never have need of it in the field. If it worked, it worked, but he'd never bet his life on it. The Yautja were too smart for that, and too inscrutable.

"Just inside the tunnel?" Snowdon asked.

"That's what I'm thinking. Not too close, but not out of sight of each other."

His display showed one red dot approaching their location from one side, the other two somewhere above and behind them. The local layout seemed complex, so it was difficult to discern just where the Yautja might emerge. What was clear was that they would be upon them in moments.

Mains and Snowdon crouched and prepared, nursing their com-rifles. He selected wide field nano-shot, having seen how effective it had been on the surface.

From behind them came the hiss-crack of the defender being fired, a heavy weapon that shot thousands of wire filaments in expanding clouds that would shred any living thing within range. In such an enclosed environment it would be formidable. Mains watched his display and saw Cotronis in close combat with a Yautja. Another three shots from the defender, a piercing scream, and then Faulkner grunted in satisfaction.

"One down."

Mains had no time to reply. Across the open space in front of him, a Yautja darted from the dark mouth of a corridor, running quickly along the slope and drawing close. Mains held his fire but Snowdon unloaded, the nano-shot seeking its target and then ripping the air apart in a thousand glaring detonations. Mains's suit dimmed his view, but the reaction time wasn't perfect. In infrared, the explosions were blinding.

The Yautja jigged to the side and slipped, sliding across the floor and leaving a trail of glowing blood behind it.

Mains zeroed on the alien, finger squeezing around his trigger.

The enemy's shoulder blaster unleashed a hail of shots directly at them. Mains's suit hardened as he ducked. Rock rained down in a stinging hail as the blasts impacted the ceiling, then a heavier slab growled as it dipped down and struck the floor between him and Snowdon. She gasped, and through the haze he saw her cloaking system fail.

It didn't matter. The Yautja already knew where they were, and as Mains dropped to his stomach and slid beneath the fallen ceiling, the alien rose in the entrance before him. Nine feet tall, heavily muscled, partially armored, wearing several trophies from its most respected kills—long golden claws, a heavily-toothed jaw, a Xenomorph skull—it glimmered with fresh blood, its own war suit sparking and letting off arcs of strange energy.

The Yautja screeched in delight as it crouched and stepped into the reduced opening, lashing out with a heavy spear.

Mains swung his com-rifle and deflected the blow, taking the opportunity to crawl quickly backward into the wider corridor. He looked for Snowdon on his display, but the reading was confused.

The Yautja slid beneath the fallen ceiling and came for him again, swinging the spear toward him, its point glimmering in the weak light. It caught him a glancing blow across the chest. His suit deflected it, but the impact knocked him onto his back. A warning chimed, and like a flipped beetle he was suddenly vulnerable. He couldn't use the com-rifle so close, not programmed to nano-shot, and as he instructed his computer to reprogram the rifle the Yautja leapt at him, claws tensed, spear raised, ready to plunge down at his face mask in a killing blow.

Light flared and the Yautja fell, torso tumbling back, the heavy head striking Mains's stomach. His combat suit, sensing no threat from a weapon, failed to solidify. Mains gasped and rolled to one side, kicking the head away. It rolled and came to rest staring at him through its helmet mask. Perhaps it still saw.

Snowdon appeared beside him, laser pistol drawn.

"Faulkner and Lieder are fighting two more," she said, holding out her hand. Mains took it, she helped him stand, and they headed back through the tunnel.

Mains checked his suit status. All good.

"Snowdon, you okay?"

"Bit banged up," she said, but she didn't run like it. She ran like an Excursionist, concerned for her friends and eager to engage the enemy once again.

Cotronis nodded as they passed her and headed in the other direction, toward the sounds of combat, the flashes, the glare and roars and screams. Mains heard the defender firing again as they skidded around a corner. Past where Faulkner and Lieder were crouched a whole section of walling disintegrated and hazed into the air.

They were at a junction of three tunnels, theirs and two others leading off at gentle angles. A few steps along one tunnel lay two Yautja. One was pulped and dead. The other was thrashing around, splashing its strange green blood up the walls. Bits of it had come off, and the entire tunnel structure around it was pocked with holes. Dust and grit drifted across the floor.

"Don't let it self-destruct!" Mains shouted.

"In its own habitat?" Lieder asked.

"We don't know!"

Lieder nodded and darted forward, com-rifle aimed at the other tunnel. She moved along to the Yautja, drew her laser pistol and delivered the coup de grace.

The third tunnel brightened, Mains's view darkened automatically, and then a volley of explosive shots slammed in around them. Faulkner was lifted from his feet as the ground beneath him erupted, striking the wall hard. Mains heard something crack.

"Just one along there?" he asked, and Lieder confirmed.

"But it's packing some serious firepower," she said.

"So are we." Mains opened up and the others joined in, lighting up the tunnel with nano-shot, laser sprays, and plasma bursts. After three seconds he signaled a cease, and they hunkered down in the tunnel, waiting for the smoke to clear.

Molten rock dribbled down walls. Dust drifted, catching light from a fire further along the tunnel. Several errant nano-shots sparked and zigged through the air, exploding in small blasts.

Mains sent instructions to one of his shoulder drones. It parted from his suit and drifted through the destruction. He switched views and checked out the drone's feed, arming its weapons at the same time. The infrared view was confused by the heat of plasma blasts, so he switched to normal view, the scene now lit by fires. The drone moved slowly, its small camera panning left and right. The tunnel floor had been ripped up, walls fractured, ceiling dripping molten rock that splashed and hardened in complex patterns.

No sign of the Yautja.

"Stay sharp," he whispered, knowing he didn't really need to. He checked his suit scan for movement, and saw only himself and the other Excursionists lit up. But this was a warren, and he couldn't afford to trust the scan fully. Back to the drone view, and the tunnel beyond the battle site grew darker again. "Looks like the target fled and—"

A shadow shifted, a clawed hand swiped, and the feed from the drone suddenly cut out.

"Son of a bitch," Mains said. He sent an order for the drone to self-destruct, but the Yautja must already have crushed it, disabling its systems. "Faulkner, Snowdon, wait here. Lieder, with me." Com-rifle set to plasma, he stormed into the ruined tunnel, Lieder close behind.

Twenty yards in, past the flames and torn-up walls, his suit scan showed no signs of movement. Even when the huge Yautja reared up before him, it showed that nothing was there.

Mains skidded to a halt. "Drop!" Lieder bellowed, and Mains fell to one side. The Yautja swung down two heavy bladed weapons, one in each hand, and he heard them whistling through the air.

Lieder fired. The plasma shot struck one weapon and ricocheted, blasting into the wall and sending the melting metal blade across the alien's chest. It screeched and swiped at its chest with its other hand, then unleashed a fusillade of shots against Lieder from its shoulder blaster.

Mains rolled onto his back and fired his com-rifle almost point-blank. The shot struck the Yautja beneath the chin, and for a couple of seconds light glared from its mask's eyepiece as the plasma charge melted into its skull and illuminated from the inside out.

The dead alien released a low, sad sigh, then slumped down beside him.

"Check for any more," Mains said.

"I've been checking, L-T," Cotronis said. "Nothing on my scans, but their signals earlier were weird, in and out."

"Yeah, they must be carrying some sort of new stealth tech," Faulkner said.

"You okay?" Mains asked Faulkner.

"Com-rifle broke in half. And a bruised ego."

"No need. We did well." Mains was breathing hard as Lieder helped him to his feet, her hand grasping his for a few more seconds before letting go. They smiled at each other, and Mains felt a sudden twinge. *It's all just a matter of time*, he thought. They'd crash-landed on a Yautja habitat, their ship had exploded, and in just an hour they'd already fought off four Yautja. How many more would come at them? How long would their ammunition last?

How lucky could they continue to be?

"L-T, you should see this," Cotronis said. "All of you. Feeding it through now." Cotronis sent through the view from one of her own shoulder drones, and while they kept one eye on their surroundings, they all gasped at what they saw.

The drone had drifted through the tunnels toward the wider, central portion of the habitat, and it hovered in the shadow of an overhang, showing the habitat's interior. It was cavernous. The interior space must have been almost a mile across and two long, roughly tubular, so poorly lit that the drone viewed through infrared.

The inner surface was far from smooth, with rocky mounds, dark ravines, and other, stranger shapes lining it all the way around. Artificial gravity was employed here—through centrifugal force, partly, although the Yautja must have been using a more arcane means to produce a result that felt so close to standard. It meant that the entire inner surface was habitable.

Here and there around the tube, settlements were visible. They seemed very small, single buildings sprouting from the uneven surface, with an occasional taller structure. Ships were moored close to some of these places. Each settlement was different, and as was usual with the Yautja, each ship varied in size and design. There were no larger buildings or ships, no places that might contain a gathering or congregation. These hunters were loners, and even though they all coexisted on the same huge habitat, still they lived alone.

"How many do you think?" Lieder asked.

"Not as many as I'd feared," Cotronis said.

"Yeah, but a lot more than we could wish for," Faulkner said.

The floor beneath their feet shook, a subtle vibration that Mains wasn't sure he'd felt until he glanced at the others. They had all sensed it, too.

"Maybe the *Ochse* did more damage than we thought,"

Lieder said. "Great. It would be a boring day otherwise."

"Snowdon, what do you think?" Mains asked.

"I think we're making history," she said. "Far as I'm aware, we're the first humans inside a Yautja habitat. Those four that came at us didn't launch a concerted, synchronized attack. If they had, they'd have taken us. Each was acting alone, and from what anyone can tell that's the way these things operate. Occasionally you'll see them in pairs—or even threes, like we did on Southgate Station—but that's pretty unusual, and it could be that was a family pack teaching a youngster to hunt. Or it might have been an initiation. This place looks like it's been around for a *long* time."

"But now a lot of the ships have left," Mains said.

"Yeah, and there are more docked outside on those mooring structures," Cotronis said. "Maybe they move their ships out there and prep them for flight."

"Right," Mains said. "So maybe we need to steal one."

Someone took in a sharp breath, but he wasn't sure who.

"Lieder?" Cotronis asked.

Their pilot took a while to reply. "I don't know," she said.

"You're the only one who'll have even a slight chance of flying one of their ships," Mains said, "and from what I can see, that's our only hope of getting out of here."

"I can do my best," Lieder said. "Snowdon can help me translate controls, perhaps. But Johnny... nothing like this has ever been done before. We've captured a bit of their tech, a few bits of bodies, but nothing substantial. And every ship is different, sometimes *vastly* different, built and modified by individual Yautja."

"I know," Mains said. "It's just a long shot, and between now and then, we've got to survive."

The floor bucked again, dust drifting down around them.

"That's if this damned thing holds together. So, let's make a plan. Cotronis, call your drone back. We've got to assume the rest of those bastards aboard know that we're here, and probably know that we've just offed their four buddies."

"Which means this silence is nothing of the sort," Cotronis said.

"Calm before the storm," Snowdon said. "They'll be getting ready to hunt."

16

GERARD MARSHALL

Charon Station, Sol System
July 2692 AD

Gerard Marshall was in a safe place. He knew that. General Paul Bassett himself used Charon Station as his main place of residence, and it had been the Colonial Marines' headquarters for over a century. In that time, no enemy action had ever damaged or killed anyone on Charon Station.

Space was a dangerous place. There had been accidents and one notable disaster, but if Marshall had been asked to choose the safest place in the Human Sphere in which to sit out a potential war, where he was now would have rated very highly.

Which was why news of the attempted sabotage had given him palpitations.

They'd caught one of the station's support staff making his way down toward a munitions store on one of the outer cells of the station. He'd been carrying a bomb. The cell was held far away from the bulk of the structure, but Marshall had heard from several sources that any detonation of the ordinance stored there would have blown most of the station into shrapnel. Any surviving portions and occupants would have been sent spinning into space, to die a slow, suffocating death.

The man had made it through three levels of automated security before being halted by human guards. They had sensed his nervousness, questioned his presence there, and then shot him when he pulled a gun.

The bomb he was carrying was still being examined, but it appeared to be homemade.

Marshall swilled a glass of single malt and stared at the view from his window. Deep space, peppered with stars. It was said that the ancients had viewed space as a dark blanket with pinprick holes to the outside, and in some ways he supposed they had been right. The real pinpricks were the dropholes, however, and they were man-made. Those stars he was looking at now were likely long-since dead, and the enormity of distance once again crushed him down.

He had been a normal child with simple desires. His mother had been a nurse on an Earth-orbit station, his father a physical educator for the military. Until his fifteenth birthday, Marshall had been a normal boy obsessed with normal boy things. He'd played zero-G soccer, sung in a band, enjoyed schooling, and had been hypnotized every time he saw Jenny Anne Francis in a bikini. Then when he turned fifteen, he was approached by a recruiter for Weyland-Yutani. His imagination was set aflame by the things she told him, and his parents had done little to douse those flames. They saw a good career for him in the Company. It was an opportunity few people were afforded, and Marshall grasped onto it with both hands.

Seven years later he was assistant to one of the Thirteen.

Seven years after that his employer died, and Marshall was tagged as the natural successor. From apprentice to one of the most powerful men in the galaxy in the space of fourteen years, and to what did he ascribe his success?

He didn't give a fuck about anyone.

Actually, that wasn't quite true. His success was due to the fact that he could convince anyone that he *did* give a fuck about them.

But he didn't.

So when General Bassett's image appeared on his holo frame, requesting contact, Marshall swilled the last of his single malt down and prepared his concerned face.

"Gerard," the General said. "I trust your mission got away successfully?"

"Halley and her people launched several hours ago, yes." Marshall frowned. "Honestly, Paul, I'm sorry I had to rip her away from her real duties, but… you know."

"Not a problem."

"And for lending her the *Pixie*, you have my eternal gratitude."

The General waved the comments aside. He looked troubled, and that wasn't a look that Marshall was used to from the old man. It made him feel troubled too.

"So, this sabotage attempt," Marshall began, but Bassett waved that aside.

"It's being looked into. My concern is that it might somehow be connected with what I have to tell you. Some intelligence just in, which I think you should relay to the rest of the Thirteen."

"Concerning the terrorist actions?"

"Concerning the Yautja."

Marshall's blood ran cold. All the talk of war, the preparations, the buzzing undercurrent of activity throughout Charon Station, he'd believed that it was all unnecessary. The Yautja were not a war-like civilization. They were barely a civilization at all. Their high level of technology was an oddity, and he wouldn't have been surprised if it was discovered that their weapons, ships, and martial technology had somehow been inherited—or stolen, from another alien species.

"The attacks?" Marshall asked.

"We're used to occasional attacks. These are just more concerted. No, what troubles me the most is Yautja ships making it into the Human Sphere."

"Only along the Outer Rim, though," Marshall said.

"They've started using dropholes," Bassett said. "They shouldn't have the ability, the tech, and codes, but somehow it's happened. Seven instances so far, and other drophole traces are being checked right now."

"Where have they dropped to?"

"They're working their way inward. A couple have been intercepted and destroyed, but others have vanished. It's an incursion. They're spreading."

Marshall leaned back and closed his eyes, wondering how he would communicate this to the rest of the Thirteen. He could see the opportunities here, as would they. The valuable knowledge they could glean from captured Yautja, alive or dead.

"It's your job to stop them," he said.

The General bristled, face turning pale. "And I'm doing just that. But I thought it appropriate to inform you, especially as we're now in a state of war."

"War can be good for progress," Marshall said. "Thank you, General. I'll communicate your concerns." He cut the link.

He sighed and took a deep breath, pouring himself more whiskey. He would have to initiate a call to the Thirteen soon, tell them the news. They were the Company, though, and each of them had individual resources spanning the entirety of the Human Sphere. If he left it a few more minutes, enjoyed his drink, and considered what the near future might bring, it was likely that they would already know.

1 7

ISA PALANT

Love Grove Base, Research Station, LV-1529
August 2692 AD

In the days and weeks following Svenlap's destruction of Love Grove Base, everything went from bad to worse. Isa Palant tried to keep a grip, attempting to coat the continuing bad news with a silver lining that might help her, and her fellow survivors, see their way through to a rescue.

When one of the indies chewed on the barrel of his laser pistol in front of them all, she could only curl up and cry, with the stench of cooked brains in her nose.

Milt McIlveen was by her side, as he had been for the past forty-four days. Any negative thoughts she'd had about him as a Company man had vanished long ago, because he gave without taking, nursing her hope even as hopelessness ghosted his eyes. He was very honest with her—he said that being positive for her and the others was the only way he could handle the situation. A classic distraction technique, he told her, but she didn't give a damn.

McIlveen was a good man. He didn't deserve this.

None of them deserved this.

On day one after the attack, the one indie who had managed to emerge in her combat suit walked the mile to the landing pad, through one of the worst storms to ravage the base in recent memory. She was gone for five hours, and they'd almost given her up for dead when she stumbled back into the network of rooms beneath Processor One. Shaking, her suit's support systems challenged to their fullest in the storm, she brought news that they'd all feared.

The *Pegasus* had been destroyed, and the resultant fire had ravaged the landing pad. She had salvaged a food bundle and dragged it across the dusty landscape behind her, step by terrible step.

On day three, two of the burn victims died.

On day five, the remaining burns survivor also died.

Day six brought a few shreds of positive news—the first since the explosions. Sergeant Liam Sharp, commanding the seven remaining indies, managed to get an old communicator working. At least sixty years out of date and probably unused since the atmosphere processors had been completed, many of its systems had corroded in the acidic atmosphere before the oxygen levels had risen. After spending days replacing circuits and making inspired repairs using an array of everyday objects, he announced that he might have enough power to send one sub-space SOS signal. They composed the message and sent it, and a couple of hours later they received a confirmation from a deep space freighter three light years away.

The communicator died soon after, but they could only hope that their situation would make it back to the Company.

That was their share of good news. Two days later, two of the indies returned from a scavenging mission deep beneath the processor and reported that their wristpads had picked up high levels of radiation. McIlveen had managed to rescue his kit bag after the initial explosions, and he ventured down several levels with a multi reader. He returned ashen faced, and said that they all had to leave... now.

They couldn't tell for sure whether Svenlap had damaged the huge atmosphere processor on purpose. Perhaps the explosions at the nearby base had caused a tremor that ruptured a sealing tank, or maybe debris falling around and into the processor was to blame, but the levels were dangerously high, and increasing. The outside might be storm-ravaged and the atmosphere unsafe to breathe for any length of time, but the *least* safe place on the planet was where they were now.

Downing iodine tablets from a first-aid kit one of the indies carried, they ventured out into the storm and approached the ruined base once again, but there was no home there. Much of it had been ravaged by fire and left open to the elements. Part of one wing still sizzled with a toxic stew of water and sulphuric acid from a bank of old-fashioned batteries, destroyed during the blaze. They spent a day sheltering miserably beneath an overhanging spread of roof structure, but when part of it collapsed during the night they knew they had to leave.

Palant knew the base and its surroundings better than anyone, but it still took some time before she thought of the storage hangars. Almost two miles south of the base, they had been used to store construction equipment and machinery during Love Grove's construction. Closed up since then, shut off, she didn't know anyone who had ever been inside. Last time she'd seen the hangars, one of the roofs had caved in, and the other was one half of a massive dune—dust and grit from decades of storms piled against its side and back.

It was a sheltered space, but little more.

Right then it was what they needed.

So on the twelfth day following the attack, seventeen survivors undertook a harrowing march across the desolate landscape and found one supply hangar still standing. The indies forced a way inside, and when they entered it was like going back in time.

Much of the construction machinery had been left behind, parked in the hangar and abandoned, some with doors still open. Tires were flat and petrified, metals were rusted, no engines worked. Stacked around the edges of the hangar were piles of rusted steel, bags of hardening compound, boxes of electrical and plumbing supplies, and other material and equipment. A clothing rack hung adorned with brittle atmosphere suits, some of them personalized by people dead for decades.

A couple of rucksacks sat at the base of the rack. No one explored them, although Palant stared at one for a long time. It contained a forgotten history, and it deserved to be left alone.

Most welcome of all, there was a wind turbine on the roof that McIlveen and some of the others took several hours repairing. They scavenged parts from the hangar for the turbine wings, long since torn off and buried in the sand. Once they were done, they were elated to discover that a low-level lighting system still worked. Everyone cheered when the lighting glowed on.

Day thirteen began with an assessment of food and water supplies. Even if the freighter had conveyed their distress signal, Sharp calculated that a Company rescue could still be at least another forty days out. It might be that a vessel closer by might come to their aid, but they couldn't rely on that. With such vast distances involved, and such extensive flight times between dropholes, few privateers could divert from their mission unless forced to do so. It was a harsh reality, but space was a harsh environment. Everyone knew their place, and accepted the risks they took.

Water wasn't a problem. The survivors rigged moisture nets across the massive dune outside, and soon discovered a dozen places throughout the hangar where water dripped steadily from the wide roof. Purifying drops were in plentiful supply.

Food *was* a problem, because they'd been unable to rescue much from the base. There were plenty of protein pills and other supplements, but hunger soon bit in.

As the days passed, survival became a routine. Though the hangar was large, most of it was a wide open space, so there was little privacy. They performed their toilet needs outside, but most of the time they remained in the building, away from the continuing storm, the violent winds, and heavy rain. Between the downpours came blown sand and grit that would scour their skin.

They made several trips back to Love Grove Base to salvage what they could, but each time they returned with less. Some wall panels soft enough to sleep on. A box of canned drinks, and a few bottles of base-brewed whiskey, which was rationed by Sergeant Sharp.

The sergeant had impressed her since Svenlap's attack. He was good in a crisis, level-headed, and serious, and he more than anyone had kept them all together. McMahon brought a board game for the two kids, and Palant felt a burning behind her eyes as she watched them playing, losing themselves for a while, drifting away from the awfulness of orphanhood, the desperation of their situation, the death that stalked them all.

A couple of weeks later, with no means of communicating beyond the base or of receiving news, there came the sound of a ship.

Palant stood and rushed toward the doorway. *They're here!* she thought, and she imagined Gerard Marshall stepping from a Company ship to rescue them all. It was a ridiculous idea, she knew, but she also knew that she hadn't been terribly rigorous in uploading her research findings. A man of endless resources, he'd still want to know what she had discovered from the two Yautja corpses.

Or maybe hunger was driving her mad.

"Isa!" Sharp called, jogging after her. "Wait!"

She wasn't the only one rushing toward the wide doors at the hangar's end. McIlveen was there, too, along with several other survivors, all eager to be the first to see the ship coming in to rescue them. They'd already ensured that there were enough signs at the base—fixed to the structure, sprayed on the exposed walls—telling any rescuers where the survivors were holed up. Nevertheless, human nature made Palant want to rush outside and wave her arms.

She skidded to a halt as Sharp caught up with her. He touched her shoulder, then turned and pressed his back to the doors, addressing those gathered there. They were panting and weak, already tired from their dash across the hangar.

They'd need some proper food soon.

"Let's wait," Sharp said.

"What for?" someone asked.

"Just… wait. You employ me and my troops to look after you. We've done that since Svenlap, and we continue to do that. Let us do our work."

Palant noticed that his sidearm was unholstered, the laser pistol's status glowing a steady green. McMahon was with them, too, her own weapon held down by her side.

"This isn't rescue," she said softly, causing a grumble of whispers from some of the others.

"Not from who we were hoping for, anyway," Sharp agreed. "It's too soon. But that's not to say someone else didn't receive our message, and decide to come for us."

The blasting roar of a ship's engine sounded from outside, closer than the base. Its tone changed, and then lowered in volume as the ship touched down.

"Maybe salvagers," McIlveen said. "They might be pissed, 'cos survivors mean they don't get the salvage."

"Or pirates," another of the scientists said.

Sharp held his hands out and lowered them slowly, pleading for calm.

"Just let us do our work. Connors, you and me. McMahon, you stay here with the others. Keep an eye on the doors." He whispered into his wristpad, and McMahon touched her finger to her ear and nodded.

Testing their comms, Palant thought. *Or he's telling her something else.* Her expression gave nothing away.

Sharp and Connors, a small, wiry woman, opened the door and slipped outside. McMahon killed the lights, and Palant pressed to her side to watch through the open doorway.

Sergeant Sharp led the way, heading away from the hangar and toward the base. The indies had set up a series of posts supporting a thick cable, a safety line between base and hangar in case someone was caught outside in a blinding storm. It wasn't needed now—the storm had abated somewhat, and the air was as clear as it ever got—but Sharp and Connors followed its line nonetheless.

Somewhere ahead of them, the lights of a landed ship glowed in the gloom.

"No comms yet?" Palant asked.

"Nothing," McMahon said. "My suit's scanning all frequencies, but all I get is silence."

"Maybe they think we're dead." It was an unsettling idea, and it made Palant more suspicious of the newly arrived ship. Maybe they *were* salvagers or, worse, pirates—in which case Sharp and Connors would have to be careful.

"Do you think…" McMahon began, but she trailed off,

words lost to the wind and Connors' long, agonized scream.

Something protruded from her back. A hundred yards away, Palant couldn't make out exactly what it was. She gasped, confused. Beside her, McMahon lifted her weapon and aimed it through the door.

"No," Palant breathed. "McMahon, no." Deep down, something was whispering to her. A truth she could not bear.

Surely fate wouldn't be so cruel?

Sharp was running right to left, taking moving shots at something out of sight.

"Sarge!" McMahon cried. She itched to get out there, but Sharp must have ordered her back.

"What is it?" Palant asked. "What does he see?" But really, she already knew. Much of her life had been spent studying them, and now in the presence of a living Yautja her bladder loosened, her limbs felt weak, and she cursed whatever luck had brought them to this place and moment.

Sharp paused and turned in a slow circle, gun raised ahead of him. He spun and crouched, and the shadows manifested into a huge shape, eight feet tall and rushing right at him. He got off one shot which went wide, then the beast thrust forward with both hands. Something glimmering burst from Sharp's back. His arms and legs jerked and shook as the Yautja lifted him high on the end of a trident spear.

Sharp screamed, and the Yautja howled a wild, exuberant war cry.

McMahon pushed forward and Palant grabbed her arm, tugging at her.

"No!" Palant said urgently. "It'll kill you, too. Don't, they're gone, and Liam wouldn't want—"

"But the Sarge!" McMahon shouted. Palant followed her gaze. Sharp was quivering on the raised trident, sliding slowly down as the points pierced and tore through his guts. He swiped out at the Yautja and caught it across the face, but it barely seemed to notice. He struck again.

The alien shook the spear so that Sharp slid further down.

"The Sarge is gone!" Palant shouted. "Listen to me. I know these things. That's my job, knowing as much about them as I can, and I'm telling you, if you go out there waving your weapons, it'll kill you. We don't even know if it's alone."

"So what?" McMahon said, snotting and crying. "We just hide?"

"We can't hide when it knows we're already here," Palant said, "but we can close ourselves inside. Try not to appear a threat."

"And then what?"

"Then we hope that it's come for sport, and not a massacre."

Palant went to close the door, but she couldn't resist one last look. It was shocking, horrific, and magnificent. For so long she had studied these creatures, their body parts and belongings, trying to understand them through dead flesh, clotted blood, and disassociated tech and clothing. Now she was looking right at one. A living, alien creature, with mysterious thoughts, histories, and philosophies, and an outlook on the universe that she did not understand. However long she studied and theorized, she would *never* understand.

At last they've come to me, she thought. More afraid than she had ever been in her life before, and more excited, Palant slid the big door closed. McMahon helped her, along with a couple of others. Then the indies moved aside and huddled together, and she could only stand on her own, shock settling coolly into her bones.

She caught McIlveen's eyes. He was standing beside the decayed hulk of a forklift, the machine slumped down like a dead beast. He was staring at her. She saw excitement in his eyes, and for an instant she despised him for that.

But then she understood. She nodded at him. *Yes, it's the Yautja.*

He leaned against the machine. His first instinct was to look at the indies.

"No," Palant said. "Milt, that's the last thing we should do. You know that."

"What is it?" someone asked. The youngest child was crying softly, picking up on the loaded atmosphere. In that moment, Palant realized that only she and a couple of the indies had seen.

The others had only heard.

"Yautja," she said. A rumble of fear passed through the survivors, the indies standing silent and sad. She realized that she didn't know that much about them. They'd always been there, friendly enough, but she didn't know where they'd come from or what they had been before. Colonial Marines, more than likely, but how long they had served together, how tight a unit they were, if and where they had fought before, this was all a mystery.

She wished she'd got to know them better.

"What are they doing here?" one of the scientists asked. He was a cosmologist, studying the effects of a quasar just a couple of light years away. They were all scientists, and not all of them researched alien life, but they *were* all employed by Weyland-Yutani. His ignorance surprised her, but perhaps it merely illustrated her own obsessive nature. So immersed had she been in her studies, she couldn't conceive of others knowing so little.

"I've heard of the Yautja," a woman said. "Horrible stories."

"They were probably true," Palant said.

"You're the Yautja Woman," the cosmologist said, almost accusatory, as if her research had brought the danger to them. "So tell us what we're facing."

Suddenly all eyes were on her.

"Hunters. Predators. Killing is a sport to them, it's their lifestyle. It might even be an evolutionary imperative. A necessity for them to continue as individuals, and a species. They're widespread in the galaxy, but relatively small in numbers, and rare within the Human Sphere. In all my years, and all reported observations made of them through the centuries, there's been no real evidence of any form of structured society. They're like white sharks back on Earth... loners until they need to mate. And we're not even sure how they do that."

"But they have technology," McMahon said.

"Yes, and very advanced, but no two ships are the same, and individual weaponry is always different. We're not sure, but we suspect their technology may be adapted or stolen from other civilizations. Species we don't even know about."

"Why are they here?" one of the children asked.

"You had dead ones in your lab," the cosmologist said.

"That has nothing to do with them being here," she said, although she wasn't sure, she wasn't *certain*. "This one might have registered the explosions, or more likely the radiation leak from Processor One, and it's come to see if there's anything here for it to hunt." She glanced at the indies and away again.

"What happened out there?" a woman asked.

"Connors and Sharp are gone," Palant said. She was thinking rapidly, and as a barrage of questions came at her she turned away, facing into the shadowy corners of the hangar.

Hands held her shoulders, turning her around.

"Isa," McIlveen said. "You know more about them than anyone. Even me. You've got to understand that."

And that makes them all look to me, she thought. Even the indies, it seemed.

"Okay," she said. "Okay." She looked at the meager weapons they had managed to bring with them during Svenlap's attack, and salvage afterward. A few laser pistols, a couple of heavier-looking guns. She knew they had also dragged a couple of cases with them, but she didn't know what they contained. Drones, perhaps, maybe even high-tech AI drones.

"They come after anyone who looks like they'll offer a fight," she said. "That's their prime motivation. If cornered, they may kill for the sake of it, but usually they relish the hunt."

"What can we do?" one of the indies asked. He was scared, and Palant was glad. They should all be scared.

"We don't panic," she said, although her heart was fluttering, and everything she knew about the Yautja should make her the most frightened person here. "To begin with, we wait. Milt and I will talk, try to come up with a plan.

Meanwhile, keep quiet, keep away from the doors. Put any weapons down, but not too far out of reach. They'll know what we're doing in here."

"How?" McMahon asked.

"They can see," Palant said. "They see everything."

From outside came a triumphant roar as the Yautja took its first trophy of the hunt.

1 8

LILIYA

Testimony

It all should have been so different. It could have been wonderful, but in my three centuries as an artificial person, the greatest lesson I've come to learn has also been the most terrible. I have come to know human nature.

I remember the day hope died.

After so long traveling in places where no human had ever ventured, the Founders were close to achieving the state they had been seeking. Wordsworth and the others had found a way to prolong their lives, with few side effects. They no longer looked entirely human, true, but in a way they had cheated evolution, so in that sense they were exploring new territories in existence as much as in space.

Their gel constructs became works of art. Those who were

shipborn respected and honored them, but in a healthy way. They weren't deified. They weren't treated as anything other than human.

Midsummer might have become our home, but that alien habitat wasn't a good place. Though it held incredible technologies which we investigated and used, and reverse engineered where we could, it was also toxic to body, mind and soul. We found only a few traces of the beings that might have built or inhabited Midsummer, and they became objects of fascination. Fossilized into the structure of the artificial moon, into history itself, the best of them was also buried the deepest. I spent lonely hours staring at this thing, looking into the deep past and endless distance, trying to make sense of what I saw.

Shreds of a thin, metallic covering still existed here and there. Clothing of some sort, perhaps. Its torso was wide and heavily boned. Withered flesh lay across protruding bones, turned as solid as stone over time. Four thick legs supported the body, while there were traces of thinner, more delicate limbs protruding higher up the torso. At the end of one of these limbs was what appeared to be a hand, fisted shut, the several digits slender and long. It was dog-like, only larger, and what remained of the head only went to reinforce that canine image.

There was only half a skull, but it had the remnants of a small eye socket, a snout-like nose, and jawbones layered with several rows of wide, flat teeth. Not the mouth of a meat eater.

I stared at that empty eye socket for a long time, wondering what marvels it had seen. I tried to imagine that thing alive and moving, riding Midsummer through the unknown depths of space, seeing and experiencing things we would never know.

Yet I knew so little that I realized these things might simply have been the builders' pets.

I said many times that we should leave that place. The *Macbeth* was in orbit, but many of the Founders and travelers had ventured down to the surface, and beneath it as well. Some said it was haunted. I saw no ghosts, but I did sense the echoes of the place it had once been. Those echoes were a language, an experience, that none of us could understand. It was as if we were listening to the thoughts of old, dead gods, whispers that we could not hope to comprehend in a million years.

It wasn't meant for the likes of us.

There are locations in the galaxy where life has had its time. It has bloomed, faded, and died away, and trying to introduce life to those dead places once more is a folly. After all, although we know that life exists throughout our galaxy, and probably the wider universe, the vast majority of places are lifeless. We are a tiny minority in an incomprehensible vastness, and we should pay heed to the echoes we hear.

Beatrix Maloney, much as I now dislike her and everything she represents, listened. She knew that we did not belong in that place, that false utopia we had proudly called Midsummer. She gathered her inner sanctum around her in secret. Whispered conversations in shadowy hallways, shared glances across empty chambers deep beneath the habitat's surface. Thus they drew their plans.

We really should have known. Perhaps Wordsworth *did* know, but could not bring himself to believe. Such infighting, such betrayal is what the Founders left the Human Sphere to escape, after all. It was our first great failure.

Deep down in Midsummer, in humid chambers that should have been left alone, we found those sleeping *things* we had been seeking for so long. *Thousands* of them. Beatrix realized instantly what they could do, and what they could become. Wordsworth marked this as the moment that the Founders should depart. The conflict between them was brief, and private, and its true nature was never revealed.

After Wordsworth's death at her hands—and I have no doubt that, even though there is no proof, Beatrix Maloney killed Wordsworth, my friend and father figure—the change was gradual but obvious. We remained orbiting Midsummer while those hibernating, chitinous bugs—those Xenomorphs— were brought on board the *Macbeth*, and the holds were adapted to contain them. Experiments were performed, incorporating research and data I had stolen from the *Evelyn-Tew*. Then the *Macbeth* and *Othello* left orbit and started their long journeys back toward the Human Sphere.

The two ships were traveling independently of each other, on the same mission but many light years apart. After the loss of the *Hamlet*, it was deemed wise.

The Founders had become the Rage, and Maloney was a preacher of hate. The transition was slow and almost imperceptible, and I berate myself for not acting sooner. I *hate* myself. That emotion feels strange, yet it fits.

It all should have been so wonderful, and when the rot set in, perhaps I could have changed everything.

Yet, to use a saying Wordsworth taught me, I'm only human.

19

LILIYA

Outer Rim
August 2692 AD

She was used to spending time alone. When Liliya had been created, more than three hundred years before, solitude would not have concerned her at all. But now, progressed as she was, evolved, loneliness was one of her nightmares.

Sometimes while resting her systems she imagined that she was the last living thing in the galaxy. All humans were gone, vanished into the void. Other species had faded into history, just like whatever civilization had created and maintained Midsummer so many millions of years before. There was only her…

…and she could not die.

It was difficult to conceive a greater hell, but while fleeing on the stolen assault ship, Liliya had only hoped that her loneliness would last a little while longer, because she knew she was being pursued.

Traveling at such incomprehensible speeds, skimming hyperspace planes that swirled and twisted toward the Human Sphere, she knew for certain that Beatrix and the rest of the Rage would have sent one of the generals to bring her back if they could, or destroy her if they could not. She even knew which general it likely would be.

Alexander was their troubleshooter. He had been at the forefront of their takeover, and she had long suspected that he might even have been the weapon Maloney used to kill Wordsworth. Big, scarred from combat with an aggressive indigenous life form on one of the planets they had landed on, his skin pale and eyes deep, dead pits, he was the least human-looking of all the generals, and he would not come alone. His two thousand Xenomorph soldiers would accompany him, nursed in their cocoons in the belly of his ship. Maloney would suspect where Liliya was heading, and she knew that Alexander's ship would be bigger, faster, and far more advanced.

The odds were stacked against her. The assault ship she had stolen was barely up to the task. She wasn't a soldier or a pilot. Her knowledge of military tactics was limited, although she'd had long enough to study and understand the ship's weapons systems.

Nevertheless, she had a head start, and the deep-set belief that she was doing the right thing.

The Rage had been traveling on their return journey for decades. They had been nurturing their weapons, creating their armies, and now, this close, she knew that the initial attack on the Human Sphere was being launched by an advance guard. She hoped that the information she had injected into her veins could be used to combat the greater invasion yet to come.

When she closed her eyes she thought of Erika, the woman she had killed, but with her eyes open, she saw only Wordsworth. Everything he had dreamed of had been trampled beneath the Rage's feet. All the good he had proposed, the advancements and progress, the evolution of the human mind he had been so desperate to seek, all had been assassinated by the people he'd sought to remove from negative influence.

Assassinated, as had he.

A synthetic with good on her side, Liliya would do everything in her power to make it back to the Human Sphere. She might yet have time to avert genocide.

Thirty-three days into her journey, the assault ship's hyperdrive failed. The computer informed her that a cease signal had been sent.

They've found me! she thought. Hurrying into the small ship's containment hold, she shrugged into a sleep suit and programmed a pod. Even she could not survive a rapid deceleration from hyperspace travel to real space, and whoever or whatever had discovered her would be waiting once the ship had slowed beneath FTL speeds.

She might only have moments to leave the pod, take control of the ship, and fend off an attack.

The vessel was starting to shake as she immersed herself. Before initiating suspension she spoke to the computer.

"Avoid contact with any other vessel, protect the ship at all costs," she instructed. "Bring me out the moment we're out of hyperdrive."

"Of course," the ship said, its voice neutral. She wasn't convinced that she could trust the computer. Though she had probed its quantum folds and examined the many levels of its mind, she had been unable to discern any loyalty programming. However, she was left without any choice. The hyperdrive couldn't reverse the cease signal without catastrophic effect, and whoever had sent it would likely be waiting.

The cryo-pod closed around her and she breathed in the suspension fluid. Time slowed to a crawl, reality became slurred. A human would be asleep by now, gone, but her mind did not allow such luxuries. Liliya remained conscious as time slowed, and then stopped around her. Frozen in a moment, her existence became a micro-second with nothing before, nothing after. All thought fled, and only a shred of consciousness remained.

Even so, each thought lasted an eternity.

Reality, the great expanse of time, the crushing depth of infinity rushed in. *"Proximity alert… proximity alert…"*

Liliya expelled the suspension gel from her insides and rolled from the pod, slapping onto the floor.

"Status?" she gasped.

"Probe approaching, distance seventeen miles and closing."

"What sort of probe?"

"Rage."

"Manned?"

"Unmanned," the computer said. "Should I destroy it?"

"Of course," Liliya said. "Why haven't you before?"

A subtle vibration passed through the ship, so subtle that a human would not have felt it.

"You did not order me to engage any other vessel, only avoid contact," the ship's computer said. "The drone has been destroyed."

"It will have…" Liliya scrambled to her feet, unsteady as her systems caught up with real time once more. She had been under for less than thirty minutes real time, but her own internal systems insisted that she had been prone for several years. She closed her eyes and did her best to ensure that sense overtook logic.

Drying and dressing quickly, she hurried through to the small flight deck. Once in the pilot's seat she accessed all system views and assessed her situation, preferring to do it herself rather than request it from the ship's computer.

Paranoia's your prize for betrayal, she thought, instantly trying to cast the idea aside. She had betrayed the betrayers, that was all. It had taken her far too long, but at last she was pursuing ideals that Wordsworth had also been following. She told herself that, remembering Erika's death in the same thought.

"Full status," she said, and as the computer ran through the assault craft's position, Liliya scanned the displays to double-check the information. Speed and location were accurate, system analysis seemed correct, and full weapons capability was confirmed.

The probe sent ahead of Alexander and his army had

disabled her drive and dropped her back into real space. He'd likely sent hundreds, and this one had been lucky enough to detect her hyperspace trace. She was still traveling at point-three light speed, but had to assume that the device had sent back a signal before it had been destroyed.

A sub-space contact would have reached Alexander, however many light years away he was, and he would be making his way toward her. Full speed, surfing the nebulous waves of various hyperspace planes, he and his army would bear down on her, and she would be no match.

She still had time, but she needed to plan a course of action that meant she could rid herself of the assault ship and go into hiding. Lost in space, she could then make her way into the Human Sphere and surrender to someone in authority.

Then it was simply a case of telling her story, and hoping that they would believe.

Liliya knew that she was close to the Outer Rim, that uncertain area of space that marked the current extent of the Human Sphere. Not a true border, it was constantly expanding as human exploration drove outward. In the two centuries since she and the Founders had left, the Sphere had grown hugely. Over the years she had absorbed as much information as she could, about how everything they had left behind had progressed.

At first she'd kept her research clandestine, but when Wordsworth had found out, he had approved, saying that just because they had left humanity behind, that didn't mean they'd broken every tie. Though he'd never revealed even the smallest desire to return, he nevertheless agreed that it was wise to keep abreast of human progress.

After all, if mankind ever created a space drive more advanced than that of the Founders, the Sphere's expansion might swallow them up.

That had never happened, but the expansion of the dropholes had been of significant interest. Capturing errant sub-space broadcasts, listening in on quantum folds, and collecting information in any way possible, Liliya had built a comprehensive picture of how the new series of dropholes worked.

She had managed to procure activation codes, and it had become a personal project to assess the complex tech required to operate them.

Shortly before Wordsworth's death and the Founders' transmutation into the Rage, she had gone to him with her results, proposing that such tech should be incorporated into their ships. He had agreed.

Part of her was glad, because it meant that her journey into the Sphere would be quicker. It also meant that Alexander— and the Rage—could follow.

"There is a ship nearby," the computer said.

"How close?"

"Thirteen million miles. Speed and direction similar to ours."

"If we've seen it, then we've also been seen."

"That is likely," the computer said. "Here you are." It flashed the details on screen, including a whole slew of vectors and comparative speeds. It was too far away for a visual, but she scanned for its drive signature and anything else that might reveal its provenance.

"Human?" she asked.

"Uncertain. It's not a ship with documented design and drive characteristics."

Liliya began thinking ahead. She could send the assault craft on a pre-programmed course across the edge of the Sphere, hopefully leading Alexander and his army on a lost cause. Then surrender herself to this ship. Impress upon them the importance of the information and nano-tech she carried.

As a plan, it was thin.

If she moved quickly, it might also work.

"All weapons offline," she said.

"Really?"

Liliya uttered a short laugh. "Yes. Really." The weapon controls closed down, and the flight deck grew a few shades darker as various drifting holo displays folded and vanished. "Send an approach vector, and record a message along with it.

"Ready?" she asked.

"Recording."

"My name is Liliya. I'm approaching from far beyond the Human Sphere, where you may have already sustained some attacks from a force that threatens the whole of the Sphere. I come in peace to help you defend against this force. I have knowledge and samples of the tech they intend to use to wage war on humanity, and I offer it freely.

"I say again… *I come in peace*."

She closed her eyes, replayed what she'd said in her mind, and then nodded. "Send."

"It's gone."

"Take us in slowly."

Thirteen million miles closed to thirteen thousand in a hundred seconds, and then the other ship suddenly slowed, swung around, and targeted an array of weapons on the assault ship.

"Countermeasures?" the computer suggested.

"No," Liliya said.

"Really?"

She laughed again, nervously. "Who programmed you?"

"I'm a warship," it said, as if that was an answer.

"War is what I'm trying to prevent."

Liliya waited, the human side of her scared and expecting the brief, shocking flare that would signal her end. Instead, the other ship moved in close, like one curious animal investigating another.

"No sign that they've received the message," Liliya said.

"They're running silent," the computer said.

"Big ship," Liliya said. "Life readings?"

"Sparse."

"Dip our nose and drift us in," Liliya said, frowning. If this were a warship, then she'd have expected more crew. Maybe humans had expanded their use of androids and other automatons. It might be that exploration had become the domain of artificial life. She found herself strangely disappointed at the idea. She had been hoping to meet someone…

Like me? She smiled. She knew that her human sensations and thoughts were genuine, because they confused and troubled her so much. Most humans she knew were badly damaged individuals.

As it turned out, there were no humans to meet.

* * *

In her many years of existence, Liliya had learned a lot. Some of it was programmed, combined with essential progressive learning, and much more had been picked up through desire or choice.

Various dialects of Yautja was one of the latter. Stranger than any human language, its multifarious incarnations and accents had presented her with a huge challenge, and its very difficulty had intrigued her. Even after she'd mastered it, though, she'd had no way of knowing how complete her knowledge had become.

When the tall, imposing figure met her as she exited the airlock onto the warship, Liliya's shock was compounded when it spoke.

"I am Hashori of the Widow Clan." A pause, a heavy silence.

"I am—" Liliya began, the words difficult in her mouth, but she got no further. The Yautja struck her across the face, snapping her head sideways and sending her smashing into the airlock door. She slid to the floor, assessing the damage the impact had caused. Some bruising, a small split in her skin.

"No talking," Hashori said.

No fool, Liliya did as she was told, taking the opportunity to assess the creature who was towering over her. Perhaps nine feet tall, torso scarred with old battle wounds, it was also virtually naked apart from a crotch piece and two wide leather belts around its upper and lower chest. No armor, no weapons, each of its clawed hands was as big as Liliya's head. Its feet were splayed and viciously tipped. It was unmasked, its wide, hinged jaws opening and closing slightly as it breathed.

Small, glistening eyes focused on her.

Liliya guessed that it was a female. There were no obvious differences that she could discern—breasts, sexual organs— and its build was muscular, broad, and as forbidding as any Yautja she had studied in holos or old books. However, there was something about its expression, its eyes.

Hashori was shaking slightly, and bleeding from a wound to her left shoulder. The silence stretched out, and Liliya decided to try again.

"I've come to—" she began.

Hashori stepped forward and kicked her in the stomach. The impact folded her in two and sent her sliding across the floor, hands clutched in to her guts.

"No talking!" the Yautja shouted, voice sharpened with anger—and something else, Liliya thought. Though she was not familiar with the Yautja tone and pronunciation, it was easy to hear the fury.

"After everything you've done, you come to us," Hashori said, spitting, her voice a guttural drawl.

Liliya didn't risk a reply.

"Whatever the reason, I don't care. It means revenge can begin sooner than I hoped." She reached down, clasped Liliya's hair, and dragged her along the dark, humid corridor.

From a wide viewing window beside the docking airlock, Liliya watched her assault ship blast away from the Yautja vessel. As the distance between them grew, it quickly shrank to a tiny spot. Just before she was hauled out of sight a brief, bright flash burst from the Yautja craft, destroying the ship in a distant glare of a billion expanding parts.

2 0

JOHNNY MAINS

Yautja Habitat designated UMF 12, beyond Outer Rim
August 2692 AD

It was their four weeks of hell.

For thirty days Lieutenant Johnny Mains and his four surviving VoidLarks fought, struggled, schemed, and hid to survive. They drew on everything they had ever learned, and learned plenty more. They relied on their wits and wisdom, their strength, fury, and fitness.

Most of all, they relied on each other.

At the end of that time, everything changed. The true indifference of the universe was impressed upon them, and the four weeks of hell they had just passed through felt like little more than a precursor of what was to come.

* * *

Day Eleven

Mains had expected that they would be hunted down and killed in the first few days.

After their initial arrival and contact with the Yautja, they moved quickly away from the site of the *Ochse*'s detonation and tried to find somewhere to hide. The plan was to attempt to board one of the Yautja ships, and perhaps even fly it out of there, but Snowdon had urged caution. She knew more about the Yautja than any of them, and that knowledge had been growing with observations they'd made since their contact with enemy ships prior to the crash-landing.

She believed that many of the ships inside the habitat weren't yet ready for flight. That was why those docking arms were protruding from the habitat's exterior. It also meant that to risk approaching and boarding a craft might be a folly.

So they found safety, and prepared.

"Really, boss, I'm ready to move."

"You look like shit, Corporal."

"Sweet-talker." Cotronis smiled, but it was a weak action, a struggle. Mains was surprised she had even survived this long.

"We'll wait another day," Mains said. "We've got a good place here, and—"

"Johnny, I don't want to die hiding." She spoke quieter, hoping the others didn't hear, but their suits would transmit her words to everyone. She seemed to have forgotten that.

Mains sighed. "Snowdon?"

"We're as ready as we'll ever be," she said. She was guarding one of the entrances to the small cave, with Faulkner at the other. Lieder was asleep. They slept one at a time, for two hours each. It was an exhausting rota, but Mains knew they couldn't let down their guard even for a moment.

"Okay, then," he said. "Let's get our stuff together. Then we'll hustle." Lieder stirred and stood. She hadn't been asleep at all.

Leaving the shelter of the small cave made him feel surprisingly exposed. Even though the habitat was more sparsely populated than they had first believed, the cave had become a safe haven. They were as convinced as they could be that no Yautja knew they were there. Their combat suits had kept them warm and fed with oxygen, their waste recycled, and concentrated food extracts from survival belts had provided sustenance. They all craved something solid to eat, but that was simply habit. Their bodies were as fueled and strong as ever, and Mains knew that Cotronis was right.

The time had arrived.

They worked their way outward from deep within the habitat, Faulkner, Snowdon, and Cotronis using infrared, Mains and Lieder relying on normal sighting. Lieder and Faulkner took point, and they moved slowly, cautiously, suit computers checking their surroundings for movement and life readings.

Their progress was unhindered until they reached a network of rough tunnels and galleries that opened onto the habitat's surface. Once through the atmos shield and outside again, the endless depths of space weighed heavily. With a docking arm less than three hundred yards away, Mains called a halt.

"They're letting us move," he said. "They must be. They *must* know we're here."

"I don't think so," Snowdon said. She clung to the idea that the Yautja were fiercely independent, habitual loners, sharks who only came together in small groups or clans to hunt or reproduce.

"I don't like this," Mains said.

"L-T, there's a ship less than two hundred yards up that docking arm," Lieder said. "Let me and Snowdon get to it, check it out. You, Faulkner, and Cotronis stay here, hunkered down. If I can fly the thing, we'll let you know. You can be with us in minutes, then we're fucking gone." She paused and looked around. "If they're watching us, it's only the two of us they'll have."

"We should stay together," Faulkner said.

"No, she's right," Cotronis said. "Johnny, we've got to take risks if we're going to get off this chunk of rock."

Mains glanced around as well, considering. Half a mile in the other direction was where the *Ochse* had landed, whatever damage it had wrought hidden around the curve of the habitat. In the other direction, the far end of the vessel was out of sight behind the curve of its thicker central section.

No movement.

They'd seen few signs of life since day one.

That troubled him. A lot.

"Okay," he said, "fast as you can. No hanging around, and stay sharp."

"You know it," Lieder said, offering him a private smile.

She and Snowdon went. By the time they had climbed the docking arm and approached the lowest ship up, Mains and the others were crouched in a wrinkle in the habitat's skin.

Cotronis was slipping in and out of consciousness, the effort of moving having drained whatever reserves of energy she still maintained. Her sickness was progressing slowly but surely, and none of them had voiced the inevitable outcome. Not even her.

"Lieder?" Mains asked. He could hear her and Snowdon's heavy breathing, but neither of them responded to his call. Maybe they hadn't heard. Maybe—

"Fucking hell," Snowdon breathed. Her voice crackled through Mains's earpiece.

"What is it?" Cotronis asked, suddenly alert.

"Faulkner, keep scanning our surroundings," Mains said, then he crawled up and forward until he could see the nearby docking arm. "Lieder?"

"We're not getting away on this ship," she said, voice calm and flat. "We're not getting any closer to this dock."

"What have you found?"

"Yautja," she said. "Ten, maybe twelve of them."

"Get out of there!" Mains said. "Back here, quickly as you can, and if they spot you we'll lay down a covering fire until—"

"No need, L-T," Snowdon said. "They're all dead."

"What? Dead how?" Faulkner asked.

"Badly," Lieder said. "Really, really badly."

Day Thirteen

Mains wanted to keep moving, not seek cover in the same place for too long. He thought that remaining still would bring on apathy and carelessness. It was his fault they had ventured into the Yautja home. He bore the responsibility, and took the blame.

They scoped out the habitat for a day first, posting three of their shoulder drones in hidden locations around the place and then retreating to a safe distance. There was no sign that it was still being used. No indication that anyone or anything had been inside for quite some time. It seemed safe, or as safe as anywhere could be in this place.

Built into the inner surface of the habitat's vast, tubular interior, it was sheltered from the massive open space by several folds of rock. The building itself was oddly regular in relation to its surroundings, though there appeared to be few aesthetic touches. A squarish block, several smaller domed structures connected around it, and a taller section atop where a ship might once have been docked. There was no ship now.

Mains hoped the home belonged to one of the Yautja they'd seen flying from the habitat. Or better still, one of those they'd taken out before crash landing.

A day after commencing reconnaissance, he declared it safe to enter.

Lieder and Snowdon went first. Mains and Faulkner followed, Cotronis bringing up the rear. By the time Mains was inside the main space, Lieder and Snowdon were already standing with their weapons lowered, breaths held, staring aghast at the wide, tall wall that might have been transported directly from hell.

"Do a sweep," Mains whispered, unable to tear his gaze away.

"Done," Lieder said. "We're alone. Except…"

Except they weren't alone at all. Mains was aware that Yautja often carried trophies of some of their kills, wearing them as medals or badges of honor, but he'd never expected this. Such pride, such care and creativity. Such horror.

The entire wall was taken up with pieces of dead things. There were talons, hands and jaws, leathery wings and razor claws, skulls and spines. Teeth of many sizes and designs speckled the whole display, and here and there clawed sculptures protruded from the wall as if to reach out for the viewer.

It was the human skulls that Mains found most horrifying. There were eight of them, perhaps ten, all thoroughly cleaned and scoured of flesh and hair, naked smashed bone paying testimony to their owners' terrible last moments. Some were holed and almost recognizable, others burnt and scorched. A couple seemed virtually whole.

"I want to go home," Lieder said. No one laughed. Everyone agreed.

"Let's get outta here," Cotronis said, and Mains did not object. He remained in the room while the others filed back out, trying to imagine the absent Yautja owner sitting or standing here looking at the same view. What would it think?

He didn't want to know.

Day Sixteen

"Faulkner, Lieder, covering fire!" Mains bellowed, cursing their luck, cursing the Yautja and their position and his inability to protect these people who depended on him. Especially Lieder. Whatever the two of them had was as close to love as he had ever felt.

"L-T, this way!" Snowdon said. She had automatically taken point, one arm around Cotronis's waist as she dragged the ailing Corporal along with her, the other leveling her com-rifle at the shadows as they ran toward the shadows that might be hiding anything.

Mains followed, grabbing Cotronis from the other side and helping Snowdon. The Corporal was out of it. Her head bobbed, and accessing her life signs on his suit's master terminal, he saw that her heartbeat was slow, blood pressure low. Her body was shutting down. It had been her screams that had brought this Yautja down upon them.

Yet they would leave no one behind.

"First live one we've seen in sixteen days," Snowdon said.

"Yeah, and it's really pissed off," Lieder added, her voice accompanied by the hiss and roar of their weapons. Ammo was running dangerously low, and they had already agreed that they'd use only laser bursts unless a target was a sure and certain hit. Charge packs in all of their weapons were still at decent levels, but nano-munitions and plasma pods were in dwindling supply.

They were heading across a wide area close to the habitat's surface, the ceiling low and glimmering with countless crystals forming part of the structure. They'd tried to avoid the exposure of the surface, or the habitat's cavernous interior, instead finding caves and fissures to hide in and bide their time. Bad luck had brought a Yautja their way.

Lieder and Snowdon were a hundred yards behind them, covering their retreat until they could find a suitable place for a stand. The Yautja was using blaster and laser, eschewing its more traditional weaponry to get closer to its prey. It also wasn't cloaking, which Mains found strange.

Perhaps it was injured. Since finding that group of dead Yautja three days before, they'd realized that there was a whole new factor to their being here.

They just didn't know what it was.

Mains believed it must have been an internal struggle. Perhaps a civil war. Whatever the reasons, it was bad news for them—and likely worse for the places where the departing ships had been heading.

"Another one!" Faulkner said. "Lieder, sweep left!"

"I see it."

Mains watched the confrontation, trying not to let it distract from where he was.

"And another," Lieder said.

"Okay, pull back to us," he said. "Three against two is uneven, pull back, reform on me."

"L-T?" Snowdon said. There was nowhere close by to make a stand, and she knew that, but there was no way Mains was leaving Lieder and Faulkner to their fate. If they were going down, they were going down together.

"Johnny…" Cotronis said.

"There, twenty yards," he said, nodding toward an uneven mound in the floor. A lot of the structure resembled a sandy rock of some kind, though they knew it was all artificial. Much of the habitat seemed to have been thrown together, rather than built, formed simply for its mass and space rather than to house a large number of inhabitants. It was as if the Yautja had attempted to build a planet, rather than a ship.

"It's not big enough," Snowdon said.

"It'll have to do." Lieder and Faulkner were falling back, alternating in ten-yard sprints before swapping and putting down covering fire. Mains heard the multiple detonations of a micro-dot spray, and a loud squealing filled their ears.

"Down?" Faulkner said, breathless.

"Just more pissed off," Lieder said.

Mains looked back the way he'd come and saw the two VoidLarks emerge from the shadows, explosions and the blood-red slashes of targeting laser following on behind.

"Johnny," Cotronis said. "Johnny, I'm going to…" Her voice faded, then came in again. At first he thought it was his suit's fault, but then he looked sidelong at his Corporal. She was pale, wan, dying. He could see that in her eyes, and when she spoke again he heard it in her voice, too.

"Johnny, give me the defender and a few plasma grenades."

"You're too weak to carry it," Snowdon said.

"Doesn't matter," Cotronis said.

Mains shook his head.

"Three of them, L-T!" Cotronis shouted, and even that effort caused her to slump between Mains and Snowdon. She was done for. She'd been finished the moment she entered the *Ochse*'s damaged engine room, and it was only down to time. They'd all known that, but none of them had voiced it. Until now.

"I'm dying, soon, so I want to die well."

"L-T..." Lieder said in his ear, and Mains glanced behind him. Lieder was running toward them through the dark chamber, Faulkner kneeling behind her and unleashing a shattering firestorm of micro-dot charges to cover her retreat. A hundred degrees of his field of view erupted into ten thousand small blasts, and in that glare he saw two of the three advancing Yautja. They protected their faces with their arms, but kept running. They would *always* keep running, and keep fighting.

"I don't want to just fade away hanging between the two of you," Cotronis said. "Please, Johnny."

"Snowdon," Mains said. She only hesitated for a second before handing the heavy defender to Cotronis. Free of their grasp, the Corporal stood upright, shaking as she took the big gun and held it in both hands.

Mains handed her his two plasma grenades, and Snowdon gave her two more.

"Go," Cotronis said. "All of you. I promise I'll die in a fucking blaze of glory, but I don't want any of you seeing."

More explosions from behind them, and then Lieder was with them. Panting hard, she moved awkwardly where her suit had hardened to protect a wound and patch a split in its skin. Snowdon knelt and fired behind them, covering Faulkner's final retreat.

"One down," Lieder said. "But the other two are—"

"Heads up!" Faulkner said. He spun and crouched, and Mains did the same, but then Cotronis stepped into their fields of fire, the defender hissing and cracking in her arms as she unloaded a full shot. The smoking, blazing air behind them blurred, and from somewhere unseen a Yautja roared in pain and rage.

"Next life, Sarah," Mains said.

He and his remaining VoidLarks ran.

Breathing hard, saying nothing, all keeping one eye on their readouts in case a Yautja appeared from elsewhere, they barely slowed. Then the first plasma grenade thumped behind them, casting their quivering silhouettes ahead toward safety.

Moments later a much larger blast knocked them from their feet as Cotronis detonated the last three grenades and the defender's charge magazine.

Struggling to their feet, they still didn't speak as they searched for somewhere new to hide.

Lieder almost died.

The wound she'd received was brutal, and it was only the rush of adrenalin and her suit's emergency repair that saved her life. After Cotronis's death the four of them had found somewhere to hide, and Lieder had started to bleed out.

Mains sat beside her for a while, holding her hand. He couldn't bear living the rest of his life without her, however short that life looked destined to be, but he was in charge. He had to lead. He would not mourn a strong woman who was not yet dead.

Administering any sort of medical aid in such an inhospitable atmosphere was extremely difficult. They couldn't remove her suit, and neither could they access her injury through the suit's hardened sections. The wound was in her upper right chest, an ugly shrapnel hole that had punctured her lung and shattered two ribs. The suit gave her painkillers and applied pressure, but Mains and the others had to watch helplessly as they waited to see if Lieder would die.

She was unconscious for days, blood loss weakening her systems. The suit continued to give her low doses of anesthetic. Awake, moving around, agitated, she would only open her wound again. The suit froze her leaked blood, stored it, and gave her a transfusion when she started bleeding some more. It cleaned and conditioned the blood in the process, and it was that more than anything that probably saved her life.

Mains, Faulkner, and Snowdon took stock and tried to formulate a plan. Already a mysterious place, this habitat was affected by something they could not understand. Even for the sparse population, there wasn't enough activity. Though the massive explosions they'd felt during their first couple of days there had ended, the slaughtered Yautja they'd found showed that all was not well.

They had to get a ship and escape, as soon as possible.

At last Lieder was well enough to move again. Though still weak, she had pulled through with her usual good cheer. The suit stopped administering drugs on day twenty-two. She walked on day twenty-four, and spent day twenty-five swapping harsh banter with the others.

* * *

Day Twenty-Six

"We don't know what we'll find up there," Snowdon said again.

"If we find more dead Yautja, we move forward," Mains said. "If there's a ship docked and we can get to it, we let nothing stop us."

"And we stick together," Faulkner said.

"Right," Lieder said. "You can't do without me."

They chose the docking arm they would target, then sent a shoulder drone ahead. After several hours they moved out of the hiding place and made their way back to the habitat's outer surface. It seemed safe and deserted and it remained so as they moved forward.

As they emerged onto the surface, space pressed down on Mains once again. This time the intimidating vastness also gave him a sense of freedom, and the idea that anything was possible. He remembered something his brother once said to him.

If the universe is infinite, or if there are infinite universes, then somewhere there's a tree that people grow on.

He took a long breath and sighed deeply.

"Yeah," Lieder said. "We'll be out there again soon."

The docking arm they'd chosen loomed ahead of them. It took half an hour of cautious advancing to reach it, then another half an hour to send in two more drones to scout the way. No sign of movement, or life. No sign of death, either. In this dock there were no bodies.

They entered and started climbing. Several hover platforms stood waiting in their wells, but they didn't have time to figure out how to use them. Mains was also worried that their operation might attract attention. Silent and cautious was best, so they climbed hundreds of stairs built for Yautja, too deep for their own legs, and soon they were gasping for breath.

Exhausted, reaching the ship they'd selected, Mains once again sent in his shoulder drone. It was weakening, charge failing, and his suit indicated that it didn't have the power for a recharge. It didn't matter. They'd be away from here soon, this place he'd started to think of as a ghost ship. There might still be Yautja here, somewhere—Cotronis's end proved that— but it felt silent, deserted, and dead.

They entered the alien ship, and once inside, Lieder went to work. It took only ten minutes for her to pronounce that she could not fly the vessel.

"Bullshit," Faulkner said. His voice was edged with fear.

"I haven't got a clue," Lieder said. "You see one single thing here that resembles anything on the *Ochse*?"

The four of them walked around the sphere-shaped room, climbing low steps set into the walls.

"I don't even know if this is the flight deck or the engine room," Lieder persisted.

"Snowdon?" Mains asked, but he already knew the answer, even as she shrugged.

"Our suit systems?" Faulkner asked.

"They're great with systems they know," Lieder said, "but I'd wager this ship's heavily personalized toward whoever owns it. Wouldn't surprise me if it was linked on a genetic level, and if that's the case, even if I *did* understand some of what we see here, I wouldn't be able to operate it."

"Shit," Faulkner breathed.

"There's more," Lieder said. "This far away from the core of the habitat, I've been able to analyze its spin and attitude. My combat suit's computer doesn't have all the data I need, but I think it's enough to say with confidence… we're fucked."

"Oh, you think?" Faulkner said.

"On so many more levels than you think," Lieder said. "Johnny, we're on a decaying orbit headed into the nearby sun."

"Great," Mains said. "Well, we wouldn't want things to be easy, would we? How long?"

"It's only an estimate, but I'd guess twenty days until the habitat starts to burn up. Of course, it might be pulled apart by the sun's gravity before then."

"Of course," Faulkner said. "Anything else? We out of coffee?"

"Just one more reason to find a way off this shithole," Mains said. "We go up to another ship. There are three more on this dock."

"Much higher up," Snowdon observed.

"We need the exercise." No one smiled. None of them could.

When by the end of the day they'd visited the other three ships, and found them all just as silent and mysterious as the first, Mains thought he might never smile again.

As they began their descent, following a wide, steep staircase, Snowdon trailed behind, and moments later she called a halt.

"L-T, take a look at this!" Mains hurried back up and across a gallery area, to where Snowdon was standing in front of an opening in the tower wall. With no atmosphere, there was no glass or other enclosure across the opening, and it was a long way down to the habitat's surface.

Snowdon wasn't looking that way.

"What the hell?" Mains said.

"Another ship."

From this high up they could see to the far end of the habitat, perhaps two miles away. Since crash landing they had remained around this central portion, fighting as they had to, hiding when they could. The docking tower was the most centrally located structure along the whole of UMF 12. This was the first time they had seen so far, and Mains cursed himself for not exploring the rest of the chamber.

"It's not Yautja," Snowdon said.

The ship was held stationary, just above the far end. If there were moorings, they were invisible from this distance.

"You're sure?" Faulkner asked.

"Pretty sure. I've never seen anything like it before."

Even looking at it gave Mains a strange feeling. It was like looking at something that shouldn't be. It seemed grown, rather than built, its smooth lines chaotic, its mass and structure uneven. It was a faint red, almost pink, and that also gave it a biological appearance.

"Those explosions," Lieder said. "Maybe they weren't to do with the *Ochse* after all."

"We've been thinking some sort of internal feud," Mains said. "But this... maybe this is something else."

* * *

Day Twenty-Eight

There was something on the habitat that was killing Yautja, and it wasn't them.

The two bodies were torn apart, scattered across the wide corridor, blood dried a crispy, deep green. They'd been dead for a long time. Blast holes scarred the walls and ceiling, and other signs of combat indicated that it had been quite a fight. One Yautja head had rolled against a sloping wall, and its jaws hung open to display shattered tusks bared in a last defiant roar.

"I'm not feeling the love for this place," Lieder said.

"Keep it quiet," Mains said. "Move in pairs, never more than fifty yards apart. We're almost there."

After seeing the alien ship docked at the far end of the habitat, they'd descended from the tower and prepared to move. Mains's and Snowdon's suits were showing signs of running down, and Lieder's controls had developed various troubling glitches since her injury. Combining assets and cross-charging had solved the worst of their problems, but there was no escaping the fact that they were running out of ammunition. Chemical supplies were also low—vital for the suits to provide oxygen, water, and artificial dietary supplements, but the Excursionists were more concerned about their ability to fight.

They moved past the dead Yautja. Sending Lieder's shoulder drone ahead revealed signs of several massive blasts within the habitat, at this end of the open area. Residual radiation suggested that they might have been caused by exploding ships.

"They suicide if faced with overwhelming odds," Snowdon suggested.

"So where are the overwhelming odds?" Mains said. "And why did we see a load of their ships fleeing the habitat?"

"They don't run away from a fight," Snowdon said. "Fighting's what they live for. That'd be like Faulkner running away from alcohol."

"Funny," Faulkner said.

"Maybe they were retreating, regrouping," Lieder said. "Left a small force behind to harry the enemy, destroy their own ships if the time was right."

"Maybe," Snowdon said, sounding doubtful. "But we've seen no evidence that they act in concert. Even in a big fight, they're on their own. They're just not like us."

"That still begs one question," Mains said. "What enemy were they harrying?"

"Let's not hang around to find out, eh?" Faulkner said.

As they moved forward in pairs, Mains mused on this. It was their job to find out what was going on here. Trapped for four weeks, reduced from eight to four, still they had a duty to perform. They were Excursionists, trained and willing to spend long years of their lives patrolling the furthest extremes of humanity's reach into the galaxy, looking out for such dangers as this. Running would be a dereliction of duty. Escape and survival was essential, but only for one reason—to deliver a message about what was happening here.

His crew knew that. Faulkner's quip had revealed his fear, but Mains knew them all better than his own family. They *were* his family.

He accessed his suit's holo view. They were four hundred yards from the end of the habitat, and beneath them the narrowing cylinder of the vessel was a solid mass. Above them, past twenty yards of solid structure, the unidentified ship was parked.

"Let's get to the surface," Mains said. "All weapons online. Cloaking active. Combat systems hot."

"I could do with a drink," Faulkner said.

"I could do with getting this suit off," Lieder said. "Four weeks without washing, and I smell like a farmyard."

"You smell like that all the time," Faulkner replied.

Mains laughed softly and started leading the remnants of his crew up to find an opening out onto the surface.

"L-T!" Lieder said.

"I got it!" His suit's holo view had suddenly speckled red, indicating some distance ahead of them. He turned left and right, one eye on the screen, to see if it was some sort of interference.

"What have you all got?" he asked his crew.

"Movement," Faulkner said. "Lots of movement. I count thirty distinct traces."

Fuck.

"Same here," Snowdon said. "We've gotta fall back, L-T."

Mains closed his eyes briefly, considering what waited for them back the way they had come. More time hiding, scurrying through shadows, just waiting to be found again by another rogue Yautja. If they retreated now—

"Johnny, those aren't Yautja," Snowdon said.

"How do you know?"

"The readings are all wrong. The way they move, and

there's something about them..." She trailed off, and as he waited for her to continue, he saw it himself.

"They're advancing in waves," he said. The red specks on his screen were closing in on them, the first line of a dozen less than a hundred yards away. "Too late to run. Dig in."

They darted left and right, Lieder and Mains close together, Faulkner and Snowdon a few yards to the left. The tunnel here was wide and low, rough, offering many places to hide. It was a good place to defend. They had a clear field of fire. He shoved aside the shattering certainty that they would all be dead within minutes, and rested his com-rifle on the rock before him.

From the shadows far ahead something screeched, a loud, sickening sound like fingernails drawn across a smooth surface.

"Oh my God," Faulkner said. "Oh, no. Oh..."

"What?" Mains demanded.

"L-T, I've heard that sound before," he said. "Xenomorphs."

The shadows ahead of them erupted into life, and Johnny Mains and his VoidLarks opened fire.

2 1

ISA PALANT

Love Grove Base, Research Station, LV-1529
September 2692 AD

Over the twelve days since the alien ship landed, and they killed Connors and Sharp, Palant and the other survivors had seen the two Yautja several times, circling the storage hangars, standing motionless in the storms, sometimes passing back and forth as if lost.

They had even given them names.

The big one they called Shamana, after a famous sportsman from the previous century renowned for his size, strength, speed, and the length of his dreadlocks. The other Yautja—the mad one, the screamer, the one that Palant knew for sure would eventually come for them—McIlveen had named Wendigo. His love of myth and legend almost a thousand years old surprised Palant, but then plenty about McIlveen was surprising her.

The Yautja knew they were there. That was for certain, but it was also a mystery, because the predators had done little to trouble them. Palant had given all the survivors, especially the indies, everything she knew about the Yautja species. How they lived, fought, interacted, and died. Their technology and capabilities. The few facts known for sure, and the many more aspects of their existence only guessed at.

She made certain that weapons were within reach, but left untouched. It was a constant trial, preventing the indies from trying to retaliate, but she'd impressed on them that it was the best way to keep safe. Whether the Yautja could see or scan inside the storage buildings she didn't know for sure, but it was a chance they couldn't take.

The station staff had arranged a schedule for sleeping and working. Most of the work consisted of collecting and purifying water from the drip points around the hangar, preparing what meager food they had, administering medicine, and trying to keep each other's spirits up. Several bodies were hidden away in a small room at the hangar's rear, wrapped in tarpaulin and with the door blocked shut.

No one approached that room.

The indies had also arranged a schedule, built around patrolling and sleeping. They did little else. The storm raged outside as it had for ten days, rain pouring down in sheets. She and McIlveen had immersed themselves in their research once again, and only a part of that was to offer distraction from the pressing dangers surrounding them. Not only from the aliens, but from the dwindling food supplies, and the growing risk of radiation poisoning from the damaged reactor.

A small part of her that she could never reveal to anyone, not even McIlveen, could begin to know how excited she was at what was happening. She had never dreamed that she would one day be this close to a living, breathing Yautja, and she could never have fantasized that she might one day be able to listen to them talking.

"Another one, there," McIlveen said, pointing. They were hunkered on the ground around an old receiver, its wiry guts spewed over the floor, clever repairs and adaptations made, a small speaker connected. It had taken three days of minute tweaking until they had found the Yautja frequency, and since then one of them had always been by the receiver's side. Usually both of them.

Palant knew that many of the survivors viewed them with distrust, perhaps even recognizing some of the sick excitement they felt at the precarious circumstance they found themselves in, but right then she didn't care. The pressure of history hung on every moment, and she could feel its deep resonance.

"Wendigo again," Palant said. She had rigged a small datapad to the receiver's speaker, loaded with a program she had been working on for some time. She stopped short of calling it a translation matrix, but after a day spent combining it with some of his own research, McIlveen had given it just that name. So far it seemed to be recognizing about sixty percent of what the Yautja were saying, even though they were speaking very little. When they did, the translation scrolled across a small screen, and was recorded on the ancient datapad device.

"Sounds more pissed off than ever," McIlveen said. "Think we should tell them?"

Palant glanced across the hangar at where McMahon was sitting with another indie. She'd taken command since Sharp had been slaughtered, and everything about her impressed Palant—but she was still a soldier. Even after everything Palant had told them, McMahon's natural instinct was to fight.

"Not yet," Palant said. "Not unless we have to. A couple of them are twitchy as hell. One of them initiates a weapon, the Yautja see, and..."

"Nothing will keep them out."

She nodded. They'd already talked about this. One blast from a Yautja shoulder weapon and the hangar's wall would be breached. It was a miracle it hadn't happened already, but the longer they listened in on the aliens' sporadic communications, the more Palant was beginning to understand.

These Yautja weren't on a hunt. They were there because they were the prey.

Hateful demons... fire lizards from... find my own... and blood.

"I wouldn't like to be inside her head," McIlveen said, reading the translation.

"I don't want to be anywhere near her," Palant said. She hadn't expected fluffy banter, but this gave her the chills. Wendigo's ranting seemed to comprise the outline of a nightmare.

"I think she's insane," McIlveen offered. In truth, neither of them could accurately discern the Yautja's sex.

"Whereas Shamana is quiet, controlled," Isa said, and McIlveen nodded. It had been almost a day since Shamana had responded to a Wendigo scream. *"Be calm... and prepare,"* he had said, yet the calmness applied to only one of them. It was what they were preparing for that concerned Isa the most.

Wendigo spoke again, that strange percussion of clicks, clacks, and guttural croaks that comprised what they knew of the Yautja language. It was a complex tongue, barely understood even by those most interested in the Yautja species. Despite the software they had created, she couldn't tell whether the translations were at all accurate. Much of what they spoke was discarded by the program and dumped in a "futures" folder.

... clan... know loss... hate hate HATE!

"She's getting worse," McIlveen said.

"Maybe," Palant said. "Or maybe she's firing herself up."

"What are the 'fire lizards,' do you think? It's not the first time she's mentioned them. Shamana doesn't seem to acknowledge them, though."

"I think it's what's chasing them," she replied.

"If they'd come here purely to hunt, they'd have forced our hand by now. They know there are soldiers in here, and weapons. And... I think Shamana is confused. He seems aloof and distant, perhaps even in control, but I think it's just a mask."

"Maybe," McIlveen said, sounding dubious. "I can't imagine anything that could hunt those things. Whatever the case, though, I think it's time to bring in McMahon. Wendigo might come at us at any moment, and then it'll be time for the guns."

"Yeah... time for the guns." Palant waited a while longer, though, listening to the soft crackle and hiss of atmospheric interference. The Yautja had stopped talking. Their silence was haunting.

"Everything we do here will help the Company," McIlveen

muttered. That surprised her. Though he was a Weyland-Yutani man through and through, she'd started to convince herself that he had come for the love of discovery. For a moment she felt back at square one, as if she didn't know him at all.

"We'll be dead before we can tell them," she said, although she wasn't sure why. She still held out hope—so maybe she'd said it out of spite. She saw his shock and glanced away, barely holding back a smile.

Hugging her knees to her chest against the cold, Palant remembered her parents and how they had always instilled in her a sense of responsibility. As Weyland-Yutani employees, they'd revealed to her some of the Company's darker workings. Her mother had borne witness, while her father had taken part in actions he believed were immoral, even criminal. Through it all they had retained their own sense of pride, and the dark deeds had weighed heavy.

They'd told her that their desire for scientific discovery drove them harder and farther than the Corporation for which they worked. If they could keep themselves apart from that— physically if possible, psychologically if not—then they would succeed. As far as Palant was aware, they always had.

She rarely dwelled on the darker episodes in their lives, instead remembering them for the love they had shared, and their passion for learning. She retained that love, that passion. Even now, listening to the words of the Yautja was opening doorways and creating a knowledge base for future generations. Isa couldn't influence how the Company would use this knowledge… but she *could* determine whether or not they ever received it.

`Not··· fault¬` Shamana said. `Leave··· alone··· wait and··· for now·`

Palant sat up, and McIlveen's eyes went wide.

"You think he's talking about us?" McIlveen asked.

Palant looked around, standing and catching McMahon's attention. Milt was right. It was time to bring her in.

The woman soldier stood, stretching.

"What's happening?" she asked.

"They're talking," Palant replied. "A lot." A few people turned her way.

"What are they saying?" McMahon asked.

"It's confusing," Palant replied. "One of them seems to be urging calm. The other…"

"The other?" another soldier prompted.

"Is mad," McIlveen said. "Insane, and if she—"

Another series of clicks and grunts issued from the speaker behind Palant, and she crouched to view the screen again. *That sounded bad*, she thought, but she waited for the translation to appear, not yet trusting that task to herself.

`··· fire lizards took··· me alone··· need blood! Need blood!`

"Oh, no," McIlveen said.

Palant stood.

"I think she's coming," she said.

McMahon and the other indies rushed to the doors. Even then they glanced back at Palant, uncertain, hands clasping by their sides as if in memory of what had once been there.

More clicking. More fury.

"Isa, she's coming," McIlveen shouted. "She's charging!"

"Yes," Palant said to McMahon, nodding down at the laser rifle propped against the wall beside the soldier.

"Everyone hide!" McIlveen shouted.

From the far end of the hangar a blast erupted, a wall panel shattered inward in a shower of metal shards, wind and rain, and a man screamed long and loud.

"Everyone hide!" Palant screamed, echoing McIlveen's words even as he grabbed her arm and pulled her toward the back of the structure. She tripped and shrugged him off, almost falling, finding her feet again, running, and then skidding to a halt and turning back.

The datapad! Everything they'd heard the Yautja saying, every translation, was recorded on that small, antiquated device. Svenlap's attack had meant there was no cloud storage and no quantum fold, only a hard disc—and she could not lose what she knew.

From her left came a shout and then a bright, sparkling burst of laser fire. Voices called out in panic, then harsh whispers as survivors hunkered down behind old, rusted equipment.

"Isa!" McIlveen hissed.

She ran. Another fusillade of fire, and the building's structure screamed and rattled where it was holed. As she reached the small bench where they'd been working there was a pause in the furious action.

Grabbing the device and ripping wires from it, Palant looked around.

McMahon and several other indies were crouching with their weapons ready, turning slow circles. She caught McMahon's eye and the woman nodded once, hard, indicating that she should hide.

Across the hangar she saw a dead soldier rise into the air, lifted by something she could not see, but was starting to know so well.

"There!" she said, pointing.

McMahon saw. She braced her legs and let off a sustained burst of laser fire. The dead soldier was ripped in two, viscera splashing across the wall as his torso was flung aside. The whole corner of the hangar was lit up as the rest of the indies opened fire.

A heavy thump sounded from somewhere and a plasma burst shone bright, the glare too harsh to look at. As Palant ran toward an old loader the shine faded, and she looked to her right to see a huge hole where the hangar's front and side walls met.

The ceiling slumped down, molten metal edges drooping, harsh steam clouds erupting where the heavy rain was blown in by the storm. Superheated metal creaked and clanged where water splashed across it.

Palant skidded to a halt behind the loader. She was alone, but twenty yards away she could see a couple of others from the station, including McIlveen. He stared at her wide-eyed, and she held up the datapad. He shook his head in disbelief.

Wendigo made herself heard.

The roar was loud and long, an ululation of rage and exultation, and if she had been injured she voiced no hint of pain. Other screams accompanied her, cries of fear from the survivors as they awaited their doom. Footsteps pounded around the hangar, thumping on the rough concrete floor, then there was clanging against the already damaged walls.

The storm howled through rents in the metal cladding. Rain lanced in, sheets of dashing light slicing across the space. Lights flickered and then died as cables were torn and smashed, until the hangar was lit only by a few low-level lamps and the stark flashing of laser bursts. Palant saw an indie close to her flip an eyepiece down from his helmet as they switched to infrared.

A moment later that same indie fell, his head parted from his body and bouncing toward Palant's hiding place.

She clapped her free hand over her mouth and used her feet to push herself closer to the loader, wishing she could crawl into the narrow gap beneath it, bury her face in her hands, and unsee every terrible thing she had seen.

The indie's severed neck gushed blood as his head came to rest against her left boot. The infrared sight was still lowered over his right eye, and she wondered whether he saw anything, just for another second.

To Palant's left, looming over her, Wendigo glittered like the star-speckled depths of space as rain was blown across her cloaked body. Her eyes were visible, piercing points of light staring down at this weak, pitiful human.

"I know what you said," Palant whispered. For that moment everything else pulled away from her, to an impossible distance that made space seem like home. McIlveen, McMahon, the survivors, the ruined base, every moment in her history and everyone she had ever known, they all became nothing in the face of her first encounter with a living creature from another world.

"I... know... what..." Wendigo growled in sickening

mimicry... and then the world exploded.

Laser blasts streaked in, screaming from the loader's chassis, knocking the Yautja back and down and peppering the wall ten yards away. The alien's shoulder blaster fired, missing Palant by inches where she had huddled down against the old vehicle's tracks. She felt the heat singe her hair and stretch the skin on her hands and cheek, and the loader's cab disintegrated in a shower of shards and molten metal.

The Yautja leapt to its feet and ran, its damaged cloaking device throwing strange sparks that seemed to reflect its whole body in motion, scattering a thousand tiny images of itself behind as it sought cover.

Two indies appeared around the front of the loader, glanced at Palant, then chased the Yautja. One of them braced himself with legs parted, and fired a plasma charge. Whatever he thought he was firing at, he missed, the charge exploding against the small locked room where they kept the bodies of the dead.

Metal warped and flew. Fire ate inward. Flesh was burnt, adding a sickening warmth to the metallic tang on the air.

"Isa!" McIlveen called, waving her over. She knew she wouldn't be any safer there than where she crouched, but she suddenly felt the need for contact, human company, and a sudden affection for the Company man made her eyes water.

She ran, glancing left and right. The fight moved to the far end of the hangar now, close to where the building's corner had been blasted open and its roof and walls slumped down to the ground. The darkness burst apart again and again, and averting her face from the glare, she looked to her right.

Standing in the open doorway, Shamana was watching her.

Palant paused in the open. A streaking, errant laser blast whipped past her, so close that her sleeve flicked and skin sizzled, pain bleeding up her arm and into her shoulder, but she barely noticed. The Yautja stared. Palant lifted the datapad, suddenly desperate to make contact in any way not involving guns and pain, bloodied blades and death.

Without looking she typed, *I know*, then whispered, "Translate." She held up the datapad, turned up the volume, and when it issued a throaty slick and a series of growls, a shiver ran down her spine.

Shamana moved slightly, tilting his head as if listening. Then he stepped aside and melted into the storm, moving away from the chaos of the hangar, not toward it.

Palant slumped to her knees.

I made contact! she thought. *I spoke to him. I reached him!* But she could not know for sure.

Someone ran toward her. An indie, her clothes burning and hands slapping at the fire that was eating into her face.

McIlveen and several others darted from cover and tripped the woman, rolling her in an attempt to extinguish the flames, but the burning material had melted in deep, and the woman issued only a bubbling groan as she grew still, then curled into a tight ball as her tendons contracted in the heat.

"Isa... here!" McIlveen shouted. She needed no more invitation. She ran to him, and they moved toward the shadows at the rear of the hangar.

As they crouched, Wendigo ran into the open. She was slower than before, trailing a slick of bright green blood that also sprayed from several points on her body. Two indies followed her, pumping laser blasts at her until she fell and squirmed on the ground.

McMahon approached. She was blooded down one side of her face, left arm held across her chest, but she still carried her rifle in her right hand.

"Step back!" she warned, the other two obeying instantly.

Wendigo wore something slick and red around her neck. Palant thought it belonged inside someone, not outside. She was laughing, a deep, throaty sound.

"McMahon!" Palant shouted, thinking of the tales of Yautja suicides. "Her hand! Don't let her touch—"

McMahon reacted instantly, raising her rifle and blasting the Yautja's hand away from her arm. It skittered across the floor like a huge spider, flipping onto its back, clawed fingers curling inward and pressing into the palm.

The Yautja grew still and silent. Perhaps dead, perhaps not, but McMahon made sure. There was no sense of victory, and no gloating in the coupe de grace. Remaining at a distance, she fired three short bursts at the alien's head. The helmet split and skittered across the floor, and Wendigo twitched once as she died.

"Regroup!" McMahon said, motioning. "You at the door, you two over at that corner! The other one could be here at any moment."

I don't think so, Isa wanted to say, but she couldn't be sure, and she would not risk anyone else's life. At least three indies lay dead. Their shelter was blasted open in several places, exposed to the inimical elements, and one of her research subjects was no more.

She glanced at McIlveen, ashamed at the sadness she felt, but from the way he looked at her, she knew that he felt it too.

"Milt, I don't think—"

"Here comes the second one!" an indie shouted, and Palant groaned as she backed away, McIlveen by her side. It seemed that in reality she knew nothing at all.

McMahon looked at Palant, exhausted and injured, and Isa began to speak. But then McMahon turned away and staggered toward the door, arm still clasped tight across her chest. Her rifle swung low and she swayed a little as she moved, but she was stocky and strong, her ginger-blonde hair flicking where it had escaped from beneath her helmet.

"Stop!" Palant shouted. "I can talk to him!" But McMahon didn't seem to hear.

"Isa, we don't know that," McIlveen said. "And there's no way you can risk—"

Gunfire erupted at the building's ruined corner, flashing through the hangar. Rain drove in almost horizontally, spears of light resembling scattered laser fire.

McMahon stopped, lifting her rifle.

The wall in front of her smashed inward and Shamana burst through, shoving fractured sheet metal aside, sweeping his clawed hand and slashing McMahon from shoulder to hip. The indie dropped her gun and tried to back away, but Shamana clasped her to his chest, spun around and leapt back through the hole.

Several shots streaked across the hangar, chasing after the Yautja.

"You'll hit McMahon!" Palant screamed. The indies ceased

fire, Shamana and McMahon vanished out into the storm, and the building was plunged into a stunned stillness. Wind roared and whistled through the countless holes and gashes in the structure, rain slashed in, but compared to the screams, shouts, and explosions of battle, the silence almost breathed.

The remaining three indies huddled around the door, scanning outside with their infrared goggles.

Palant ran to them. They glared at her as if she were the enemy, eyes wide and shocked, one of them openly shaking.

"I can communicate with it!" she said. "If you go out there after it you'll be killed."

"You expect us to let *you* go?" one of the indies said.

"Do you give a shit?" she spat back. Palant was terrified and excited at the same time, heart thumping, and her fight-or-flight instinct pulled her both ways. Every animal part of her wanted to hide away from the danger, yet the intellectual heart of her—the part that drove every action she'd taken as an adult—craved to venture out into the storm and find the Yautja. Talk to it. Communicate with the alien in a way that had never been attempted before.

"Please," she said, and then the long, high scream came from out in the storm. It was horrible, an expression of pure pain that could not be feigned.

An indie moved to rush outside. Another one stopped him.

One more scream, long and loud, ending suddenly.

And then Shamana roared in triumph. Somewhere in the storm, another trophy was being taken.

"You want to communicate with *that*?" the indie said to her. He sounded defeated now, almost resigned to his fate.

Palant had no answer. None that made sense to her, at least. She had just listened to another good person die.

The hangar was a ruin. One end had slumped to the ground, its walls were holed from laser fire and explosions, and there were more bodies, with nowhere to keep them.

The remaining three indies were edgy and careless, stalking inside and outside the hangar with weapons at the ready. To Palant, they now seemed dangerous rather than protective. They'd lost their leader, lost their friends, and this relatively safe, comfortable posting had changed into a version of hell. She was certain that they would flee, if there was anywhere left to go.

But there wasn't. Radiation levels were rising from the damaged reactor, and the storm showed no signs of abating. So the mercenaries prowled the area, waiting to fight, waiting to die.

Palant and McIlveen gathered the survivors and together they built what shelter they could in the undamaged end of the hangar, away from the ruined corner and the stench of burning bodies. There was very little food left. Drinking water was heavy with radiation, but they had little choice. They all took the maximum doses of radiation drugs, but the longer they were exposed, the more they were merely delaying the inevitable.

While the others gathered and salvaged what they could to survive, the two scientists saved as much of their research material as possible. Palant felt a little shamefaced doing so, yet it felt like the one good thing that could come of this situation. Whatever happened to them, if she could preserve everything she and McIlveen had discovered about the Yautja, independently and together, then perhaps their work might live on. Benefit humanity. Maybe even form the first uncertain foundation on which peace might be built between species.

Thinking of Sharp's death, and McMahon's drawn-out scream of terror and agony, she had to wonder whether this might ever be possible. Yet she was still convinced that the Yautja were scared, and had been chased here, essentially cornered. If she and McIlveen ever found the time and facilities to analyze their recordings in greater detail, perhaps they would be able to confirm it.

I want to know, she kept thinking. *We're so close to something amazing, and I want to know more.* Yet she felt the tightening noose of time, the crushing weight of fate, and the idea that she might die before discovering more made her feel wretched.

"I tried speaking to Shamana," she said. McIlveen glanced up from the mess of wires and components their translation machine had become. Palant still had the precious datapad, and she was keeping it safe.

"During the attack?"

"When the indies were fighting Wendigo. I used the datapad as a reverse translator, its onboard speaker to broadcast. And I think I got through."

"How can you know?" he asked, shaking his head. He almost scoffed.

"If I hadn't, I think he would have joined in the fight." She nodded at the remaining indies, even now stalking back and forth inside the damaged hangar's front wall, weapons held high. "He'd have taken them by now."

"What did you say?"

"I said, 'I know.'"

McIlveen blinked at her, frowned, and for a moment she saw a look in his eyes that she had seen so many times before, from other people. That confusion, that sense of, *Are you mad?*

"He killed McMahon."

"Revenge for Wendigo, maybe."

"I don't think we can assume we know anything about them," he countered. "I think we're fools if we do."

They gathered the rest of their equipment and returned to the other survivors. The fires burned down, and the storm raged outside.

Three days later, just around dawn, another ship arrived.

"More of them!" someone shouted, and the indies took up firing positions. "There's more!"

Palant's heart sank. Someone started crying.

"That's a Colonial Marine ship!" the indie wearing a combat suit said. "They've come for us!"

"The Company sent Marines?" McIlveen asked, but he was smiling at Palant, the sense of relief on his face mirroring everyone else's.

Palant went to the hangar's smashed doors and stood with the others, watching distant lights as the ship dropped slowly through the rain. The raging storm had calmed over the past day, allowing them to attempt basic repairs on the hangar. It did little to give them any better shelter, but keeping busy seemed to have lifted the mood a little, and the effort made them feel better.

Now it seemed as if their hopes had not been in vain.

"We should stay here," the suited indie said. "Wait for them to come to us. No point putting ourselves in danger now."

"We haven't heard a thing from him in three days," Palant said. "He might even have left during the storm."

"Yeah, we might not have heard his ship," McIlveen said.

"It's still there," the indie said. "My suit's got a fix on it. Nothing's changed. That Yautja bastard is still out there, hasn't touched its ship since landing."

"Maybe we should warn—" another indie said, and then the shooting began.

Flashes danced across the landscape, strangely silent because of the distance and remnants of the storm. The ship was out of sight beneath a ridge, so the flashes resembled lightning strikes, occasional rumbles rolling in like thunder.

They're killing him, Palant thought. She had the datapad in a backpack. She hadn't put it down in three days. It was still fully charged. *They'll kill him, and I might never be so close again*.

She ran. McIlveen shouted behind her, and other voices echoed his pleas to return, but she shut them out and ran toward the fight, carrying everything her parents had ever lived for—that passion for discovery and knowledge. At that moment if she'd died she would have died content that she was chasing her dreams. People with guns discovered nothing, they merely destroyed. That was why the Yautja were still a mystery. Perhaps if she substituted datapad for gun, she might learn something amazing.

She passed the remains of one of the indies, little more than a mass of tattered clothing and torn flesh washed pale by days of heavy rain. She didn't look too closely, and she had no wish to know who it was.

Splashing through standing water, slipping in mud, trying to stick to high ground in case she became bogged down or fell into a deeper pool, she closed quickly on the scene of combat. The sounds grew as she approached, and the weapon discharges were very different from the laser rifles she'd heard over the past few days. As she ran she shrugged the rucksack from her shoulders and opened it, drawing the datapad out. She had to be ready to use it, and several times she slowed, debating what to say and how.

At the top of the final rise, looking down at the newly arrived ship and the fight taking place around it, she tapped in a simple message. Then she went down the slope, sliding in the mud all the way to the bottom.

Two Colonial Marines spotted her and split from the ship, running quickly toward her position. To her right she saw Shamana sprinting across a small slope. His cloaking device had failed, and the bright glare of blood splashed around him. Heavy weapons opened up and bright points of light flicked from his torso, drawing the fire and confusing the Marines' weapons.

Palant skirted sideways, away from the approaching Marines and toward the fight.

"Hit the dirt!" one of them shouted, weapon raised, but Palant ignored him. Her whole future was ahead of her—not a space of unknown decades filled with stories untold, but this single entity, this one alien creature hunting and being hunted. Everything she had worked toward was concentrated there, in this one moment, this one being.

She watched as he was taken down.

The shot came from behind the ship, a heavy fusillade of bright red points that seemed to slow as they surrounded him, and then they all exploded in a blooming flower of white-hot fire.

Shamana roared and splashed across the sloping ground, his blood speckling the sand, helmet slipping off and smoking in the mud.

Palant ran faster. She was aware of shapes approaching her, but she had the lead and would reach him first. Her future might consist of fewer than ten seconds.

She focused and sprinted, touched the green button on the datapad's screen, and the sound of an electronic Yautja voice crackled across the landscape.

The writhing alien stilled.

"Don't kill him!" she screamed, trying to distract and confuse, and then she was standing between Shamana and her rescuers.

His hands were raised and he stared up at her, his glowing yellow eyes revealing nothing. She looked at the control sleeve on his left hand. Its cover was open, access board glimmering. One touch and he could detonate a blast that would take them all out.

She touched the datapad again and the message repeated.

She hoped it said, *Don't move, don't die, I know why you came*. The next few seconds would determine just how much of what she knew was right.

Shamana stiffened, then relaxed back into the mud. His wounds were horrific, and his limbs shook with shock. His clawed hands remained raised, in threat or supplication she could not tell.

He spoke. She looked at the datapad.

"Please tell me you're Isa Palant," a woman's voice said behind her, as Palant saw Shaman's words appear on the screen.

You cannot know.

"I am," she said, without turning around, "and I need to talk to this Yautja. This isn't all that it seems."

"You're the Yautja Woman, but if it shifts one inch I'll blow it—and you—to atoms."

"Who are you?" Palant said, still without looking.

"Major Akoko Halley, thirty-ninth Spaceborne."

Palant crouched down beside the dying alien and placed the datapad on her thighs. She hoped he could understand her. She hoped the basic translation program would recognize his words, phrases and dialect, through a damaged mouth and a flood of blood from internal injuries. All she could do was hope, and try.

What are the fire dragons? she typed and played.

Shamana coughed green blood. It might have been laughter.

You fled them.

We… nothing! Only a… retreat… attack again and…

Your companion seemed scared.

… only young.

Have more of your kind retreated?

Many.

Palant blinked softly, trying to see into his eyes. If they were the windows of the soul, then perhaps the Yautja were soulless. She thought of other such Yautja encountering other human settlements, and what the result of that might be.

You didn't wish to attack us.

`I don't… the weak and feeble.`

I want to know you.

A bloody cough again, this time accompanied by a groan of pain. In her peripheral vision Palant was aware of the newly arrived Colonial Marines taking up firing positions all around. She didn't want to see Shamana die, and for a moment she considered lying close to him—but she could not bring herself to do that. Though the Yautja fascinated her, and this moment might well have been the highlight of her life, she knew that they were as inhuman as a shark, or a slug, or a bird. They were unknowable to her, and this basic interaction was only confirming that more.

Stay with me, she said.

`… surrender.`

She frowned at the screen, confused, wondering whether it could be that easy. Then Shamana laughed again, the sound easily identifiable now, and Palant was left with the decision of a lifetime.

Try to prevent him doing what he was about to do… or run.

Self-preservation took over, and as Shamana's clawed right hand moved toward the control sleeve on his left arm, she backed away and covered her eyes, hugging the datapad to her chest with her other hand, tripping over a rock. She hit the ground hard on her back. The air warmed and then burned around her, and the deafening sound of death smothered all other senses.

Palant squeezed her eyes shut and curled into a ball, and even when hands touched her and offered rough comfort she tried to keep herself away from the world. She wanted to hold onto that last moment of contact. It had been amazing. It was what every moment of her life had been heading toward.

When at last she looked she saw only the tattered, meaty remains of what had once been a living thing. One of Shamana's tusks had sheared off when his head was blasted apart, and now it protruded from her left calf. She issued a single loud sob that might have been a laugh.

The woman she assumed to be Major Halley knelt beside her. She was wearing the full Colonial Marines combat suit and was heavily armed, as were her soldiers. Behind the skin-tight mask her face looked strangely inhuman. Or maybe it was simply her cold, impersonal manner.

"You could talk to that thing?"

"A little," Palant said, looking at Shamana's remains, steaming where the rain struck.

"Good," the marine said. "That might help. I've been sent here to save you, so we need to get moving."

"Right," Palant replied, but she was glad when Major Halley stood and moved away again, leaving her with the Yautja's remains. Then pain kicked in, her leg felt like it was on fire, and as she heard someone shout, "Medic!" the whole world receded into a deep, dark dream.

2 2

L I L I Y A

Yautja ship Zeere Za, *Outer Rim*
August 2692 AD

Even long ago, when she had betrayed the people who had
made her and fled the Human Sphere with Wordsworth and
the Founders, Liliya hadn't been the most advanced synthetic
in existence. Though a new model, she had been one of many
rolling off the Company's production lines in those vast lab
and factory complexes scattered throughout Brownlee Major,
a system given the nickname "The People Factory."

She was indistinguishable from a real person—on the
outside, at least. Inside things were different, and although
altering her own physiology was forbidden, Liliya had
embarked on an enthusiastic series of upgrading, installation
of new programming, and downloading of any new update,
patch, or improvements for her specific model.

She called it "learning."

During that time, she had also been presented with one of the most profound choices available to an android synthetic. They were all given the nervous system of a normal human being, the rationale being that a android synthetic needed a way to detect its own damage and degeneration. They were also given the ability to determine whether or not they would feel pain.

As an abstract concept, it was built into them that their systems would transmit pain signals to their central hub— or brain, as most synthetics chose to call it. Once there, there were many ways in which the signals would be translated and addressed. The most basic arrangement was that it would arrive as a stream of information providing an instant analysis of the location, severity, and treatment required at any origin point the signals identified.

The hub would process the information and provide a solution. It was a clean, efficient way of protecting the biomech bodies into which consciousness had been uploaded, and the fact that it closely mimicked the true human nervous system was—as the Company tech people said—simply added value.

When given the choice, Liliya had chosen pain as her signal. Many synthetics did, as they believed it made them more real. The term "artificial person" was coined, but always in the background of their minds—in the deep, complex portions of their hubs created from quantum computing technology allied with biological circuits—lay the desire to lessen the term "artificial" as much as possible.

For the first time, Liliya was starting to regret that choice.

* * *

The chains swung in again. They caught her across the right shoulder, neck, and jaw, and her head flipped to the left. The initial pain was mainly shock, brought on by the bruising and splitting of skin. The residual pain bloomed through her, merging with agonies from other injuries, adding to the large conflagration her whole body had become.

Then the secondary pain began to kick in. The chain being wielded by Hashori of the Widow Clan appeared at first glance to be a traditional rope of smooth, oval, interlocked shapes. Yet these were the Yautja, and their entire existence seemed to be devoted to the hunt. This chain was spiked in a hundred places, and each spike was tipped with the egg of a small, horrific creature.

The spike punched through skin, the egg compressed and hatched, and the insect was left inside the wound, suddenly woken by the violence and given freedom to writhe, crawl, and eat.

Liliya screamed again.

Her throat was raw from shouting, her left eye swollen mostly shut. Her blood flowed, and at first Hashori had been surprised at its color and viscosity, white and thinner than human blood. This had only caused her to pause for a few seconds, however, before she went to work with even greater enthusiasm.

Liliya's skin was slashed in and around the impact wounds, her clothes shredded, and inside some of those wounds she felt the insects eating her alive. Much smaller than the nail on her smallest finger, still they felt like burning, blazing rocks moving within her body. She hoped they would choke on her biomech flesh, that they would drown in her blood.

"Why are you...?" she managed to breathe, but Hashori turned her back on her bound victim. She had been doing so for the past hour of torture, any time Liliya spoke. "Speak to me!" Liliya cried.

The Yautja walked across the room and dropped the chain on the floor. She paced the chamber's perimeter, disappearing behind her prisoner, reappearing again on her right. As she repeated the motion, again and again, her footfalls were soft, claws clacking on the metal flooring. Her breathing was heavy, rasping, and Liliya suspected she nursed a wound more serious than the fresh injury on her shoulder. Something internal.

Good, Liliya thought, surprising herself. Such uncharitable thoughts were unusual and went against her natural programming, but anger gave her some small measure of control over the situation, and she welcomed it.

Eating her... alive... slowly chewing, consuming, passing and moving on... and it couldn't be long until the terrible insects made it to somewhere vital, the heart of her that was unlike any human heart.

Hashori paused where she had dropped the chain. She shifted it around with her foot, knocked spiked links together. One of the bulbous yellow eggs split and the glistening insect emerged. She shifted the metal aside as it unfurled itself, exposed to the universe for the first time. From several yards away Liliya could see no details, but she imagined chitinous legs stretching, multiple eyes opening and closing behind a milky film.

The Yautja moved her foot, lifted her largest toe, and pressed it very deliberately and slowly onto the insect. A subtle crackling sound and it was dead, little more than a smear.

Liliya started laughing. It felt good.

"You think that's intimidating?" she asked through her laughter, using the Yautja tongue as best she could. They had no words for surrender, weakness, or pain.

"I'm thinking," Hashori said.

"So you *can* think?"

The Yautja turned and regarded her, head tilted slightly to one side. Liliya took the opportunity to look more closely at her shoulder wound. It was a ragged cut, the skin rough and the wound uneven. An attempt had been made to clip the wound's edges together, but blood still seeped through, forming a dark green scab in those places where it had dried. Elsewhere, it dripped.

Liliya hoped it hurt.

"You were sent to destroy the *Zeere Za*," Hashori said.

"Is that the name of this ship?" She shivered. A plume of pain consumed her right hip as an insect there chewed through a nerve. She bit her lip and tasted blood.

Hashori did not reply. She came closer, leaving the chain on the floor behind her, but that didn't put Liliya's mind at rest. The Yautja could inflict equally heinous injuries with her hands, her clawed feet, her tusked mouth.

"You were sent to destroy," her captor continued. "But your pathetic ship is now a cloud of atoms, and you will suffer every death you have inflicted on my species."

"My pathetic ship, which approached with all weapons offline," Liliya said. "What happened to your species?"

Hashori lashed out. Liliya's reactions were fast, and she relaxed herself at the last moment, her head rocking on her neck and the impact blurring her vision. She gasped, coughed, spat blood.

I don't even have to ask, she thought. She knew what had happened. It was obvious in the little Hashori had said, and the wound on her shoulder bore testament. She had recognized Liliya's vessel and the drive tech it carried, and had associated it with the aggressors who had attacked her species. The Rage had already gone to war, storming in toward the Human Sphere and testing their horrific army against those they found in their way.

The Yautja.

It seemed ironic that such a violent species had been subject of what amounted to target practice.

"I've come alone to try to stop them," Liliya said. "I have information—"

The blow came from her blind side, and for a while afterward all her senses receded, leaving only the pain and the grim realization that this might be the end of her voyage. Everything she knew—all that she brought with her to share, to end the mind-numbing violence to come—might go to waste here at the hands of this being.

Liliya coughed an agonized chuckle at the uselessness of it all, and Hashori picked up the chain.

For the first few days there were no questions, no demands. Only violence.

It was always Hashori. She said little, asked nothing, and Liliya could only guess at why the Yautja was singly responsible for her torture. Perhaps it was something to do with her membership in the Widow Clan. It might be that widowhood had landed on her very recently, and she thought of this as some sort of sick revenge.

After the first day the chain disappeared. The insects it had implanted were neutralized with the sweep of a sensor rod across her body. It seemed the Yautja didn't want her to die too quickly.

It was replaced by a small, silvery device that resembled a simple metal ball. Hashori rolled it across Liliya's body—it defied the ship's artificial gravity, moving up her stomach and chest, across her throat, over her shoulder, down her back, around her hips—and everywhere it touched, it felt as if her skin was being ripped apart, her flesh minced, and the pain reached deeper to her bones and organs, grinding and pulping.

Liliya screamed aloud until she almost passed out, even though she knew the pain was false, the effects only imagined. Her sight fooled her, showing her ripped flesh and spilling blood. Her nose betrayed her, presenting the stench of insides turned out and the burn of an android's skeleton melting into smoke and gas.

The damage was all in her mind, in her hub, but she had made the choice many years ago. That meant it could not be turned off—her pain was very, very real, and for the first time in her long existence Liliya wished that she would die. At the same time she had something to live for. She carried the information and means by which humanity might yet be able to defend itself against the Rage, and understand the weapons they brought with them.

"I've come to help," she told Hashori again and again. "Not to destroy."

Still the torture continued—the pain, the screaming, until her senses edged toward madness and she almost shut down. She wondered whether Hashori even understood these attempts at her Yautja language, because she very rarely replied. If she did it was only to mock Liliya, to tell what the next moments and days would bring.

More torture. More pain.

"I haven't come to destroy," Liliya said again, and she wondered whether this declaration was the reason for torture. For the Yautja, the hunt was their rite of passage, and killing provided the meaning of life. Perhaps telling them that she came in peace somehow diminished her in their eyes.

"I can help," she said, and the torture ball curled around her chin and across her face, melting her lips against her teeth, crushing her nose, scooping her eyes from their sockets and setting acid into the hollows left behind.

Her face remained.

The pain went on and on.

At last Hashori sat against the far wall and stared at Liliya. Her tusks settled, her shoulders slumped. Her eyes drifted shut.

"I know who did this to you," Liliya said. It was a change of tack. Hashori hadn't asked a single question about the information the synthetic claimed to carry. No, this was torture for its own sake, not an attempt to glean intelligence.

"I also know," Hashori said. "They are close. Bringing the fight to me." She seemed to shiver in the delight of grim expectation, standing again and shaking away any dregs of fatigue.

"They're coming?" Liliya asked. She knew all along that Alexander and his army would find her. It was destined to be. A single artificial person couldn't hope to cheat the Rage. Beatrix Maloney would have her way, and capturing or killing Liliya was merely a distraction en route into the Human Sphere.

"How many of you are left?" Liliya asked.

"Many glorious brothers and sisters fell in battle," Hashori said. "Survivors are ready for further conflict."

"You can't win."

Hashori uttered something that might have been a laugh.

"I can help you fight them," Liliya persisted.

This time it was obvious laughter, and the Yautja flung her head back, the metal slips in her dreadlocks glimmering as if in reaction to her mood.

"You can keep me occupied, while I await their arrival," Hashori said. She cast the torture ball aside, and Liliya breathed a sigh of relief.

Hashori left the room. It was the first time Liliya had been alone since being brought here. She was weak, tired, damaged, bleeding, and wretched, but she did everything she could in the short time she had. Tested her bindings. Flexed her legs and arms, expanding her muscles, straining harder than any human could against the metal straps that held her there. Her skin beneath them split, but the agony was nothing compared to what she had already endured. It was the pain of trying to fight back, and there was something clean and pure about it.

But there was no escape. The chain was too solid, the bindings too tight.

The Yautja returned moments later, leaving the door behind her open. Two more Yautja stared in. One was even taller than Hashori, darker skinned, tusks chipped and yellowed, one side of his face and head horribly scarred. The other was smaller and fully dressed, heavy with weaponry and breathing fast, as if working itself up toward a fight. Its skin was a pale yellow color, speckled with reddish spots across its face and chest. Liliya realized how little she knew about these beings.

"Ask me something," Liliya said. She was surprised at what she felt—the sadness, the frustration, the sense of hopeless at being tortured for the sake of torture.

"Your friends will be here soon," Hashori said. "Will you enjoy watching them die?"

"They're not my friends!" Liliya shouted. Her artificial heart thumped hard, her wounds dripped white.

Hashori returned to the door and took something from the tall Yautja. When she turned, Liliya saw a thin, long creature squirming in her grasp, the barbed spines along its length, the rounded head filled with the silvery gleam of countless tiny teeth.

"You're all going to die," Liliya said. The Yautja language felt strange in her mouth, and she knew that no true human would be able to speak it as well as her. Their jaws weren't built that way, their throats and vocal chords unable to be molded and manipulated the way she was doing with hers. It was a feeling she was usually successful in hiding away in the vastly complex depths of her quantum computer brain, but sometimes humans felt like children in her care.

Even though she didn't think she could, Liliya began to cry.

After seven days on board the *Zeere Za*, the Yautja ship that Liliya still knew nothing about, Hashori entered and closed the door behind her.

She wore full armor now, and all her weaponry. Her feet were encased in metal-strapped sandals, her limbs bore muscle-hugging, supple armor, and her torso was similarly adorned. It must have been her own personal combat gear, scarred and battered from old fights, each scorch or impact mark the memory of some past conflict. Her helmet hung from one hand.

On her left shoulder a blaster drooped inactive, ready to be paired to the helmet when she put it on. Her left forearm was bulky with the control panel that most Yautja carried into battle, a system which allowed them to control weaponry, communicate, and which also contained vital medical equipment and drugs. Guns hung from her hip, ammunition from a bandolier around her shoulders, and on her back was fixed a vicious spiked weapon, its handle probably home to other blades and throwing knives.

She presented an intimidating figure, a self-sustaining fighting machine with a fearsome countenance and the desire, the *craving*, to kill. Evidence of victories hung on a heavy wire around her neck—scraps of flesh, leathery and dried, of differing shapes, colors, and sizes. Liliya thought they might be tongues.

"The battle will begin," the Yautja said.

"And me?"

"You're one of them. The first to die."

Liliya started laughing. It came from deep within, not a calculated reaction but something instinctive, something so very human. She shook in her restraints and tears formed beneath the laughter, pain and wretchedness at the agonies she felt and what had been done to her. The whipping chain, the insects now dead and bloated within her flesh. The torture ball, discarded against the room's curved wall, its reflected glimmer promising more pain.

The snakelike creature, now curled on the floor as if absorbed in an innocent sleep. There was nothing innocent about its shape, nor its intent. Her throat lacerated from its many prongs, her stomach ruptured, and her complex recovery systems were working overtime to repair damage that should have killed her.

If I were human, she kept thinking. She had spent most of her existence struggling to be just that, and this was another reason why she hated what Hashori had done. Torture, pain, and trauma had revealed just how unhuman Liliya was.

Suddenly a blast rumbled through the ship.

"If you kill me, then they'll kill the rest of your people," Liliya said. "You have no idea of their power, or the weapons they will use."

"I understand well enough," Hashori said. "The fire dragons are an ancient subject of our hunts."

"Not like this," Liliya replied. "How many Yautja are dead already? How many ships, homes, planets have been overrun?"

Hashori tilted her head at the term "Yautja," perhaps not understanding.

"Numbers of dead don't concern me," she said.

"Not even if you're among them?"

"I will die well."

"Did your mate die well, Widow?" Liliya knew nothing about their mating habits. She wasn't even sure this creature was female.

Hashori took a step forward, then paused. She looked aside, as if ashamed of some emotion or thought, but Liliya saw nothing different. The Yautja was an enigma. To survive this, she had to play to that mystery.

"I can help turn the fight around," she said, "but only if we survive this."

"You're scared," Hashori spat.

"Fuck you," Liliya said. She wasn't quite sure whether the expletive translated correctly, but from Hashori's reaction it seemed close enough. "You've seen my blood. You've smashed my insides. You know I'm not something that feels fear."

And yet… Liliya thought, because a very human fear had been at home in her for days, months, even years. The terror that everything she had come from was threatened. That here and now, the idea that her own meaningless death might put the Human Sphere even more at risk. In truth, the fear was almost crippling.

Even so, she was a synthetic, and she was able to hide her thoughts and emotions.

"I'm going to fight," Hashori said. "Perhaps I'll survive. If I do, we'll talk some more."

"Oh, good," Liliya said. "Well that makes *perfect* sense!"

Hashori paused, seeming to consider what she'd said. It

appeared as if Yautja weren't well-versed in sarcasm.

So she left, and she closed the door behind her. For a while—a short while—there was silence.

Then Liliya heard the sounds of battle.

Several massive explosions rocked the ship, sending great groaning creaks through the walls, thudding the floor, making Liliya feel as though she were spinning. Perhaps it was rapid deceleration, or a blast interfering with the artificial gravity. She strained against her bindings for the thousandth time.

After the blasts there was silence for a while. She heard only her own breathing, a sound usually unnoticed. Her heartbeat filled the room. Groans, sighs, and the occasional grunts as she tried to break the straps holding her in position—these were the only noises keeping her company. They almost belonged to someone else.

A little while later the sounds of combat returned nearby. Blasters coughed, and walls transmitted the *thuds* of multiple impacts. Something roared, a Yautja shout she recognized so well. Then something else screeched, long and loud, and the acidic stench of burning filled the air.

They're here, she thought. *So close, so terrible, and I never thought I would witness something like this.*

The door smashed open. Hashori stood there for a while, uncertain, breathing so hard that her breath condensed before her. She stepped back into the hallway and looked left and right, shoulder blaster tracking her movements. It smoked. She carried her pike in her hand, one end of it deformed and slick, like melting ice.

"You killed one," Liliya said.

"They're different," the Yautja replied.

"I can tell you—"

"Don't speak." Hashori came forward, touching the control panel on her left forearm as she came.

The bindings that had held Liliya for so many days melted away and she fell, her body barely believing that she was free. She shook her head and pressed her hands to the floor, feeling a constant, strange vibration. It was as if the *Zeere Za* itself was shivering in terror.

Just as she raised her head, Hashori grabbed her around the neck and lifted her.

Liliya tried to cry out, but her throat was compressed. The Yautja darted to the doorway, holding Liliya beneath her left arm as if she was no weight at all. Her feet did not touch the ground. She grasped at Hashori's big, clawed hand, but the Yautja's fingers squeezed in tighter, breaking skin.

Then for the first time in days Liliya was outside the room. To their left a Yautja fought, shooting and hacking at a dark shape that thrashed around the corridor beyond. The Yautja issued an ululating battle cry, then a screech tore at Liliya's ears, and the Yautja screamed.

As Hashori turned to hurry in the opposite direction, Liliya saw the unmistakable gleam from a Xenomorph's skull as it bent over its floored enemy and bit into his head.

Beatrix Maloney had sent her full might to capture or kill Liliya, and although she had always known how terrible the Xenomorphs would be in battle, she had never realized how beautiful and graceful they might be, as well.

Hashori moved surely, running along curving corridors,

crossing open spaces, her heavy feet barely making a sound as they slapped at the floor. Liliya could hardly breathe, but in truth she didn't need to. She could survive for hours without a breath. It was just another way to make her seem more human.

They rounded a corner, and ahead of them stood a Xenomorph. Beneath its feet lay the remains of a Yautja, head smashed apart, acrid smoke rising from across its chest where its killer had bled upon it. The beast hissed, long and loud, and Liliya felt her unnatural blood running cold.

She could see the regimental markings on the side of its head. This was surely a beast of Alexander's army, and the general would be close.

Hashori dropped Liliya and stepped forward to fight.

The Xenomorph powered toward the Yautja, its clawed toes kicking up sparks from the floor. Hashori's shoulder blaster fired and the beast jigged sideways, the blast impacting the wall thirty yards beyond.

Hashori crouched and fired again, angling the shot upward this time. She missed a second time, but the blast struck the ceiling just behind the charging monster, bringing down a rain of metal and molten parts. One chunk of material struck its tail and it slowed, only a little but enough for Hashori to leap to her right, swinging her pike around in a powerful arc.

The Xenomorph ducked to avoid the blow, but Hashori unleashed another fusillade of blasts from her shoulder cannon, striking the creature's abdomen and legs. One limb ricocheted back along the corridor. The creature screeched and thrashed, splashing its acidic blood.

Hashori growled and fell back, scrabbling at her mask

where it smoked and ran from the acid's destructive touch. Liliya also saw speckles of bubbling skin across her throat and shoulder, and her body armor was distorted.

The Xenomorph looked directly at her.

Paused. Tensed.

It knows me!

Then it leapt, wider jaw opening to reveal the deadlier, slicker mouth inside.

Hashori grabbed its tail and, using its own momentum, swung it sideways into the wall. It struck hard and thrashed around, finding its remaining feet again quickly and leaving melting patches across the floor.

As it tensed for another spring forward, Hashori jumped across the corridor and pinned it to the wall with her pike.

The Xenomorph screeched. The pike had pierced its body behind and below its arced head, and already its blood was melting the impeding weapon.

Hashori gestured with her hand, and Liliya pushed herself back along the corridor. The Yautja followed for a few steps, then zeroed its triumvirate of targeting lasers directly onto the beast's domed head.

"Be careful, when it dies it will—"

The blast came. Liliya closed her eyes and protected her face.

Dead, the Xenomorph burst apart as if destroyed from within. Its parts bounced from walls and ceiling, acidic blood splashing all around, and Liliya stripped off one leg of her already torn trousers when they started to smoke. Her skin beneath was raw and blistered, a new wound almost lost among those Hashori had given her.

The Yautja picked her up again, arm around her waist this time, slinging Liliya beneath her arm and leaping past the dead invader.

"How many are there?" she asked, but Hashori didn't reply. So Liliya just hung on. The Yautja had saved her once, and hopefully that was a sign that she'd listened to what she had been saying.

A series of small explosions shook the ship, echoing along corridors and blasting air their way. A loud, mechanical screech sounded somewhere, and several booms vibrated the air. Another big explosion and then Hashori slipped and fell forward. Liliya's stomach rolled, and her senses confused up and down, left and right.

The gravity generator had been hit, and they were weightless.

From behind them came the frantic scratching of claws across metal, and Liliya feared they were being pursued. But it was two Yautja, heavily armed and armored and rushing after Hashori.

The three of them conversed, using a dialect or a level of language that she did not understand. Yet another aspect of the Yautja that was a mystery. They seemed to be arguing, the two of them gesticulating at Liliya still hung beneath Hashori's left arm.

"I'd like a say in this," she said, and the other two glared at her as if she was a rock that had spoken.

Hashori said something, and the other two nodded fiercely. They touched each other's shoulders in a surprisingly intimate gesture, then Hashori turned and pulled herself through a doorway, still carrying her captive. They emerged into a stairwell, and Hashori expertly pulled them down, grabbing stairs to give leverage and aiming them at the next contact point.

From above and behind them came fresh sounds of fighting. Blasters, metal scoring metal, screeching, the gnashing of terrible teeth...

Moments later they passed through a circular opening into a small hangar, where a ship hung ready from two mountings. It was a small ship, perhaps an attack craft, sleek and smooth, and it was here that Hashori pushed Liliya away from her.

The Yautja shoved herself toward the ship, and Liliya arrested her own movement against an upright.

She had a terrible, sinking feeling.

"Hashori," she said.

The Yautja had reached the ship. As she approached a section of hull turned clear and then disappeared, a doorway forming before her.

"I've carried you this far," Hashori said. "Boarding the ship is your own choice."

"Just the two of us?"

An explosion somewhere nearby sent fire and debris into the far end of the hangar, the fire strange and beautiful in zero gravity. The mechanical screech rose again.

"Another hull breach," Hashori said, and she pulled herself into the ship.

Liliya prepared herself, aimed, and then pushed off from the upright. For the few seconds it took her to drift across the hangar, she expected the doorway in the ship's hull to solidify again, causing her to bounce off and meet her destiny elsewhere, but she grasped onto the doorway's edge and pulled herself inside.

The ship was small, intimate, and beyond anything that Liliya could understand. Hashori was in a seat that seemed to have congealed from the floor. She was using controls that appeared from the walls and ceiling around her the instant she reached for them.

"Sit," she said, and a second, smaller seat appeared beside her own.

"What changed your mind about me?" Liliya asked, pulling herself into the seat.

"The news of what is happening to my people." She whispered something beneath her breath, and liquid metal closed around Liliya and herself, holding them close. "This will hurt," she said. Then she muttered another phrase, and Liliya's perception exploded outward in a bright, blinding light.

It felt like forever, but was probably only several seconds later when she opened her eyes. Part of the hull had cleared to offer them a wide view of space. They were pulling quickly away from the *Zeere Za*, and stationed around the Yautja ship were seven vessels that Liliya recognized so well.

Blooms of fire and escaping atmosphere speckled the *Zeere Za*'s surface like rapidly growing fungi.

"They'll follow," Liliya said.

"We're cloaked."

"They know of cloaking technology."

"Not like this." Hashori glanced across at Liliya, and there might even have been something resembling a smile in her eyes. "I built it myself."

* * *

An hour after leaving, Hashori announced that the *Zeere Za* had been destroyed. She whispered to herself, a prayer or a promise, and Liliya closed her eyes and left the Yautja to her grief.

She waited some time before asking, "What have you heard?"

"Tales of fighting, sacrifice, and glory."

"And more," Liliya pressed.

Hashori was silent for a while. It was strange in that small space, uncomfortable, and Liliya wondered how long they would be in here together. The ship hadn't looked large enough to have many other spaces.

"Destruction," Hashori said. "Many Yautja killed." The term she used to name her species wasn't easily translatable, so Liliya heard it as 'Yautja'. "Several habitats have been destroyed. A planet I once called home, fallen to the aggressors. The memories... The history... We treasure that more than any physical thing. Every Yautja death is a tragedy, wiping out centuries of experience and history. Every death takes away part of that story. Now, the Yautja story is more denuded than it ever has been before, in all living memory."

"I'm sorry," Liliya said.

Hashori was silent for a while, before saying, "You have the means to fight them?"

And you almost destroyed me, Liliya thought, her body still bleeding, wounds merging to form a pulsing background pain. But it would serve no purpose to say that now. She wasn't even sure the Yautja would recognize or admit to her mistake. The torture had been relentless, but now things had changed, and Hashori was following the direction of that change.

Liliya could only do her best to heal herself, and not to show the weakness and pain she felt. She was damaged, torn, leaking blood, but she could repair. Her systems were already doing their best to mend what was broken and bypass places or circuits that could not be fixed. She would be left with scars—and she was glad.

"Yes," she replied. "In my veins. A technology being used to control and weaponize those bug-like creatures… we call them Xenomorphs."

"We call them fire lizards."

"As good a name as any. Where are you taking me?"

"Where many of my kind in this part of the galaxy are regrouping to fight back. Into the Human Sphere."

2 3

AKOKO HALLEY

Love Grove Base, Research Station, LV-1529
September 2692 AD

While her small DevilDog crew gathered the survivors together and assessed their condition, Major Akoko Halley grabbed Isa Palant's arm and dragged her back to the *Pixie*. The Bolt-class ship wasn't huge, but it was fast, and it looked like it had got them there just in time. Dropping down into action had invigorated the DevilDogs and seen away any remaining anger Halley felt at being sent on this mission.

Now she had the woman she'd come here to save, and it was time to find out just why. Palant was thin and drawn, dirty, scared. She looked hungry and confused, but there was also an excitement about her. A sense of urgency.

They boarded the ship and Halley guided the woman to the small table in the rec room. Sitting her down, she poured some energy drink and dug out a few sachets of power bars. They tasted like shit, but they'd give her an instant boost. It looked like she hadn't eaten properly in some time.

Halley knew there must be one hell of a story here, but her first task was to prepare a sub-space message for Gerard Marshall. The thought of speaking with the odious man sickened her, but this was her mission, and this was her duty.

"I have to speak to someone in command," Palant said. She sipped at the drink, then downed it, staring at the opposite wall but seeing into a much farther distance. "It's urgent. It's important."

"I'm composing a transmission to Gerard Marshall, he in command enough?"

"Why did you come here? For me?"

"He told me you'd have some value in the fight against the Yautja."

"This is happening elsewhere?" There was a desperation to Palant. She was coiled like a power spring, ready to flip and fire—and she'd been bent over the injured Yautja, seemingly talking to the thing using the device she still grasped in her hand. Maybe that's what Marshall meant when he said how important she might be. Maybe she could communicate with the things.

"There's an incursion," Halley confirmed. "No one wants to call it an invasion, because there doesn't seem to be that many Yautja, but there's enough of them penetrating the Human Sphere—attacking settlements, and taking and using dropholes—to make it feel more serious than an isolated incident. We're edging toward war, and that's why I was sent out here to see if you were still alive. Apparently you might know something that'll help us beat them." Halley shrugged.

As far as she was concerned they had everything they needed to push back the Yautja, and track and kill those who didn't run. It was a situation that she and her DevilDogs had trained for many times, and she resented the idea that Marshall didn't feel comfortable under their protection. That he needed more.

"So what is it you know?" she asked.

"I've been studying the Yautja my whole life," Palant said.

"And now you can talk to them."

Palant glanced down at the device in her lap. "In a limited way, but I know something about why this incursion is taking place, and I really need to communicate that to the Thirteen."

"Let me get my communications guy here and we'll do just that." Halley turned away, troubled. The woman was strange, like only a part of her was here. She touched her comms bracelet and called Gove back to the ship, then turned back to Palant.

"How many survivors?"

"Fifteen," she said. "A couple of indies, the rest of us from the base."

"Indies," Halley scoffed.

"They saved our lives!" Palant glared at her, going up in Halley's estimation. Halley knew she was an intimidating personality, yet this woman was confidently standing up to her. She guessed the scientist had been through a lot.

"I'm sorry," she said. "I'm sure it's been tough."

"Tough," Palant said, snorting. She wiped her eyes. "So this communication?"

As Gove appeared in the rec room, a chiming sounded through the ship. Palant raised her eyebrows.

"Guess he wants to talk to us more than we want to talk to him."

"That's Marshall?" Palant asked.

"Message incoming, so could be," Halley said. "Gove, comms room ready?"

"Good to go," Gove said.

Halley nodded toward the doorway leading onto the flight deck. "Come on. Let's see what the Company has to say."

As it turned out, the message wasn't from Gerard Marshall, but General Paul Bassett himself. When his image flickered onto the holo screen he had Gerard Marshall sitting behind him, and Halley couldn't shake the idea that Marshall could use even the General as a puppet. The Company man smiled softly as Bassett prepared himself.

Halley wondered whether Weyland-Yutani had something on the General, too, and then she snorted a silent laugh. Of course they did. They had something on *everyone*. That was where they found their power. Through all their ups and downs, the Company had remained constant on that, at least.

"Are we on?" Bassett asked, and someone out of the picture must have nodded. "Major Halley!" Basset said. "By our estimation you should have reached LV-1529 by now. I trust your mission has been successful, and Mr. Marshall and I are awaiting your report, I hope imminently. In the meantime, I felt the need to appraise you of how events have advanced since your departure.

"Your DevilDog battalion has reached the Addison Prime system and rescued the survivors from the Spaceborne frigate. More survived the terrorist act than was first thought. The 39th are now en route to Addison Prime itself, where it's rumored several Yautja have landed, and news across the north-east-alpha quadrant of the Sphere is much the same. The initial seventeen occasions of sabotage we talked about is now more like fifty, the worst of which was on Spaceborne 17th's orbital in the Jackson system." Bassett's face dropped. "The saboteur got hold of an anti-matter loop and exposed it in the orbital's drive hall."

"Oh my God," Halley whispered. She was aware of Palant glancing at her, but her focus was on General Bassett. A man hardened to war, veteran of many conflicts large and small, and someone who had reputedly killed with his bare hands when he was a grunt during the Quailed Wars, he now seemed almost too shocked to go on. Halley wished these sub-space communications could be real time. She wanted to offer condolences, and share the grief.

"Nineteen thousand men, women, and children," Bassett said. "Almost the entire compliment of the 17th, along with their support crews and families. There's nothing left of the orbital. At least they felt nothing."

Marshall leaned toward Bassett and said something unheard. Without looking back, Bassett snapped at him.

"Major Halley has a right to be appraised of our situation, Marshall!"

Halley smiled at the General's outburst, but in it she also saw a shaky reserve.

"That's just the instances of sabotage," Bassett said. "Many other saboteurs failed, but none have been captured alive. They either killed themselves, or entered into conflicts with Marines which ensured their deaths. It's not yet known what organization initiated the attacks, but we have to believe it's connected with the Yautja incursion, which has grown in seriousness. We have over a hundred reports of Yautja attacks, spread all across the quadrant. It appears as if they have no preference over where to land and attack. Research stations, mining bases on moons and asteroids, orbitals, military transports, scientific missions, independent stations, pirate ships—the Yautja are assaulting wherever and whenever they can. We've launched countermeasures, and combat is underway in scores of sites. We're keeping track of everything we can, but with the sub-space lag and distances involved, we're a little…"

Lost, Halley thought. Everything for which the Colonial Marines had been established, centuries before, was happening now, and their commanding officer looked lost. Maybe it was a hidden weakness he had never displayed before, or perhaps it was because the Company had taken notional control of the Colonial Marines, turning them from a protective force into a police force.

Bassett suddenly looked up, blinking, obviously aware of Gerard Marshall seated behind him. The Company man had said nothing. Perhaps his presence was enough.

"The Colonial Marines are up to the task," Bassett said. "While many contacts have been reported, and we suspect more are ongoing that are as yet unreported, our main concern remains the Yautja possession and use of a greater number of dropholes. Seven dropholes along the Outer Rim were assaulted and taken by aliens, and their ships have been dropping through ever since. Some of them were intercepted when they emerged further into the Sphere, most were destroyed, but some have disappeared. Once they've dropped a second time, the number of places they can emerge is increased tenfold.

"They're also suiciding whenever they are trapped or mortally wounded. News I have is… horrific. Massive death tolls among Marine units, as well as civilian populations. So few Yautja, but such massive damage."

"I know why they're doing it!" Palant said, and Halley held up her hand. Didn't the fool realize this was a one-way conversation?

Gerard Marshall rose at last and stood beside the General. Palant hated him. Undoubtedly an important man, she also believed him to be a monster. Not a killer—at least not with his own hand. Not an animal, but a man who put personal gain, and the good of the Company, before anything else. Even now, with General Bassett relaying news of tens of thousands dead and violent contacts with the Yautja across this quadrant of the Human Sphere, Marshall would be assessing how Weyland-Yutani could benefit from the war.

She was sure of it.

"We need to know if you found Isa Palant and Milt McIlveen alive," he said, "and if you did, we need you to transmit all of their research and knowledge of the Yautja, securely. A lot might depend on what they know."

"We're considering offering a ceasefire," Bassett continued, "but we have to do it from a position of strength. Otherwise they won't even respond. We still don't know the Yautja's intent, and our analysts have found no discernible pattern in their attacks. They seem almost random, yet the more we know of them, the more we can threaten them with.

"I look forward to your report, Major," he concluded. "Be safe."

The picture shivered and clouded, and just before it faded to black Palant saw that unsettling smile back on Marshall's face.

"Major, I think I know what's happening here," Palant said. "I don't think they're launching an invasion."

"It sure looks like that to me," Halley said. "Did you hear what General Basset said? This is a war, and while you were talking to that bastard thing out there, Marines were dying."

A sound from behind made her turn around. Gove was still there, standing at the communications unit, eyes wide and Adam's apple bobbing as he tried to swallow away tears.

"Private Gove?" Halley said.

"The SpeedSharks," he said.

"Yes, the 17th. All of them, the General said. A saboteur working with the Yautja."

"That's not true!" Palant said.

"My brother is a Corporal in the 17th," Gove said. He tried to say more but his voice failed.

Halley took a step forward and grasped his upper arm. "My condolences."

"I haven't seen him in seven years. You know, it's so difficult, distances so… and I usually spend my leave on orbitals or…"

"I'm sorry for your loss," Palant said. "We've all lost. A

good friend of mine died when our base was blown up, but the saboteur wasn't a Yautja, and didn't have anything to do with them. I don't know why she did it, but I do know this— the Yautja are fleeing from something. McIlveen and I listened to the two Yautja who attacked us, talking about them, and when I spoke with Shamana—"

"Who the fuck is Shamana?" Halley asked.

"The Yautja you blew away out there."

"Before it blew us all away."

"He and his kind have been attacked by something he called the fire lizards. They've retreated to regroup, fight back. It's not an invasion. They're entering the Human Sphere because they're running away."

"And attacking military and civilian outposts as they do so."

"I can't pretend to understand their motivations," Palant said.

"I thought you were supposed to!" Gove said, anger in his voice. "We came all this way to rescue you because you *do* understand them!"

"More than most, probably," Palant said, "but that's not saying much."

"What do you mean by that?" Halley asked. The woman's circling talk was getting on her nerves. She had a report to prepare and send to General Bassett, and they had plans to make. The *Pixie* wasn't a big ship, and to contain the fifteen survivors of LV-1529 they'd have to work some magic in the cryo-pod bay. She didn't have time for this.

"They might appear almost humanoid," Palant said, "but they're as similar to us as we are to a fish. Perhaps they're unknowable, but we have to use what I do know to try to stop this situation getting any worse."

"How?"

"Your general spoke of brokering a ceasefire."

"And?"

"I think I can compose a message in the Yautja language that they'll understand. McIlveen knows enough about their tech and communications systems to prepare a general sub-space message on one of their open frequencies."

"Saying what?"

"Saying that we know why they've fled, and we don't want to fight them anymore. We want to help."

Halley smiled, then frowned, realizing that Palant was serious. The silence hung heavy. The gravity of Gove's loss was a weight inside her, and she knew that such grief would be falling all across the Sphere.

Palant stood, and for the first time Halley saw past her frailty to the strength and determination underneath.

"Major," she said. "If there's something bad enough out there that the Yautja fled from it, don't you think we should be concerned?"

Akoko Halley had been out of her comfort zone the moment the *Pixie* had taken off from Charon Station. Leaving the bulk of her DevilDogs behind had been a wrench, and although she had a good crew with her—most importantly her right-hand man, Sergeant Major Huyck—their absence cut in the further she was from them.

What Isa Palant was asking her to do made her even more uncomfortable—and yet, deep down, she knew that the scientist was right.

"If we ask permission of your general to do this, he'll waste time consulting his experts, his advisors. And if Gerard Marshall finds out, it will become politicized. His interest is in the Company and himself, and whatever our reasons for sending the signal, this will place both of those interests above our own."

Halley hadn't been surprised that Palant knew Marshall, and the scientist's dislike of the man made her like the tough little woman more.

But it was a heavy decision to make, a bold step. Especially as Palant and Marshall's man, McIlveen, had by their own admission only a very cursory knowledge of the Yautja language.

"So how can you guarantee that this device will do what you say?" Halley touched the small datapad that rested on the table between them. It was dusty and scratched, as if it had been through as much as its owners. Palant and McIlveen sat across from her, Huyck to her left and Nassise to her right. Nassise was a good man, strong and quiet, and had been under her command since she was a corporal. He'd saved her life once, and once she had saved his. That had formed a strong bond between them. She trusted him, and though he'd refused any offers of promotion and remained a private, she valued his opinion above most anyone else.

"We can't," Palant said, "but we think we can word the statement simply enough that no mistakes will be made. We'll use words and phrases that are tried and tested. You've seen everything we've recorded since the two Yautja arrived here, and you were present when I was speaking with Shamana."

"Before he attempted to nuke us all," Nassise said. His voice was always quiet, but always carried. Perhaps that was why his opinion bore weight.

"Like I said, they're unknowable," Palant said. "But it's worth a try. It could be that the Yautja incursion, as you call it, is just a prelude to something much, much worse."

Halley nodded slowly, never taking her gaze from the scientist. Palant stared back. At last Halley's lips twitched into her version of a smile.

"Put your message together. Tell me when it's done. I'll vet it, along with my crew, and then we make a decision."

"*You'll* vet it?"

"Unless you want to send it to General Bassett for approval?" Halley asked. *And thereby to Marshall*, she thought, though she didn't need to say that. "It's my own reputation I'm risking here."

"After what you just heard, you're worried about reputation?"

Halley did not reply. In truth she was not, and she was quite certain that Palant knew that. She was a perceptive woman. A good woman. It remained to be seen if she could achieve everything she hoped.

"It'll take us half an hour," McIlveen said.

"I'll get you restricted access to *Pixie's* computer," Nassise said, but Palant shook her head and touched the datapad.

"We've got everything we need right here," she said. "And... thank you."

Halley nodded once, stood, and left the rec room, marching back down the ramp and back into the storm. Bestwick and Sprenkel were helping the survivors gather their meager belongings in the ruins of the hangar that had been their home for so long. Gove was heading back toward her from the direction of the devastated base, his suit shimmering where it had thickened against the heavier radiation readings coming from that direction.

Halley wanted to be away from this shithole as quickly as possible.

She spoke to her crew, organized a brief search for anyone left behind, then returned to the *Pixie*.

She'd been gone less than twenty minutes.

Four hours after landing on LV-1529, Akoko Halley authorized a transmission that might change history.

She should have felt scared giving the go-ahead, because it was probably the end of her career, but it was the support of her crew that carried her through. Every one of them—the taciturn Huyck, the quiet Nassise, loyal Gove, and Sprenkel and Bestwick—had agreed that this course of action was the correct one. They had quietly absorbed Palant's and McIlveen's thoughts and ideas, listened to the brief message they planned to send, and then given Halley their approval.

She thought perhaps a lot of that was because of their respect for her, and their realization that she was behind the plan, and that was good enough.

"You sure these sub-space plane levels are right?" Palant

asked as she and McIlveen sat before the *Pixie's* main communication board. Gove was with them, guiding them through the process.

"Sure as I can be." McIlveen was nervous, but excited. Halley knew that he was a Company man, sent here by Marshall to oversee Palant's work. Yet he was ready to bypass one of Weyland-Yutani's Thirteen in order to send this transmission. That fact solidified her opinion that this was the right course of action.

"Okay, we're good to go," Gove said. "Message is uploaded. Just press 'send'."

Halley expected some sort of pause from Palant, a loaded moment heavy with the potential for objection. Instead she stroked the SEND button and sat back, and on countless planes below and around that in which they existed, the sub-space message spread across the galaxy.

We understand what has happened to you. We know why you are traveling into the Human Sphere. We know about the fire dragons. For our good, and for yours, we must call an honorable truce and confront the threat together.

2 4

JOHNNY MAINS

Yautja Habitat designated UMF 12, beyond Outer Rim
September 2692 AD

"Cover!"

"Eleven o'clock!"

The rattle of nano-ordinance spitting from a com-rifle, the roar of a thousand sparkling explosions, the screech of a target being shredded and killed, the hiss of shrapnel blasted by superheated gas, the thuds of stones impacting combat suits.

"L-T, *drop!*"

Mains reacted even before his suit could process and analyze the thought, folding his knees and rolling as Snowdon unleashed a glimmering spray of laser fire inches from his head. The suit indicated that it was armoring his entire left side, hardening around muscles yet still monitoring his muscular electrical impulses, allowing movement.

A weight slammed down onto his legs and thrashed at him,

heavy blows across the upper legs and torso that pummeled him down again and again into the ground. His com-rifle slid across the gritty surface and he reached for his sidearm, suit glitching as it attempted to keep up with the chaotic movement. The squirming attack by the injured Xenomorph pressed him down.

He grasped the laser pistol's grip and his arm was pinned down by spidery, chitinous hands.

Another spray of laser fire and the hands fell aside, severed from the arms.

Mains felt the patter of fluid across his body and the suit reacted, its surface consistency altering at microscopic levels in an attempt to shed itself of the spatters and slicks of deadly acid.

He rolled and shoved the dead alien away from him, kicking the steaming, leaking parts. Its blood splashed and smoked across the floor, separate limbs still twitching. Then it seemed to erupt from within, showering him with slick parts and a film of acid. His suit hummed as it struggled to shed the deadly layer, and encased as he was, he still smelled burning.

"What the hell just happened?" Snowdon shouted.

"Two on your left!" Faulkner called.

"I'm going for that rock!" Lieder.

"Plasma!" Snowdon warned, and Mains's suit visor darkened as she lit up the attacking Xenomorphs with two grenades.

Screeching, screaming, they looked like giant insects thrashing in the flames, spitting acid and shedding body parts that skittered across the floor leaving patches of melting ground, still blazing, still deadly.

Mains ducked right and crouched beside Snowdon.

Before them lay a scene of devastation. The wide, low space was burning, walls and ceiling pocked and blasted from the unleashing of their com-rifles' full fury. Dead and dying Xenomorphs formed bizarre sculptures within the flames, casting shivering shadows and sometimes still moving, still striving to reach their prey with their last shreds of life. As they died, they burst apart, spilled blood sizzling and splashing.

Beyond the shadows and the flames, a second wave appeared and charged.

Mains opened fire. His com-rifle shook and bucked as he sent several spurts of nano-ordinance toward the enemy, then his suit display indicated that he was out of that ammunition. On instinct he switched to micro-dot munitions, more dangerous than nano—especially at close range, because of the risk of errant charges.

His vision flowered with a thousand explosions and a Xenomorph came apart. Another ploughed through its showering remains, hands clawed and reaching, its body slick and streamlined, glimmering with the promise of a painful, bloody death.

A plume of laser fire came from his left and the creature fell in two.

"Head to the surface!" Mains shouted. "There's an opening at ten o'clock."

"Too many of them!" Faulkner said.

"I'm out of nano," Mains said, but his suit indicated that Snowdon and Lieder still carried a small supply. "Lieder, Snowdon, clear a path."

He and Faulkner moved to the right and forward, picking

off Xenomorphs as they scampered forward, and allowing their comrades the opportunity to open up with sustained bursts of exploding ordinance. The ground shook and a great swathe of ceiling crashed down, hazing the air with dust and smoke.

Mains instructed his suit to drop a sensor-based schematic of their location. If his vision was lessened, he could rely on the suit's sensors. He didn't *like* doing that, because he'd always been one to trust his own senses. Suits could go wrong.

"Single file!" Mains shouted, leading the way along the scorched path.

A shadow jumped ahead of him and he took it down with a laser blast. He jumped over it, emptying another shot into the domed head as he did so. Wet internal matter splashed across his feet and legs, and he cringed. He knew what Xenomorph blood could do. He'd never fought one, but he knew Marines who had. Many of those who survived were in veterans' homes, melted and scarred by such encounters.

Their suits were designed to withstand Xenomorph blood. So far, they were holding up, but his suit's power was down to seven percent, challenged and drained by the demands he was putting on it.

This is our last engagement, he thought, and the idea was terrifying. They had to get to the surface, out through the atmosphere skin and into vacuum. The Xenos couldn't follow them out there—at least not in theory—and they'd have a chance to make it to that docked ship. It was their last chance to make it off UMF 12.

Someone shouted. Lieder, calling instructions.

A scream. Snowdon.

Mains had just reached the opening in the wall and he turned, weapon up and ready.

Snowdon had tripped and was squirming beneath two Xenomorphs, their tails lashing out at Lieder and Faulkner where they stood beyond.

Mains took a step forward and a tail caught him across the legs, taking them from under him, slamming him on the ground. The suit took most of the impact but he gasped a breath, briefly winded.

"L-T!" Snowdon screamed, and then he saw one Xenomorph holding her head still between its massive, spidery hands, while the other bent close.

He brought up his laser pistol. Too late.

The creature's inner jaw slammed down, ripping through Snowdon's suit mask and caving in her face.

"No," Mains breathed.

"L-T, roll!" Faulkner shouted, and he obeyed. He rolled three times and was presented with a flickering view of the two aliens—along with Snowdon's body—consumed in a blast of plasma fire. From within the conflagration came two wet explosions as the dead beasts burst apart.

Lieder grabbed his arm and pulled him upright, rifle held out in her other hand. Snowdon was gone. There one moment, nothing the next, wiped from existence, every experience and memory and personality quirk halted in a moment too brief to measure.

Losing one of his crew felt like losing a sister, or a child.

Lieder held onto his arm and dragged him after her into the opening in the tunnel wall. "Faulkner!" she shouted, and he appeared behind them. He'd lost his com-rifle and held onto a laser pistol. His right arm was a mashed mess, slashed from shoulder to elbow and swinging from a few shreds of flesh and a shattered bone.

"Jesus," Mains said, but Faulkner shook his head.

"Suit's doped me up. Just don't ask me to look at it."

"Between us," Mains said, shrugging off Lieder's hand and pulling Faulkner between them. "Lieder, take lead. I'll back up behind us. This crack's too narrow for more than one of them to—"

The opening back into the blazing tunnel grew dark, and he lit it up, spraying laser blasts and cringing as the thing there came apart, acid raising smoke from the walls and floor.

"Lieder, let's go!" he shouted. "Follow the schematic, up and out."

Lieder moved quickly. Mains kept one eye on his own schematic display, never dropping his attention from the opening that was receding rapidly behind them. More Xenos came in, and they fell beneath his concentrated fire.

He checked ammo. Not looking good, and Faulkner was badly wounded, only the drugs the suit had administered keeping him going. Shock would drop him soon.

"L-T, got to climb a bit here, then we're out," Lieder said.

"Let's do it."

Faulkner groaned, but said nothing. Lieder went first, Faulkner next. Mains waited until Lieder was at the top of the low wall, checked his suit scanner for movement, then slung his rifle over his shoulder and climbed.

"Atmos shield," Lieder said, and as they moved toward the

milky opening onto the outside of the habitat, Mains never thought he'd been so pleased to step out into vacuum. Leaving the claustrophobic interior and tunnels behind, he stared up at the ship docked against the end of the Yautja habitat.

Where had it come from? Who or what crewed it, and why had the Xenomorphs come with it? All important questions, but they were questions for later.

Right now, survival was their prime concern.

"Status?" he asked.

"Ammo low," Lieder said. "I've got one more plasma charge, some micro dot. Laser pod's pretty decent, but my suit's power's not looking good."

"You've got more than me," Mains said. He looked at Faulkner, swaying slightly where he stood, looking into infinity as if readying himself to go there.

"Faulkner!" Mains said.

"L-T…" the injured man said, blinking slowly, swaying some more. "I'm good. Suit's sealed up at my shoulder and pressurized. Keeping me pain free. I'm good."

"What the hell's going on here, Johnny?" Lieder asked.

"Beats me."

"That ship…"

"Yeah. Never seen anything like it."

"Xenos don't have tech, do they?"

"Not that we know."

"And they seem to have some sort of auto-destruct when they're killed."

"So someone brought them here?"

"They're marked," Faulkner said.

"Huh?" Lieder grabbed his arm.

"Not now!" Mains said. He was eyeing the atmosphere shield they'd just penetrated. Even though their suits were pressurized and feeding them oxygen, he wasn't sure whether those creatures might not break through anyway. Charging into the line of fire didn't seem to bother them, so why should pursuing the enemy into a vacuum?

"It's our last hope," he said, and neither of the others replied. They had known for quite some time.

An instant after they started walking toward the ship, Mains's suit chimed a warning. He turned and saw several Xenomorphs crossing the habitat surface toward them. Ice was forming on their shining black carapaces, their limbs moved sluggishly, and one of them slipped and fell, clasping at the ground as if to dig its way back inside.

Mains pulled his antique pump-action shotgun and put the others out of their misery. Their blood froze as it fell, shattering across the ground. He didn't believe that they hadn't known the results of pursuing their prey out onto the surface, and he wondered what might have driven the creatures to suicide.

Mains's shoulder drone had been lost during the recent battle, so he instructed Lieder to send hers ahead and set it to transmit on open frequency. All three of them needed to see what was coming.

"Never seen a ship like it," Lieder said softly. There was an edge of fear in her voice, and a level of respect.

"Not sure anyone has," Mains said. It was an amazing vessel, with no clearly definable bow or stern, no certain shape. It was as if it had grown from the habitat rather than docked here.

There were three docking arms connecting it with UMF 12. One of them was blackened and open, apparently damaged during an exchange of fire. The other two were whole.

"We don't have a chance," Faulkner said. His voice was monotone, soft. His energy was fading, and soon even his suit wouldn't be able to hold back the shock of his shattered arm.

"It's our *only* chance," Lieder said. "We've got to report what we've seen here." The certainty that they could never escape this place remained unspoken by any of them, but heavy in the air. Excursionists weren't trained in suicide missions. They would fight to the last soldier, the last drop of blood and gasp of air, but they weren't so stupid that they could not see the truth.

"That first docking arm looks clear," Mains said. "No sign of movement."

"It'll be defended," Faulkner said. "By *them*."

Mains did not reply. There was nothing left to say.

They moved across the habitat's surface, expecting to be fired upon at any moment from the ship, or attacked by Xenomorphs from hidden atmos shields. Then there were the Yautja that might still be alive, and hungry for revenge against whoever or whatever had launched this assault.

Mains was troubled that the ship was still there. If the assault had been successful, why would the attackers remain docked on the habitat? There was no sign of activity. The Xenomorphs they'd fought hadn't seemed to be performing any task other than keeping still, silent, watchful, until they had a target.

He wasn't even sure they could pilot it, but the ship might have communication technology they could use, and that became Mains's prime concern.

All seemed quiet. As they neared the docking arm, he expected his suit to chime warnings of movement. Still there was nothing.

"L-T, we'll have to go back below the surface to access the docking arm," Lieder said. "It's been blasted through the habitat's surface and sealed."

"Not too keen on going back down there," Faulkner said.

"No choice," Mains said. "How's your ammo?"

"Low."

"Me too," Lieder replied.

"Okay, we'll move quickly. Concentrate on your footing and moving forward, let your suit watch out for danger. We'll know if something's coming for us."

Lieder and Faulkner nodded. Faulkner looked pale, wide-eyed, like a man trapped in a vehicle's headlights. He was waiting for the pain and shock to bite in.

Mains took point. They found a nearby atmos shield and passed back through the milky field and found themselves in a wide space, their suits allowing for the additional oxygen levels. The air here was warmer than elsewhere, a heavy heat that seemed to pulse from the strange structures covering the walls, floor, and ceiling.

"Okay, now what the *fuck* is *that*?" Lieder said.

"Hold," Mains said. He interrogated his suit, requesting an analysis of this strange place. They'd seen nothing like it on the habitat before.

"Xenomorph nest," Faulkner said. "I knew a guy in the DevilDogs who'd seen this shit before."

"Nest," Lieder responded. "Fan-fucking-tastic." They kept moving.

"Check motion detectors and life sensors. We're almost below the docking arm." Mains consulted his suit's schematic, a confused image that seemed to blur and flicker, as if the true dimensions of their surroundings were difficult to discern. "Ten yards."

He ran, and the others followed. They jumped over ridged protrusions in the floor, ducked beneath structures drooping from the ceiling, and just as they reached a wide opening above them, their suits screamed warnings.

The Xenomorphs came from the walls. Black, glinting shapes flashed before them, confusing sensors, dashing through shadows, casting ghostly images on their infrared visors.

Faulkner fired a nano-burst point blank above them, blasting two Xenomorphs apart and showering them with body parts and acid. Even the blasted parts seemed to melt down to nothing. Faulkner groaned. Mains saw his damaged arm steaming and bubbling, and as the three of them ran, Faulkner reached across and ripped the remnants of the arm from his shoulder.

His suit must have been pumping him with dangerous doses of phrail, because he never even broke step.

They advanced, fired, regrouped, forming a defensive triangle that no creature breached. Below the intrusive docking arm at last, Mains instructed Lieder to start climbing. The tunnel above them was wide, criss-crossed with thick structures similar to the open space below.

Lieder reached back and helped Faulkner. Mains waited

until they had a good start, turned quick circles—taking out one more Xenomorph with his shotgun—and then it fell silent.

He kicked at the remains of a smooth, curved head steaming at his feet.

They're marked, Faulkner had said, and now Mains saw that he was right. A stamped image was partly hidden by a splash of acidic brain matter. Mains scraped it aside with his boot, crouched down, and took in a deep breath.

Patton, it said.

"What the fuck?"

"Johnny, we're close to the ship," Lieder said from above him.

"On my way." He started climbing, querying his suit computer as he pulled himself up through the honeycomb structure inside the docking arm.

General Patton—a 20th-century American military leader.

"Guys, you wouldn't believe what I've just seen," Mains said.

"You and me both," Lieder whispered.

Mains climbed faster, one eye on his suit readout. No movement, other than Lieder and Faulkner above him. No life signs. It was as if the Xenomorphs were ghosts, sweeping in to haunt them, then fading away again to nothing.

Patton.

They climbed into a wide space, walls smooth and uneven, the whole vessel's structure seemingly grown rather than built. There, they found the dead.

A battle had been fought. It had been a while ago, probably when the ship first arrived and the Yautja started to leave.

Those left behind had come here to fight, and the destruction was immense.

Scores of blasted Xenomorph bodies lay strewn across the whole area. Lit by their suit lights, the scattered, strange limbs cast shivering shadows across curved walls. Acid blood had spilled and burned. Structure had melted and set again, around and across the Yautja bodies that also lay here and there. Some of them had been torn apart. Others were whole apart from holes smashed through their helmets and into their skulls by the Xenomorphs' powerful jaws.

Every Yautja corpse was minus its left arm, torn off to prevent any of them from suiciding.

"Some fight," Lieder said.

"Yeah." Mains walked among the dead, and here and there, where enough of the Xenomorphs' heads had survived the weird self-destruct, he saw the same markings.

"Seen it?" Faulkner asked.

"Seen it, but having trouble processing."

"Someone's using them as weapons," Faulkner said. "Someone naming himself after an old general."

"Weirder and fucking weirder," Lieder said.

"And more reason than ever to get to a communications unit," Mains said.

"At least it means we'll probably be able to use it," Lieder said. "Johnny... whoever's done this is *human*!"

"Maybe, maybe not," he said. "Either way, let's see what we can find."

They moved deeper into the ship. Away from the scene of the big battle, they encountered nothing, and no one. There was an atmosphere here, but their suits still had to filter it and supplement them with extra oxygen.

Faulkner struggled on. Mains was amazed at his resilience. He knew the big man would grind to a halt soon, and that his suit's ministrations could not continue indefinitely, but Faulkner's doom was simply a more visible manifestation of their own. None of them would survive this.

Lieder took point and probed ahead, and ten minutes after entering the strange ship and forging onward and upward, she held up a hand.

"Johnny. Bridge."

"And?"

"Another battle." She disappeared through an opening, and Faulkner and Mains followed.

The android was pinned to the wall at the far end of the bridge, several yards from the floor. A wide, heavy blade had pierced its chest and held him there, its handle heavy with hardened drips of his pale gray blood. His head hung low, chin touching his chest.

The android's legs had been ripped off, one arm crushed, stomach slashed open and emptied, so that his complex insides hung below him like some sick decoration.

It looked as if it had happened some time ago. Yet still his eyes watched them approach across the bridge.

"Who the hell are you?" Mains asked.

The android smiled. It wasn't particularly human, neither in appearance, nor in that small movement. It had basic humanoid features, but there had been no real effort to give it a personality. This thing had not been made to fool anyone.

"Patton?" Mains asked.

The thing stuck on the wall tried to speak. Its jaw was broken and its tongue had been pulled out, teeth smashed in by a heavy weapon. It snorted.

Scattered around the bridge were a score of blasted, melted Xenomorph corpses. At the feet of the android were many more, a slick of destruction piled on and around the body of the one Yautja that had made it this far. Mains couldn't help but admire the Yautja. Its body was hideously wounded and acid-burnt, and he guessed many of those had been inflicted while it was still alive. Its left arm was a pulped mess, its clawed right hand clotted with clothing and pale, raw flesh.

Before dying, it had pinned its aggressor to the wall and slashed him to pieces.

"Johnny!" Lieder said, staring past him at the android. "Comms unit."

"Can you work it?" Everything here was strange, yet recognizable.

"Yeah, think so. It's weird. This ship's like nothing I've ever seen, but lots of the symbology and language on the control panels... it's old English."

"We'll worry about that later," Mains said. "Prep a sub-space transmission to all Colonial Marine units. Open frequency. We want everyone to hear this."

Faulkner sat gingerly next to Lieder, resting his head back against the unit she worked at.

"Why did you come here?" Mains asked the ruined android.

"Who sent you? What are you doing?"

But Patton was mortally wounded, and between his fluid snorts and the quivering of his broken jaw, Mains saw nothing that made sense in those eyes. Perhaps given time, they might be able to wire up his head, give it a voice, and interrogate it.

But not yet. Now, there was a warning to send, accompanied by a mystery that others would need to work on and solve.

"Channel open," Lieder said.

Mains waited until his suit signaled readiness for his message, and then he began.

2 5

ISA PALANT

Independent Research Vessel Tracey-Jane, *Drophole Gamma-116*
September 2692 AD

She was told that it had become the most famous and historic sub-space transmission of all time.

General Paul Bassett's immediate reaction had been to initiate a mission to hunt down and capture Akoko Halley, her small crew of DevilDogs, and the survivors they had picked up from Love Grove Base, announcing them as deserters and conspirators with the "Yautja Incursion." He'd even gone so far as to pull together seven crews and ships for the mission, but two hours after the message was received all across the Human Sphere, the Yautja attackers had signaled a ceasefire.

Palant's message had been listened to over three billion times within the Sphere, and Gerard Marshall had already held a conference with the rest of the Thirteen.

He instructed Bassett to welcome Halley and Palant as heroes.

What happened next was even more out of the ordinary.

"You sure you're ready for this?" Halley asked. She had hardly left Palant's side since their arrival on the *Tracey-Jane*. Seven days' travel and a drophole jaunt had lifted them nine light years across the sphere, to this ship orbiting a planet which was unexplored, in a system barely touched by humanity. The *Tracey-Jane*'s crew were roughneckers, independent contractors, salvagers.

Pirates, Halley had said, though the name held many connotations, depending on who spoke it.

Whatever they were, theirs was about to become one of the most famous ships in the galaxy.

"Absolutely not," Isa Palant said.

"Nope. Not ready. Not at all. Very, very unready." Milt McIlveen had also rarely left her side, though she suspected that was more for his own reassurance than hers. A Company man, still he'd never felt this much attention before.

Certainly not from the Thirteen.

"Well, *they're* ready," Halley said. She was a no-nonsense woman, and the idea of pausing for a deep breath didn't seem to appeal to her. She swiped her hand over her datapad, and around the small, scuffed dining table in the *Tracey-Jane*'s galley, thirteen shimmering holograms appeared.

Palant had seen their images before, and had conversed with Marshall, but she'd never believed she would one day be in the presence of the Thirteen. It shocked her, conversing in real time with people spread across hundreds of light years of space. Yet it did not surprise her. The Company had always been rumored to have technology that could bring sub-space communication closer to face to face, without the frustrating time lag of processing, transmission, and receipt. That it kept such tech to itself only reinforced her opinion of Weyland-Yutani.

"Isa Palant," Gerard Marshall said, "and Milt McIlveen. I'm so pleased to see you both well. You've been through a lot, but if I may intrude upon you again, myself and the rest of the Thirteen have a few things to discuss before today's conference."

I'll just bet you do, Palant thought. McIlveen held her hand, surprising her. They both squeezed.

"After all," Marshall continued, "along with my old friend Major Halley, you do seem to be the history makers."

The "history makers" made their way toward the *Tracey-Jane*'s hold.

It had been cleaned out for the meeting. There were other places they could have met—in rec rooms, on the ship's cramped bridge, and in bedrooms or storage spaces scattered around the huge central area—but the hold was what this ship, a transporter, was built for, and a sense of occasion and grandness was desired. After the Yautja had requested the meeting to be on neutral ground, the *Tracey-Jane* had been the best the Colonial Marines could find in the time given to them.

Though cleaned out, the hold could hardly be called pristine. A stale stench lingered, perhaps old cargo burst from packaging, or the torn metal and leaking fuel of salvaged ships.

The floor was rough and scarred, the walls tall and rising into shadow. The hold would have held the *Pixie* five times over.

Colonial Marines were in evidence everywhere. They were heavily armed, and a few of them appeared jittery, but all weapons were stowed or holstered, and Palant could see that Akoko Halley engendered a huge amount of respect from these warriors. They weren't from her DevilDog regiment, but the Snow Dog's reputation seemed to precede her.

At the hold's center, a strange scene awaited them. A large square of plastic flooring had been laid out, programmed to show a gentle green, like close-trimmed grass. Several heavy seats had been removed from the bridge and dragged down, arranged in a rough circle with a round table in the center. Drinks and food were waiting on the table. Behind these seats were ranks of smaller, less comfortable chairs.

All of those currently present chose to stand.

Four Yautja stood in a line behind one of the big chairs. Fully armed, exuding menace and bearing scars old and new, they held their hands down by their sides. Their helmets hung from their belts, exposing their peculiar, grotesque faces. They looked around, moving slowly, jaws flexing as if always on the verge of speech, but they remained silent, and Palant guessed it was in deference to the much older Yautja who was standing before them.

He held onto the back of one of the big seats, and if some chose to see that as a sign of weakness, Palant knew they would be mistaken. Her heart skipped a beat when she first saw him. She had already been told his name and position, but even if she hadn't she would have recognized him as the leader among them. He carried himself with pride, displaying a cool intelligence and even grace. He exuded age and knowledge, and a simmering violence which was as much a part of his existence as breathing. He was the star around which those in the room—Yautja and human alike—were now orbiting.

Violence hung heavy in the air, and Palant breathed it in. This was not a peace conference. It was an invitation to embark on an even deadlier war.

His name was Kalakta, and his weapons were older than those carried by the others, all of them shining and bladed. He seemed to wear no blasters. Unlike the four Yautja behind him, he wore a bandolier of trophies across his right shoulder. As Palant drew closer, she realized that at least one of these was a human jawbone.

On his left shoulder was affixed a cleaned, pristine human skull.

McIlveen walked beside her. He carried the datapad they had been using. They'd rejected the idea of using a different machine. Although the program they'd developed had been copied and uploaded to a quantum fold, they both agreed that the original computer should be used. It wasn't like Palant to be superstitious, but this machine had saved their lives.

Now if only this old bastard speaks the dialect we've come to know, she thought, and she let slip a manic laugh. She bit it back, glancing sidelong at McIlveen. He, too, seemed on the verge of hysteria. Neither of them was meant for this, but at the same time she realized that this might well be the culmination of her dreams.

Halley remained behind at a respectful distance, and as

Palant and McIlveen stepped onto the temporary flooring, she recognized what a task they had been given. It should be military leaders or politicians doing this, she thought. A complex negotiation even when conducted in the same language, a ceasefire discussion had the potential to go sour at any moment.

Kalakta had asked for them.

Their conversation was being recorded and transmitted by several sources, but its conduct was down to her and McIlveen.

The four Yautja and their leader watched them approach, every part of their expressions exuding aggression. As they drew near, Kalakta spoke, his words deep and grinding, more like industrial machinery than a voice.

Palant closed her eyes, breathed deeply, and hoped that they were as clever as they thought.

`I am Kalakta… six hundred and seventy-seventh Elder clan.` The words appeared on the screen. They continued, missing some of what he said but still managing to make sense.

It's working! Palant thought, almost slumping with relief.

`… born long… ten thousand suns. My parent group… Ascendance was on your Earth, in a city of… and heat. A man with dark skin… worthy opponent. I have hunted through… and taken many human trophies.`

She glanced up at this, meeting Kalakta's gaze. It did not waver. Not a challenge, but also shameless. He continued speaking.

I have risen through the clans. I speak…
all Yautja civilization, and have… respect
for them to listen to me. Right now we are at
a ceasefire. This… give us time to prepare.
We are always ready to fight. One wrong move…
humans… begin again. A greater darkness.

He made a gesture behind him, one of his companions touched his forearm, and a holographic projection appeared from nowhere between them. Palant took a step back, but then the image darkened into a starscape, and she could only watch the awful scene unfold.

The footage shifted and bounced, as if taken from a combat camera of some kind. A planet or moon, desolate, whipped by cruel winds. Several low buildings, angular and functional. Two ships, probably Yautja, some distance apart.

The view shifted upward as the viewer lifted its head, and then the sound came in. A loud roar accompanied a dark shape approaching quickly from the blood-red sky. It parted clouds, growing rapidly in size and then slowing to a standstill.

A hundred small objects dropped from the vessel in bursts of smoke or steam. They were compact, falling quickly toward the ships and buildings.

Palant cringed, expecting explosions. But none came.

The barrage landed in showers of sand and stone. The viewer drew a weapon that shimmered past the camera, and from the left a trio of lasers cast about the clouds of dust thrown up by the impacts.

Several shadows emerged at the same time, scampering across the rough ground toward the camera. One of them went down, struck by a blaster, but there were a dozen more to take its place.

The image twisted and turned, and a loud screech was cut off as the hologram flickered to nothing.

`You said that you knew… fire lizards,` Kalakta said. `Speak of what you know.`

Palant tried to set her shock aside. Now was the time to see whether she knew enough to maintain this ceasefire, and perhaps even turn it into something different. Only a day ago, just before her audience with the Thirteen, Akoko Halley had played her a transmission received from an Excursionist unit. Trapped on a Yautja habitat for weeks, reduced from their usual contingent of eight down to three, they had witnessed something horrific and intensely troubling. Their story, and the footage she had just seen, at last gave a name to the Yautja's fire lizards.

She typed.

"We call them Xenomorphs," the datapad chimed. She saw recognition in Kalakta's eyes, and a gentle nod. Such human characteristics gave her pause, but only for a moment. This was important, and every moment wasted might mean more lives lost.

She wrote what she had gleaned from Shamana back on LV-1529, about how the Yautja had been attacked, how they had traveled to regroup. She did not use the word retreat—she doubted there was such a word in the Yautja language. The last thing she wished to do was challenge some personal or species pride.

Kalakta nodded slowly as the datapad translated and spoke, but he said nothing.

The Thirteen were being relayed the conversation through their secretive two-way sub-space tech. In her ear she heard Gerard Marshall's voice.

"Tell it we know where their home planet is."

Palant felt a flush of shock pass through her, and she looked down at the datapad to try and hide it. *No one* knew where the Yautja home planet was. She had long suspected that their planet of origin was lost in the mists of deep history, and that they were a nomadic species, spread far wider across the galaxy than the humans they sometimes chose to hunt. So much about them suggested that they were older, *far* older than humanity.

If Marshall and the Thirteen did know, it was knowledge that they had kept to themselves.

"I'm instructed to tell you we know where your homeworld is," she typed, and the machine spoke.

"You knew of this?" she whispered harshly to McIlveen by her side.

"No," he said. A pause. "It's bullshit. Has to be."

"Maybe."

Kalakta's expression didn't change, but his bearing altered subtly. He seemed suddenly taller, wider, as if he had puffed himself up ready for conflict. His hands dropped slightly toward his belt, where weapons almost as long and heavy as Palant hung.

"And tell him we'll nuke the fuck out of his homeworld if this ceasefire doesn't take effect immediately," Marshall said.

Palant paused. She could almost sense Marshall's anger as he watched. Because she had no doubt that he *was* watching this exchange, somehow, along with the rest of the Thirteen.

"We hold you in great respect," the device said as she typed. "Some of my kind hate you because they don't understand you. Others fear you for the same reason. I fear, but I also want to learn more. You fascinate me."

"Palant!" Marshall said. She took the small pod from her ear and dropped it on the floor.

"The Xenomorph army are driven by something else, a greater power. On their own they are formidable. With organization and order behind them, they might be unstoppable."

Kalakta nodded again, slowly. Then he knelt before Palant and McIlveen, groaning like an old man as his knees clicked and popped. The long spear on his belt touched the floor and he grabbed it, leaning on it as he sighed heavily. He had brought himself down to their level.

We have lost much. Several habitats. Many ships. Two moons, three asteroids, one planet. Not… homeworld… settled millennia ago. Your elders… threaten war, which we… But this threat… all of us.

"The enemy of my enemy is my friend," Palant replied. Kalakta stiffened as the datapad read the translation. Then he tilted his head and actually laughed, a soft, rattling sound.

We have… only enemies, the Yautja elder said. But some… worse than others. So… work together.

Palant smiled. She hoped Marshall could see and hear this. She doubted the Thirteen's intentions and their word, but she hoped that they appreciated the honor here, and the historical decision this moment had inspired.

Kalakta leaned forward, reached out, and closed his hand around the back of Palant's head.

She sensed people bristling behind her, and behind Kalakta his accompanying Yautja brought their weapons to bear. But she, and he, did not shift their gaze from each other's eyes.

He pulled her head toward his and their foreheads touched. She smelled his breath, warm and spicy. She felt the heat of him, and the depth of years and experience in his eyes. His trophy belt swung before her, and she could have reached out and touched the skull of a human she had never known, or the jawbone of a creature from beyond the Human Sphere.

The ceasefire… is sealed, Kalakta said. Yautja… humans… together.

"Thank you," she replied. There was little more to say.

Kalakta released her and stood, speaking rapidly to the four warriors behind him. They lowered their weapons and all took three steps back.

"Wow," McIlveen said. "Er… you dropped this." He handed her the earpiece she'd cast aside, smiling apologetically.

She put it back into place.

"Palant, have you any idea what you've done?" Gerard Marshall bellowed. "A pact with the Yautja? You were here to assert our power over them, not give them a place at our table!"

"I know exactly what I did," she said, trying to remain calm. "I just saved your life, and the lives of your wife and children, and their children, too."

"You think you can—" But then Marshall was interrupted, falling immediately silent when a new voice cut in.

"Time for this later."

It was a voice she knew, but had never expected to hear in person. This was James Barclay.

"Well done, Palant," he continued. "That was inspired. It's good to have you on our side. Now, Major Halley will need the translation program developed and expanded so that she can communicate with the Yautja and plan our defense."

"Of course," Palant said.

"And thank you, Isa. McIlveen, too. Your actions might have saved a lot of lives."

Palant did not reply, and soon the sub-space connection was severed with a long, deep sigh.

Akoko Halley approached, warily eyeing the Yautja in the middle of the huge hold.

"I'm not sure what I feel about this," she said.

"You heard the Excursionist transmission," Palant said. She remembered how Lieutenant Johnny Mains's voice had made her shiver, and the knowledge of where the message was coming from—deep space, way beyond the Outer Rim, on a ruined Yautja habitat—would haunt her dreams for a long time.

"Yeah," McIlveen said. "Worse things coming."

"At least we might have time to prepare," Palant said. "And now, maybe, we have access to Yautja knowledge of whatever's been happening out there."

"Dark times," Halley said, then Palant saw her smile for the first time. "Exactly what I'm trained for."

2 6

JOHNNY MAINS

Yautja Habitat designated UMF 12, beyond Outer Rim
September 2692 AD

A day after they transmitted their warning, Faulkner died.
Lieder and Mains moved his body into a side room away
from the flight deck, then sat close together in two of the big
seats, staring at a viewing screen that still showed an image
across the end of UMF 12.

Beyond, the sun toward which they were slowly spinning
appeared at the edge of the screen, blazing across the habitat's
surface, its glorious beams acting like claws to clasp the vessel
and never let it go. It was the most beautiful, most terrifying
sunrise ever.

They'd tried to take control of the alien ship, but nothing
worked. Lieder guessed there were some genetic triggers she
could not possibly fire.

The android still pinned to the wall was no help. It moved

occasionally, but they'd been unable to get any sense from it. Sometimes its facial muscles ticked and flexed as if it was trying to talk, but it could not form words. Even if they'd had the tech required to try and access its memory banks, Mains suspected they'd find only madness inside.

He called it Patton. Its one good eye seemed to focus slightly the first time he spoke the name aloud, then it hazed again, staring into distances he could not understand.

"Always thought I'd go out fighting," Lieder said. Mains looked across at her, sunlight piercing the gloom and lighting her face, reflecting from her eyes. Their suits remained on but with lowered power, non-essential systems idling. Her mask was almost clear.

"We have," he said. "We've been fighting ever since we landed here. We can climb back down, if you like. See if there are any more Yautja or Xenomorphs to tangle with."

She smiled. "I'm quite enjoying this."

"Enjoying," he echoed, and he found that he was, too. This quiet after the storm, this intimate moment with the woman who had become his lover. He wasn't sure if it was love. He was almost certain it wasn't, because love couldn't come easily to people like them, who eschewed the normal human existence to explore and travel beyond, the safety of those left behind always at the forefront of their minds. Affection was the most they could wish for, he supposed—but he felt affection for all of his crew.

His dead crew.

With Lieder, it was a little bit more.

"I wonder where they come from," he said. He glanced

back at the android, stuck on the wall by a Yautja spear, torn and tattered. It had hardly moved for hours. Perhaps it had finally died, or whatever it was androids did.

"I've never seen anything like that," Lieder said. "I mean, that thing's just... functional. It's barely human. Maybe centuries ago they made them like that, but I don't know."

"And they've militarized the Xenomorphs," Mains said. "The Company has been trying to do that for as long as its known about them. They even had a queen once, so it's rumored, but that ended badly. Whoever has done this must have been out there for a while. Researching, developing the tech, and... why? For this?"

"Taking out the Yautja," Lieder said.

"Maybe."

"I've always wondered what goes on in places we don't know and can't see. You know, way beyond the Human Sphere. The Sphere's huge, but just a fraction of the galaxy. Yautja have a deep history about them, Johnny. I mean *deep*. They might have been out there forever, when we were just crawling from the water and sprouting fingers."

"Yet whoever did this is human," he said.

"Has to be. Old Patton there proves that, with his face *and* his name."

"And the Yautja ships we saw launched fled inward, toward the Sphere."

Dawning broke over Lieder's face, just as the full glare of the sun touched them both.

"We've warned them," she said. "They'll be ready. If whoever made Patton is going for the Sphere, the Company and the Colonial Marines will be ready."

"Maybe," he said. He jumped up and approached the strange control panels. "We've figured out the comms, we know we can't fly this thing, but what else is there?"

"What are you getting at?"

"Deep space scanners. Sub-space monitoring, quantum fold webs. Anything to find a link back to wherever this ship came from. We have to discover whatever we can, for as long as we can, and message it back. Every scrap of information might be priceless."

Lieder was looking at the blazing sun crossing the viewing screen at unnatural speed, as if counting down the days to their demise faster than ever.

"We might be dead in a day or two."

"All the more reason not to sit here doing fuck all."

Lieder jumped up beside him, and she surprised him by kissing him on the cheek. Then holding him tight, pressing her face against his neck.

"Sorry. Sir."

"You're forgiven. Private."

Mains smiled, and the two of them went to work.

They'll come up here and kill us, he thought. He was convinced that there were still many Xenomorphs down in the habitat, and perhaps more in the bowels of this strange ship, but he had no inclination to put themselves at risk by exploring further. *Soon, they'll storm the bridge and we won't be able to fight them off.*

Yet the more time that passed without them being attacked, the more he began to wonder. Down in UMF 12, he and his remaining crew had approached the Xenomorphs and woken them from whatever slumber they might take. Their attack had been defensive, perhaps reflexive.

With Patton dead or dying, it could be that their commander had been lost, but still the threat of potential Xenomorph attack hanging over them made him and Lieder work quicker.

In truth, there was little Mains could do other than operate some of the tech. He monitored their suits, too, and when his own levels looked dangerously low he went to Faulkner's body, extracting some of the chemicals and systems that would help while trying not to look at his dead friend's face. He hadn't died in pain—the suit had made sure of that—but he had passed away knowing how much more there was left to do.

"Johnny, get back here," Lieder said urgently. Mains happily turned from Faulkner's corpse and dashed back onto the bridge. He glanced at Patton as he went, the android motionless and silent.

"What is it?"

"I've got some sub-space systems up and running. At least, I think that's what this is. There's a sort of grid of contact coordinates, like a network of sub-space transmissions already opened and waiting to be used. It's pretty radical stuff, and way ahead of anything I've seen before."

"We can analyze it?"

"It's way beyond me. If we had a full tech crew here, and time to take the ship apart, maybe we could reverse engineer.

But it's not that it's here that troubles me, it's what it shows."

"So don't keep me in suspense."

"There are ship traces out there that are familiar."

Mains frowned, trying to understand. The flat holo screen on the unit before them glowed a gentle blue, and scattered across its surface, and deep down, were at least a dozen pulsing red specs. Each had a list of figures and numerals beside it. He could read them, but none of them made sense to him.

"How do you know them?"

"I don't. My suit does. It's uploaded with some of the latest navigational software, and I added some of my own improvements. I've got several dips into quantum folds that the Company would probably prefer I didn't. It's the least important one that's flagging up these ship traces."

"Which one?"

"Historical. Johnny, at least seven of the traces I can find here are Fiennes Ships. They're all coming back toward the Sphere, heading for drophole locations."

"They were never meant to come back."

"Right, and they're moving at speeds way, way beyond their capabilities when they were sent out. This one, the *Susco-Foley*, left the Sphere almost five hundred years ago. The *Aaron-Percival*, fifty years before that. And the others... none of them should be here, Johnny."

He closed his eyes, because it was all becoming horribly clear.

"Nurseries," he said.

"Yeah. That's what I was thinking. Those Xenomorph bastards have to be born somewhere."

"How many people did those ships carry?"

"*Susco-Foley* was the smallest of them, and old records suggest almost seven thousand passengers in cryo-sleep."

"And there's seven of them."

"That I can see, yeah."

"Holy shit." He shook his head. "Holy *shit*. Okay, prepare another transmission. We've got to warn whoever we can."

Behind them, the speared android Patton made a noise. It was a strangled, gurgling, sickening sound. Mains went closer, trying to make out any words. But the android was not attempting to speak.

As Mains heard the chilling scratch of countless claws approaching from below the flight deck, Patton began to laugh.

ABOUT THE AUTHOR

TIM LEBBON is a *New York Times*-bestselling writer from South Wales. He's had over thirty novels published to date, as well as hundreds of novellas and short stories. His latest novel is the thriller *The Hunt*, and other recent releases include *The Silence* and *Alien: Out of the Shadows*. He has won four British Fantasy Awards, a Bram Stoker Award, and a Scribe Award, and has been a finalist for World Fantasy, International Horror Guild, and Shirley Jackson Awards. Future novels include a new thriller from Avon, *The Rage War* (an Alien/Predator trilogy), and the *Relics* trilogy from Titan.

A movie of his story *Pay the Ghost*, starring Nicolas Cage, is due for release in 2015, and several other projects are in development for TV and the big screen.

Find out more about Tim at his website
www.timlebbon.net

ACKNOWLEDGMENTS

A big thanks to the whole team at Titan. It's wonderful to work with a gang of such passionate and professional people who are, above all, fans of the genre. Thanks to Fox, especially Josh Izzo and Nicole Spiegel. A big thanks to everyone who let me use their names in the book. Apologies for killing some of you. But what a way to go, in the depths of space fighting some of cinema's most iconic monsters…

ALIEN

OUT OF THE SHADOWS

Tim Lebbon

As a child, Chris Hooper dreamed of monsters. But in deep space, he found only darkness and isolation. Then on planet LV178, he and his fellow miners discovered a storm-scoured, sand-blasted hell—and trimonite, the hardest material known to man.

When a shuttle crashes into the mining ship *Marion*, the miners learn that there was more than trimonite deep in the caverns. Hoop and his associates uncover a nest of Xenomorphs, and hell takes on new meaning. Quickly they discover that their only hope lies with the unlikeliest of saviors...

Ellen Ripley, the last human survivor of the salvage ship *Nostromo*.

TITANBOOKS.COM

FOR MORE FANTASTIC FICTION, AUTHOR EVENTS, EXCLUSIVE EXCERPTS, COMPETITIONS, LIMITED EDITIONS AND MORE

VISIT OUR WEBSITE
titanbooks.com

LIKE US ON FACEBOOK
facebook.com/titanbooks

FOLLOW US ON TWITTER
@TitanBooks

EMAIL US
readerfeedback@titanemail.com